IT'S JUST US

R. PHOENIX

CHRIS MCHART

It's Just Us

Copyright April 2019 by R. Phoenix & Chris McHart

CHAPTER ONE

CARTER

Tables moved to the side? Check. Thick mats covering the floor? Check. Drinks ready? Since this was a regular bar, they always were. So, check. What else was there to do?

I turned around to Rick, who was fiddling around with the corners of two mats. They refused to lay flat on the ground, so he bent them until they did what they were supposed to do.

"Anything else? Or are we ready?"

We didn't have much time left. The first visitors would arrive soon. They were all eager to come to our monthly meet, so some always arrived a few minutes before it officially started.

The bar we rented belonged to someone who wasn't into the lifestyle, but he was very open-minded and didn't have any objections to us rearranging his bar for a night. We made sure to push the tables back to where they'd been at the end of the night, but the pups needed some room to run and play. It prevented injuries if they didn't have to do that around table feet, chairs, or us sitting there. Sometimes, they tended to forget themselves, and it got a bit rough when they played. Plus, I didn't need a ball in my drink, just because someone threw it in the wrong direction.

Rick seemed to have won his fight with the mats, so he stood up, viewing his work. "I think we're ready. Did you check the door?"

Right. There was something missing. "No, I haven't. I'll do that now."

"Perfect. Then I'll drive home and get Sean. He's probably half-crazy with excitement."

I laughed. "Most likely, yes."

Rick's little loved the get-togethers, and he was always beaming with joy — which was the whole reason his daddy didn't bring him to get the bar ready. Having a little around here was no help at all, especially since Rick tended to forget we had work to do when he was around. He'd rather watch his partner play. I could relate, even though—

I stopped myself. No need to go there now.

"Okay, you do the door. I'll get my boy. See you soon." Rick nodded in my direction and made his way to the door.

I followed him, much slower. I didn't have to go home again since I had my clothes with me. We all needed to be dressed decently, so I'd just brought a change of clothes instead of the sweaty jeans I currently wore.

I put the sign on the outside of the door: "Private Party." It had always been enough to stop anyone who wasn't aware this was a fetish meet-up from entering. The same procedure went for the fire escape. We couldn't lock it, for obvious reasons — the same ones why we all had to stay decent — but the sign would do the trick, too. No vanillas would walk in here to see more than they ever wanted to. I'd prefer to lock the door and have our pups and littles run around naked or in their favorite clothes. But laws were laws, and no one wanted to get in trouble for indecent exposure — or for locking a fire escape — so it stayed open.

So, the doors were done. Time to get changed.

When I grabbed my bag from behind the bar, my eyes caught the basket I'd stashed there. The first few times, I'd brought it with me when we met and taken it home too, but the bartender had finally offered for me to just leave it. Even though it wasn't his kink, he didn't mind a basket with binkies and sippy cups and all the other stuff a little might need. A short glance revealed everything was still stocked up, so I went on my way to freshen up and get ready.

The kid was clearly shocked. Not like the cute kind when he got a surprise party as a kid, but more like he'd woken up naked in Central Park after a long weekend of fun and had no idea where the fuck his clothes were. This didn't look like fun at all.

Clearly the kid had no idea what the hell was going on. What was he doing here then? Had he planned on coming here?

Not wanting to startle the guy, I made my way around the edge of the bar and headed over to the door.

This was the very fucking reason the door should be locked, but laws weren't something I could change. Now I had to deal with either a newbie, which would be cool, or some random stranger, which would suck. Calming down some guy who'd managed to accidentally stumble into this party wasn't really my idea of fun. But no one else had noticed him yet, so I'd take care of that. Obviously. Because they were too busy playing.

I drew closer, getting a better look at his clothes. He was dressed in pressed jeans and a button down shirt, which made him way too overdressed. Well, overdressed if you planned to attend our party.

He was still staring around, giving the very famous deer-in-headlights expression. Yep. Most likely the wrong door, or the wrong day, or whatever. Not a curious newbie, in any case... Just someone unlucky enough to see things he might not have wanted to see. Well, I'd get him on his way, unless he left before I reached him. Right now, he was frozen on the spot, though.

I stepped around Adam and his little, who were lip-locked right there, and stopped next to the guy. "This is a private party.

Probably not your scene. I'm sorry if you just expected a regular evening at the bar."

He stammered something, but I didn't understand it.

"Sorry, I didn't catch that."

He brushed a few strands of dark hair back behind his ear, and without the hair in his face, I could see deep green eyes. They were trained to a spot somewhere on my chest.

"I'm... I'm so... I am so sorry."

I had to strain my ears. His voice was weak, but soft and sweet at the same time.

It was kind of cute.

Okay, no kidding. Big eyes, pleading look? Right up my alley. Still, the stranger had walked into the bar, where he'd seen things he couldn't have expected. So, damage control, then getting him out of here. Then again, maybe I just had to get him out of here without much damage control needed. "It's all right, darlin'. No harm done. We're a friendly bunch, just not what you're probably expecting."

His hair had fallen back into his face, covering those green eyes. I wanted him to push it back behind his ears. Or better yet... my fingers itched. *I* wanted to put it behind his ear.

A pretty little thing like him shouldn't be hidden away.

"I..." His eyes darted past me to take in the others, all dressed in gear he probably hadn't seen before. "No," he admitted. A few of the regulars had cast glances at the new guy, but they'd gone back to talking when they'd seen I was on my way. Even though he didn't exactly relax, he looked relieved. "I was supposed to meet..." He grimaced, then sighed.

His shoulders slumped, and his whole posture changed from intimidated and insecure to absolutely, completely dejected.

"Yeah. I'm sorry again. I should go."

His eyes were trained to the floor, but not in the way a submissive would avert his eyes. No. He was just devastated. Something had happened here, and it wasn't just accidentally walking through the wrong door.

"You can stay," I blurted out. Damn. Talk about subtle and not scaring him away. This was a nice way to do that. He was inside a bar, surrounded by strangers in weird gear, and I was telling him to stay? Perfect. Just perfect. "If you want to stay, that is. We're not shy. You can look around, ask questions. If you're interested."

I raised my hand, giving in to the urge to touch him. He seemed to be so fragile. Inches before I would've made contact, I let my hand drop. Would that be too much?

"I..." He drew in a deep, shuddering breath.

I wanted to see those eyes again. Currently, they were trained on the floor, like he expected to find answers there.

"I—" He bit his lip, cutting himself off again.

This time, my hand didn't stop before touching him. Something about seeing this lost boy pulled at me. He startled as my hand made contact with his shoulder, but at least he raised his eyes and looked at me again. They were such an intriguing shade of green, way too big as he tried to look at me and the scene behind me at the same time.

"I'm not sure what to ask about," he admitted. He looked past me again, this time more obviously, then looked back at me. His cheeks took on a nice shade of red. What had he seen that had affected him so much? Littles? Pups? All of it?

"Most people would have questions the first time they run into BDSM in real life. It's not exactly like an episode on one of those cop shows. And it's certainly not like it's portrayed in some books."

A faint smile appeared on his face, but it was gone before I could really admire it. Then he was back to looking... rejected? Sad? Miserable? I wasn't sure. "No, it's not."

This had to look strange for anyone who wasn't into the scene — daddies and masters with their littles and pups, playing and coloring. Everyone might've been fully dressed, but it was still more than obvious it wasn't just an average party in a bar.

"Are those... What are they?" He nodded in the direction of a master playing fetch with a pup.

"A pup and his handler. Or master. You've never seen pups playing before?"

Green eyes met mine again. God, they were still so big, so innocent. How the hell could someone look so innocent and sexy at the same time?

"Yes. No. I mean, the… real, furry ones. Should I have seen people-puppies?"

I chuckled. It wasn't a term I'd heard yet, though it was accurate enough. "I don't know. You can find anything on the internet, if you search for it." I chuckled quietly as I imagined him in front of his computer, staring at a pup.

"Not something I've gotten my google on with," he replied.

There went that fantasy. Still, his innocence was sort of adorable.

"Hands-on learning is better anyway, if you ask me." My fingers gently rubbed over his shoulder. Since he hadn't tried to move away and didn't indicate he was feeling uncomfortable with my touch, I just let my hand stay there. Totally unselfishly, of course. "What do you think of the pups?"

A lot of newbies to the lifestyle had been drawn to the puppy play side lately. Evidently, if you shared a few hot videos online, people were more than willing to try all kinds of things. But as fun as it was to watch pups, and sometimes even throw a ball for them, they weren't the side of the lifestyle I'd been drawn to.

"Um." He looked past me again. "They're… interesting."

"Interesting?"

"Yes," he said. His eyes got a bit harder, as if he was trying to dare me to correct him. Cute. "Interesting."

I smiled and nodded. "I can see why you'd think that. A bit of a rowdy bunch, though. I'm more of a daddy. I'd rather cuddle with a sweet boy than endlessly throw a ball."

"That sounds a little bit like you're throwing some shade," he noted. A small smile tugged at his lips again. This time, it lingered there, almost like it was genuine.

I laughed, shrugging. "It's not shade if it's true. Everyone knows there's nothing cuter than a boy with his binky curled up in his daddy's lap."

The smile vanished, melting away into confusion. "A what? You mean…" He eyed me for a moment. "You aren't some kind of… pedophile, are you?" he whispered.

Ah, there was the question that always came. How could I expect someone not in the lifestyle to understand the difference between being a pedophile and being into age play? By now, I didn't even get offended anymore, but it somehow hurt coming from the kid.

"No. Think role play with consenting adults. It's a form of domination and submission. A daddy is a type of dominant that wants to take caring for his submissive to a whole different level. This has nothing to do with actual kids, and that's something no one here would tolerate."

His large eyes stared at me, somehow mesmerized and disbelieving at the same time. The last time a boy had looked at me like this when I'd explained the lifestyle had been with Nicholas. That had been a lifetime ago.

Ruthlessly pushing back memories that had no place there and then, I forced a smile. "Littles are a type of sub who like playing and coloring and doing things that let them relive simpler times when they didn't have to make any decisions. Haven't you ever thought for just a moment how wonderful it would be if someone else could make the decisions for just a few minutes?"

"Maybe. Sometimes?" he asked, tilting his head. "To a point, I guess. Doesn't everyone?"

Now those were precise answers. But some of the sadness had ebbed in the wake of his curiosity. He also seemed to be less nervous. My hand still rested on his shoulder, as if he liked it there.

Maybe wanted it, even.

That might've been wishful thinking, though. All he was doing was standing there.

"I think so, at least to a degree. But littles actually get a chance to experience it and have a daddy or mommy who take care of them." I took a stab and guessed that he was from the college. "Picture a long day of classes and studying, but then getting to come home to someone who would make dinner for you and give you a bath, then let you relax and color or play with blocks or dinosaurs, until it was time for... say, your daddy to tuck you into bed. No decisions, just someone there to take care of you and watch over you."

"Blocks and dinosaurs," he repeated, tugging at the bottom of his shirt. "I mean, everything else just sounds like... a relationship or something, or how they're supposed to be, right?"

"Yes. This is just a different way to experience a relationship." I allowed my fingers to barely caress his shoulder, so lightly he might not even realize what I was doing. "Just one where the daddy makes the decisions because that makes them both happy."

"Usually when one person makes decisions for another person, it's not a great thing," he said.

Even though I didn't like the implications, I couldn't help but smile at him.

"I mean, it seems like it'd be pretty hard to just... let go and let someone else do the thinking for you. It sounds good in theory, but... not so much in practice."

Nodding, because I could see where he was coming from, I pointed across the bar. "Look at the two guys over in the corner booth."

I wasn't sure what he saw when he looked at the two men. I saw love and a relationship that had been meant to be from the first time they'd looked at each other.

"Do you see my friend Sean? He's the little sitting on his daddy's lap and racing the car around the table. Does he look like he's unhappy?"

He studied them for a moment, taking the question more seriously than I might've expected. Finally, he shook his head.

"No…" He paused, then added slowly, "He looks like he's having fun."

"What about his daddy? How is he looking at Sean?" Could he see the love between them? Or was it just me, with my outlook filtered through the expectations of the lifestyle? And was he okay with it, or was it too much for him to take in?

"Like he's everything," he said softly. Did he sound like he wanted the same? Or was that just my brain, telling me that he'd look more than cute in Sean's position?

"Because to his daddy, he is. His daddy's entire world revolves around making sure his boy has everything he needs to be happy." They'd been together for years, and even though watching them had been painful in my darker moments, I'd never begrudged them their happiness.

"It's really sweet," he said. He swallowed hard, looking away from them.

My heart ached, for my own losses and for the boy in front of me who looked like seeing their happiness was painful. I could relate all too well.

It was probably reckless of me and would clearly be pushing the kid out of his comfort zone, but I did it anyway. "How about you stay? Get a feel for it?"

Insane was my middle name.

He stiffened, and his eyes widened again.

I continued quickly, "No pressure, and I won't push, but why don't you let me show you how it feels to let someone take care of you? Just a little bit? A few minutes, half an hour?"

"I…" He was a little pale, but I saw it when he gathered up something — courage, defiance, *something* — and nodded slightly. "Okay."

I hadn't actually expected him to agree. What a leap of faith. It took a lot to just jump into that when you accidentally walk into a party like this.

"I'm proud of you." Then I smiled. "If I'm going to be your daddy for the evening, I should probably know your name."

"Oh!" He looked a little startled, like he hadn't even realized we'd been talking this long without exchanging names. "Micah," he offered.

"I'm Carter. It's nice to meet you." He gave me a little smile, and I squeezed his shoulder again. "I've got a few things behind the bar that I'd like to fetch. We can use them tonight. And how about sitting down with my friends then?"

He paled a little. "Um. Your friends. Right." He peered past me. Everyone was talking and laughing, enjoying getting to be free in a way Micah didn't seem to be comfortable with — yet.

"It'll be easier than you think. I'll introduce you, and you don't even have to talk if you don't want to. Then you either relax with me or play with Sean. I happen to know he loves sharing his cars." Sean loved playing with other littles, and I had a feeling this wouldn't be any different.

"Cars. Right." He squirmed beneath my hand.

"There's no pressure," I told him. "If you don't want to, you don't have to." I'd be disappointed, but I also didn't want to make him uncomfortable. This was about showing him how good it could feel to relax, after all.

"No, no. I want to try. I just don't think I'll be very good at this. I have no idea what to do."

"There's no 'being good' at it. It's just what works best for you." I gestured back at Sean. "Just relax and see what happens."

"I…" Micah took a deep breath then nodded. "Okay. You just might have to walk me through a little of it. It's… been a while since I played with cars."

I smiled. "That's the easiest part. Playing comes back to every-one. You just have to figure out what toys are your favorite. I know some littles who love to color and watch cartoons. I know others who absolutely love blocks and being read to. There's no right or wrong way to play."

"I never really played much," he admitted slowly. "I read a lot, but I don't really remember playing a whole lot."

My heart clenched at the quiet admission. "We'll start slow

then and take our time. But remember what I said. There's no right or wrong way to be little." He clearly didn't believe me, but I didn't mind a skeptical little as long as he was open-minded. "Come on in and we'll hang out for a while."

I slid my hand over his shoulder until I was resting at the small of his back. Putting the slightest pressure on it, I moved us forward toward the bar.

"Short detour to the bar and then we'll be all set."

Feeling the tension in his body, I decided to keep talking. Maybe it would distract him. "I know I have a couple of different coloring books back here, as well as a few toys."

I glanced over to see an unasked question on Micah's face.

"You want to know why?" When he nodded, I grinned. "Because I believe in two things: one, always be prepared, and two, little boys will always forget their binkies and cups in odd places. It's better to have more than you need. Better than having not enough."

"Binkies and cups," he repeated. "Coloring books and toys." He sounded like it would make more sense if he repeated the words. Even though he shook his head a little, but he didn't seem repulsed by the idea. More... baffled.

Maybe I could show him why some people found them appealing. More and more, I wanted to get this skittish boy to sit down and just... relax.

As we got to the bar, I had to remove my hand from his back, which I hated. It was warm, and right, and I wanted to let it be there. Micah leaned against the bar as I walked around and pulled the small basket out from behind the counter.

"Okay, I've got a couple of questions for you. No right or wrong, just tell me which one catches your eye first." I held up two coloring books. "Animals at the zoo or oceans?"

He looked between them, nibbling on his bottom lip. "I... I don't know." More nibbling. That poor lip. "I don't want to pick the wrong one," he finally admitted.

"There's no right or wrong," I reminded him.

Micah looked skeptical all over again, but he nodded. "The… oceans, I guess?"

He could have asked for blank paper and I would've done my best to find it for him, but he couldn't know that yet. "Good boy. That will be fun to play with."

He blushed, but a small smile curved onto his lips.

Looking in the box, I started to pull out a couple of things, but stopped. Asking him about these things might not be the best way to approach this. "Okay, how about I pick out a few things and you just see how they feel? That way you don't have to make any decisions — because Daddy is in charge." I gave him a grin. "Well, Daddy for a little while."

Relief flooded his expression. "Yeah." He nodded, more confidence in that than anything else he'd shown. "Please."

With that decided, I picked out a sippy cup and filled it with apple juice, then grabbed a binky, crayons, and a little stuffed bear — just for the hell of it. "Okay, ready. Let's go."

He watched the items with a curious but hesitant expression, one that I'd seen before on new littles. People had to actually try these things to understand. It would either work for him or it wouldn't. There was nothing I could do to change it if he didn't, but I'd do everything in my power to give him a positive experience.

Not giving him time to worry, I came around the bar and started moving us toward the back of the room.

His eyes widened as he watched the pups run around on the mats covering the floor. "What are they doing?" he whispered to me. Was he afraid of being overheard and… well… *judged* for his ignorance?

"Playing." I shrugged. "Think of it as another way to role play and relax, but pups have even less responsibility during playtime than littles do." I dodged a tennis ball that was bouncing across the room. "They do a lot of the same activities that biological dogs do. Have you ever just relaxed with a dog on your lap and felt how calm it made you?"

Micah nodded. "I'm still not sure what you mean, though. Not with people," he admitted.

I thought about how to explain it. "For the handlers or masters, it's that they get someone to cuddle with and play with who's just focused on having fun without any of the baggage that comes from being in a relationship. You can't complain that the dog hasn't done the dishes, so all the kind of regular stuff that can drive us crazy… is left behind when they get in their roles."

"Do people do this… all the time?" he asked, his eyes on the pups as they raced around on the mats, trying to catch their toys. "Be in those roles, I mean."

I shook my head. "Mostly no. It's usually just an occasional part of their relationship. A lot of the pups have incredibly stressful day jobs. So when things have been really tough, say a doctor had to give someone bad news, or things went really wrong at work in some way, they can come home and tell their loved one or call up their handler and say they need to let every-thing go."

"Oh." Micah looked like he was mulling things over, his head tilting slightly to the side and errant locks of hair falling into his face. This time I did reach out to tuck them behind his ear. He started, but he only looked up at me with a small, sheepish smile. "Yeah, it does that," he said shyly, gesturing to his hair.

"You have beautiful hair, but we can't let it cover your eyes. You need to be able to see where you're going." His hair really was incredible, soft and nice and long. I had to force myself to keep my fingers from running through it and making him uncomfortable.

He blushed, and I was glad I'd brushed the hair from his face to see the lovely red tint to his cheeks. "Thank you?" The words were more like a question.

I chuckled. "You're welcome."

As we finally reached the back table, I put everything on it, then I scooted back a chair and sat down. Since I wanted to show Micah how it could be if he didn't have to make any decisions, I took his hand in mine and gently pulled him to my lap without asking him first. I gave him plenty of time to say no or reach for another chair, but he followed my lead. Even though his eyes were even bigger than before, he stiffly stepped closer and sat down on my lap.

I tried to find a good spot for my hands, not really knowing where to put them. On his hips, as I'd hold a little? Maybe too intimate. But what was less intimate? Thighs, surely not. Waist? Worse.

Finally, I settled on resting them on his hips, making sure it wasn't a sexual touch in any way. Not that I didn't want to, because, hell, there was a hot cutie on my lap, coloring and trying being little, but I wanted him to be comfortable — not getting groped by someone he just met.

Sitting on my lap had to be a huge step for him, so I wouldn't push it.

Hoping to get Micah to feel comfortable, I looked across the table at Sean and his daddy Rick, who were clearly trying not to look too curious. "This is my new friend Micah. He's going to hang out for a while and try being little."

Micah's blush deepened, but he didn't comment. Instead, he busied himself with flipping through the coloring book, looking at each picture before going on to the next page. He finally settled on one, smoothing the book down so he could properly get to the page, then reached for the crayons. He hesitated a little when he picked up the blue one, eyes darting to me, but I only nodded. He slowly brought the crayon closer, then made a tentative swipe within the confines of a wave.

I watched him color for a moment, seeing the way he carefully made sure not to color out of the lines. He was still tense, even though he colored. I wanted to make him relax, truly relax, before the night was over. He looked like he needed it.

Being little wasn't about being perfect or doing everything right. It was about letting everything else fade away until only the joy of being cared for remained.

CHAPTER TWO

MICAH

I couldn't have felt more ridiculous if I'd tried.

I'd expected conversation and drinks, not to be sitting on some random guy's lap while I colored ocean waves. Then again, I hadn't really thought I'd be stood up — and I had the sinking suspicion that I'd been completely set up, too.

Maybe if I'd just noticed the sign on the door…

But at the same time, some part of me was glad I hadn't. As embarrassing as the whole situation was, it was better than going home in tears because I'd been the subject of some fucked-up prank. It still hurt, but the knowledge that I was going to come out of here with a new experience counted for something.

Didn't it?

"Am I doing okay?" I asked after a few minutes, staring studiously at the paper. I didn't want to see his disappointment for the way I'd gone out of the lines a few times on accident. He'd let me use his coloring book — which was an odd thing to keep at a bar, really, but I wasn't in a place to question that at the moment — and there I was, fucking up the picture.

He moved his hand so it was resting against my back and started slowly stroking it up and down. "I think the picture is absolutely fridge-worthy, but are you having fun?"

Fridge-worthy.

I almost had to laugh, even though I knew that was far from the reaction I should've had. But I was starting to wonder if this was a part of the grand prank. Was this all just some game meant to truly humiliate me?

Part of me wanted to get up and leave without another word, but a larger part of me wanted to believe this was actually real.

"Um… sort of," I said awkwardly.

Before he could respond, a tiny race car plopped down in the middle of my picture. "I'll let you play with my car if I can color too. I love fishes, but Daddy said no fishes at home, and Uncle Carter wouldn't let me have the fishy coloring book 'cause he says I have too many at home already. But you really can't have toooo many. Right?"

"Wait, what?" I looked up to see an innocent-looking expression staring down at the coloring book like it was a treasure and he wanted some too. "I…"

What was I supposed to say to that? This was a grown man offering me a toy car and trying to get me to share someone else's coloring book. What the hell had I walked into? Were my so-called friends going to jump out from somewhere, aiming their cell phone cameras at me? Or were they going to continue until I was humiliated even further?

I looked up, on the verge of slipping out of Carter's lap. My eyes met the ones of the guy with the car — Sean, right? — He looked so… calm. Happy — and like he really just wanted me to share the coloring book. Could this really be part of a prank?

I shook my head slightly, then nodded. Then shook it again. Hell. If they were pranking me, I'd play along. And if not, I'd just enjoy the evening. Coloring.

It was nice, after all.

Sean's excited eyes met mine again. He was practically bouncing on his daddy's lap.

"I should probably ask… Daddy, if it's okay," I said, testing the word out. This was one of the weirdest things I'd ever done. Not that I'd done that many weird things, really.

A part of me was on the verge of freaking out, but at the same time, I didn't have the slightest idea of how to behave so Carter would approve. His hand was still running along my back, warm and comforting, and I finally got up the courage to glance at him.

He was smiling, seeming perfectly content watching me. It was… weird. Even if this could be called some kind of screwed-up first date, no one had ever looked at me like that. Carter glanced over at Sean, shaking his head like the man was a handful or something.

Sean's… daddy just laughed. "That one's a sneaky little thing. He really has entirely too many coloring books because his daddy doesn't tell him no. So you only have to share if you want a friend to color with."

He wasn't going to color the same picture I was, was he? I looked at Sean with mild alarm, unsure if I could handle the idea of a kidlike guy coloring all over the page like a toddler might. It was my picture, and I wanted it to be as close to perfect as possible for my… daddy for the night. It still sounded weird in my head.

"Um. We can try another picture," I offered, though I was still cringing inwardly at the idea of watching him potentially wreck a perfect page.

Carter chuckled and I had a feeling he'd guessed some of what was going through my head. "How about we try this?" He flipped several pages then turned the coloring book sideways on the table. "This way you each get your own picture and then Sean can take his home later if he wants to."

I was a little embarrassed over my protectiveness of the picture I'd started, like it somehow belonged to me. It was… well, childish, but I couldn't help myself. Calling him Daddy, even only in my own mind, seemed to mess with my head. Not in a bad way, but it did, since I got defensive over a picture.

"Okay," I said, but really, I was afraid to say anything else. I didn't want to look like an idiot in front of these people. I shouldn't have cared what they thought about me, but then, I always cared what people thought about me.

Which was how I'd ended up here looking like I'd worn jeans to the Prom. Just… in reverse.

Sean gave an excited squeak and reached across the table, grabbing for the red. "I love fishies."

His daddy seemed to have other plans though. One hand came down on Sean's greedy fingers, and the man cleared his throat.

Sean stilled then peeked up at the man. "Yes, Daddy?"

"Is that how a good boy behaves?" The smile in his eyes said he wasn't surprised or upset, but it was still weird to see him correcting his… little boy.

Sean sighed. "No, Daddy. I'm sorry."

He didn't seem sorry, though.

Carter laughed. "Brat." Glancing up at him, I noticed he was looking between both of us with a smile still on his face. "Be nice to my boy or I'll tell him he can't share."

My boy.

The words sounded strange, and I squirmed a little on Carter's lap. I couldn't figure out how I felt about that, about him, about any of this. It all seemed beyond anything I could understand, yet it was appealing somehow. It was nothing I'd ever thought about before, but it felt nice.

Of course I hadn't thought about it. I hadn't even known this sort of thing existed, but I was starting to see the appeal.

"He's being nice," I said. I offered him the blue crayon to go along with the red one. "For your fishies," I tried, looking at Carter again instead of at Sean. Was I doing this right?

Carter's smile widened. "You're a nice boy. But he likes being a brat, so don't worry. If he's not nice, his daddy will make him behave."

Make him behave? That sounded a little ominous.

Then he looked down at the coloring book again. "I'm going

to get a bigger box of crayons for you, if you decide to come play again. This one doesn't have enough blue ones for you, boy."

If you decide to come play again.

I wasn't sure if the thrum that ran through me was from terror or anticipation — maybe a little bit of both, really, but I couldn't decide which was more prominent. "Um." That was all I could manage, and I closed my mouth. I grabbed the purple crayon and started to color the plant on the page, deliberately avoiding looking at the other three men.

Sean chatted a lot as he colored, but I stayed silent, just listening. It was a marvel, listening to someone who looked much older than me ramble on like a child, free and unabashed, while he colored in a coloring book made for kids a fraction of his age.

After a while, I set my crayon down and just rested back against Carter, feeling oddly relaxed. It seemed so unlikely, given the start of the night and how out of my depth I was, but at the same time... There I was, and it felt surprisingly good.

Carter slowly wrapped his arm around me and pulled me closer until I was resting against his chest and his hand was stroking my side. His voice was warm and quiet as he held me. "You look like a boy that's had a very long day. Let's see what we can do to make my boy relax a little."

Reaching out, he grabbed the bear and sippy cup I'd forgotten about — or maybe I had just refused to acknowledge them. Carter put the teddy bear in my arms and slowly brought the cup to my lips, like he was giving me time to figure out what I wanted.

"It might seem different because it doesn't come out very fast, so you have to suck hard. Just relax back and have a drink, baby."

All I could think of was the double entendre of his words. Were we really talking about the sippy cup, or was he using it as a euphemism? Was he setting me up for another proposition later that night?

What would I do if he was?

A whole lot of nothing. There were reasons I was 0 for 0 in the dating department.

I nodded, not trusting myself to speak for fear I'd burst into nervous laughter, and when the spout pressed against my lips, I opened my mouth. He held it up a little to help me, and I sucked — hard — as my mind went to other places.

"Good boy." Carter's fingers continued to stroke my side as he held me. "Close your eyes and just relax. There's nothing to worry about and nothing you have to do."

His praise did something unexpected to me, making me flush with warmth. I wasn't used to it. Certainly not from my parents, at least, and I'd had rotten luck with friends. They always liked to tease me for looking just a little too feminine, acting just a little too tentative — and I couldn't do a damn thing about it.

I sucked a little slower on the sippy cup as I relaxed against him, closing my eyes as he'd bidden me. I was aware, distantly, of a whole bar filled with people like Carter and Sean and pups that ran around chasing tennis balls, but in that moment, it felt like it was just the two of us.

Until the moment Sean burst the bubble around us. He started wriggling around so much that he rattled the whole table.

His daddy chuckled. "Potty time for wiggly boys. Come on, brat. Let's go to the bathroom."

My eyes flew open as I was startled out of the quiet reverie, and I stared at the two of them.

What the hell? Sean couldn't even go to the bathroom by himself? I felt a little queasy and a lot weird about it, but I didn't know what to do or what to think. I'd settled into the role of a *little* pretty easily, but I hadn't thought about things like… going potty, or whatever this was.

I watched as Sean's daddy picked up a small backpack then took Sean's hand like he really was a kid and led him toward the back of the bar, where a long hallway had to lead to the bathrooms. Sean bounced along like a kid with the case of the wiggles and giggles and laughed as they waded through the puppies and their handlers — at least, I thought that was what Carter had called them.

I couldn't stop myself from staring, my thoughts racing as I tried to make sense of what had just happened.

Once they'd disappeared from sight, I sagged back against Carter. It was less stressful now that they'd gone. Other people had stared at me for a while when they thought I wasn't looking, but now everyone was doing their own thing — which made it so much easier to do mine.

"Well then," I mumbled, pushing the sippy cup away a little so I could speak. "This is… interesting." I couldn't think of another word to describe it.

Carter chuckled. "It's a different experience, I agree, but I'm enjoying spending time with you."

"Is that because I don't talk a lot?" I asked dryly.

His fingers dug into my ribs, tickling me and making me squirm and cry out with laughter. He didn't give up, tickling me to the point until I couldn't hold back from crying for mercy.

When he finally let up, he pulled me close again as I collapsed into him, completely out of breath, but still chuckling a bit every once in a while.

"Every little is different, so there's nothing wrong with being quiet or a chatty brat. It's whatever feels right to you. Your little side seems like it would be cuddly and quiet while you just enjoyed Daddy taking care of you."

"I have," I admitted. "I didn't really think I would, but it's been… nice." It really had been too long since I'd been touched, but I wasn't into casual touches. Usually, it had to mean something — which was why I was a virgin. It was hard to get a lot of experience when the guys around me just wanted to score, especially when I yearned for something… different. More. Better.

Something I'd started to think didn't exist.

"I'm glad. When you first walked in, I thought you would leave in a panic, but I'm glad you stayed." Carter's hand came up and stroked over the back of my head then along my back. "I like hanging out with everyone here, but there's just something about spending time like this. It's my favorite way to relax."

"I'm glad I stayed too," I said slowly, and I was. I hadn't expected to. I'd thought this would be just... something I'd done to spite the guys, to try to make the best of the situation they'd put me in. "I..." I squirmed a little, not sure how to put what was going through my mind. I hated how fragile my voice sounded when I said softly, "Please tell me this isn't part of their joke."

If it was, it was going to devastate me. I couldn't have an evening of utter peace, of feeling wanted in a way I'd never felt before, only to have it be used against me.

Carter shook his head, something sparking in his eyes. Then he leaned in and kissed my forehead. "Never, baby. I thought you might have been confused or lost when you came in, but it never occurred to me that someone would deliberately set out to embarrass you."

I closed my eyes as his lips brushed my skin. "It was..." I said, trying to keep the misery out of my voice. "I..." I sighed. "I should've known better."

But I hadn't expected something like this. In high school, sure. But we were in college now. I'd thought people who claimed to want to hang out with me actually had. I hadn't thought I'd be the subject of another cruel joke.

"Sometimes you take a leap of faith with people and it doesn't work out, but don't blame yourself." He hugged me tight, bringing me back to his chest. "It might not have been what you thought you'd be doing tonight, but I'd like to think we've made the evening a little more interesting for you."

"More comfortable than just going to a regular bar, too," I said, relaxing against him. "I'm not really the bar-going type." I was pretty sure he'd gathered that much. I stuck out like a sore thumb. "But this has been nice."

He nodded. "I come here because I've known the owner for years. It's comfortable to hang out here because most understand

BDSM or are into it themselves. Otherwise I'm a stay home and cuddle on the couch kind of guy."

"You're a good cuddler. I've never enjoyed sitting in someone's lap before," I offered, which was true.

Carter's hand started stroking along my back again. "Thank you."

"You're welcome," I said. Was that the right response? I could feel my cheeks turning hot as I blushed, and I faltered because I didn't know what else to say. This was already strange enough as it was. Calling attention to it happening was just... making it seem stranger.

"I like having you here on my lap." Carter shifted and relaxed back in the chair, pulling me tighter against him. "This is one of my favorite parts of having a little in my life."

I wanted to turn around and bury my face against his shirt, to breathe in his scent, but I thought that might've been a little too much. But I was so relaxed there, so much that the rest of the bar seemed to fade into the background. It was unimportant that anyone might be watching us.

"Do you have one?" I asked.

His arms hugged me close for a moment longer before relaxing. "No, I've been single for a while."

I didn't understand how someone like him could be single, not when he'd been damn near perfect the entire night, but I wasn't going to press. "So am I," I said, not even sure why the words escaped me. I instantly blushed. "I mean... I..."

"I'm glad. I've enjoyed spending time with you." He smiled and started slowly caressing my back again. "Tonight hasn't gone how I expected, but I'm glad you showed up even though the circumstances weren't ideal for you."

I liked his touch more than I should have. It was comforting. "I'm glad too," I said shyly. It would be nicer thinking about this night knowing he'd come to mind — not the assholes who had set me up and sent me inside, knowing what I was walking into. "But I... probably have to go soon," I said reluctantly.

Carter nodded. "I know we've given you a lot to think about, but did you have fun?"

"I did," I said, a little surprised by how true the words were. "I didn't expect to, but… I'm glad I gave it a chance."

And oddly enough, it was even true. I still didn't know what to make of the situation, not really, but I'd been able to relax despite my hesitation. I couldn't remember the last time I'd settled down that much, especially not with another person… least of all a total stranger.

"Good." Carter finally seemed hesitant as he paused for a moment. "I know you need time to process everything, but would you like to meet for coffee or dinner sometime?"

I blinked at him. It took my brain a moment to fully understand what he'd just said, let alone the entire situation. He wanted to see me again? Would he want… *this* again?

Did *I* want it again?

"I…" I was pretty sure I wanted to, but I wasn't sure where this would lead. Was it somewhere I wanted to go?

Yes.

"I would really like that," I said slowly, offering him a shy smile.

I would. Something about him had drawn me in from the start, and I'd liked the careful touches to my back and the way he'd treated me like I was his… little.

I'd liked how it might feel to be his little, too. I'd never thought about it before, but if I'd known it had existed…

I might have sought it out before just to feel like this.

Maybe.

"When can I see you again?" I blurted out, blushing furiously when I realized what I'd just done. I shouldn't have been so eager — and even if I was, it had been stupid to seem like I'd be looking forward to it that much. I didn't want to look desperate.

But this wasn't something I could just leave up to fate. It was bold of me, bolder than I usually was, but I wanted this decision made before I left.

I wanted to have something to look forward to beside the smirks on my supposed friends' faces the next time I saw them.

"What do you think about having dinner next weekend?" Carter's hand moved up my back and rested on my shoulder. "I'd like to get to know you more."

Next weekend. My heart skipped a beat, and there was a part of me that wanted to ask him to make it sooner. Or further away. Or now. Or never.

But I was sure he had his own life and demands on it, and I didn't want to seem pushy or wishy-washy.

"I'd like that," I said, and for the first time, I let myself turn and press my face against his chest. He smelled as good as I'd have expected, spicy and clean all at once, and I inhaled deeply.

He gently ran his fingers through my hair, and I closed my eyes. I could've stayed there forever.

CHAPTER THREE

CARTER

I'd never walked into a date before not knowing if the guy would show up or not, but I was running two steps behind Micah, if not three.

"It's just dinner. He knows that. You're just finding things to worry about," I told myself. I looked in the rearview mirror and frowned. "It's not too fast, and it's not too much. He's going to be fine."

But he'd given mixed signals, and he'd been anxious, which made it hard to figure out how this evening would go.

Pulling up in front of the small mom and pop pizza place I'd chosen, I tried not to let the doubts take over. We were just going to enjoy a casual dinner and get to know each other.

Parking the car, I turned off the engine and climbed out. My first instinct had been to pick something fancier for him, but as I'd thought about it, I'd realized something more casual might be easier on his nerves.

Hopefully I'd been right.

It'd been a long time since my last real date. Starting again at forty wasn't a way to make me feel younger. Micah had to be about half my age. While I usually loved the difference, I doubted myself today.

Even though he was nervous and anxious and uptight, he was young, gorgeous, sexy. He could have everyone, especially someone closer to his age.

Yes, some boys liked their men older, some littles liked their daddies older and some simply didn't care, but I still couldn't get rid of the small voice telling me that he could have anyone he wanted. Why should he pick me? Because I'd put him on my lap and made him relax? He'd enjoyed that, of course, and he'd seemed eager to meet me again, but still.

Neither of us could deny the age gap. Nicholas had been 12 years younger than me, and he'd sometimes... No, he hadn't wanted a different partner, but it had been an issue sometimes, especially when we'd fought.

Of course, being younger hadn't saved him.

Pushing the gloomy thoughts out of my head, I scanned the parking lot. I didn't see Micah. Would he come? I resisted the urge to reach for my phone for the thousandth time and just made my way to the door instead. He'd said he'd meet me, and I would believe him.

My palms grew sweaty, and I wiped them on my jeans. He wasn't going to just let me stand here. We'd texted back and forth a couple of times during the week, but he wasn't really chatty. It had mostly been agreeing on a place to meet. That made it way harder for me to determine if he'd really show up. Not that I didn't want to text more, but... I wasn't up to date on how to behave these days when you were dating.

Damn, now I sounded twice as old as I actually was.

My eyes moved over the parking lot again, and I spotted someone climbing out of a small compact car on the other side of the lot. Thank fuck.

My shoulders sagged, and a breath I hadn't realized I'd been holding escaped as Micah came into view. With another deep breath, I tried to calm myself so I wouldn't scare him away by being too excited. Scaring him off was the last thing I wanted.

"I hope you like pizza. This is one of my favorite places."

His hands were in the pockets of his nice jeans. The dress shirt he wore seemed oddly formal, and his whole body was on high alert. He looked wound up tight, but I was pretty sure the smile on his lips was genuine when he nodded. "I love pizza," he assured me. "I've never been here before."

"It's not something the college crowd usually visits, so I'm not surprised." We walked to the door, my hand itching to rest it on his hip, but I stopped myself. That was too much, too soon. I'd been so familiar with him at the bar, but I didn't know how he'd handle it in another setting. Instead of touching him, I reached for the door and opened it for him. "It's one of those places you have to hear about from a local because I'm not sure they've ever heard the word advertising here."

He smiled as we made our way in.

One of the waitresses walked up, greeting me with a wide smile. "Hey, Carter. How are you doing tonight?"

I glanced over at Micah, feeling my face go hot. "I may eat here too often," I said conspiratorially, grinning before I looked back toward the server. "Great. How are the kids?"

"Oh, crazy as ever. Table for two?" She raised one eyebrow.

At least she managed to hold her questions back. For now.

"Yes, please, in the back, if possible." I wanted privacy tonight so Micah and I could talk without being overheard. The back was usually quieter, which should help him relax.

She cast a knowing smile in our direction, her eyes wandering from me to Micah and then back to me. "Of course. Come on."

Micah was quiet as we followed her through the small tables to the back of the restaurant. The booths allowed for more privacy. He was still radiating nervous energy, but at least he hadn't run.

He cast a glance over his shoulder every two seconds, and I made sure to look at him. I wanted to show him I was still there and very much interested in having dinner with him — that I wasn't like the asshole friends who'd set him up when he'd walked in the bar last time.

When we were seated — next to each other in the booth, but with entirely too much space between us for my liking — and she'd taken our drink orders, I smiled at him. "So how was your week?"

"It was good," he said, peering up at me and briefly meeting my eyes. "I was…" He hesitated, shifting around in his seat, then went on slowly, "I was looking forward to this." He winced a little, like he was expecting me to tell him that was wrong.

"That makes two of us." I wanted to reach out and touch him, maybe put my hand on his, but that was probably too much. "I'll admit I held back. Otherwise I'd have texted you more this week. It's been a while since I've dated, and I had no idea when I'd cross the line into being annoying."

He blinked owlishly at me, the tiny smile returning to his lips. "You can text me," he said. "I was sort of afraid to text you. I didn't want to be annoying either."

"I thought I'd look a bit stalkerish." I shrugged. "Since we didn't have the most conventional start, I figured I had to be on my best behavior."

"Were you on your best behavior the other night, too?" he asked, tilting his head as he looked at me.

I got lost in the green of his eyes. How could they be so big and innocent and —

Focus, Carter.

I swallowed, bringing my brain back on track. That was a hard question. "I think so. Although I probably should've given you a bit more personal space. So let's say I was fairly well-behaved?"

"You make it sound like you're partially housebroken," he said. Then he paused, flinched, and hung his head, like he was afraid I might get angry for those words. "I'm sorry. That was rude. I was just joking."

I smiled at him. "I'm not upset. I think you're cute."

His shoulders lost a bit of their tension, which I probably wouldn't have noticed if I hadn't watched him so closely. But this was the only way to have a chance at figuring out what was going on in his mind.

"I just have a hard time deciding how to respond to you. Part of me wants to pull you close and tell you everything will be fine no matter what the problem is, and the other part is trying not to scare you off because I know how new this is for you." My eyes met his, which were staring at me like I'd just told him a secret. He didn't react otherwise, so I continued, hoping I didn't mess that up completely. "So I go back and forth and keep questioning what to do."

"You sound like me," he said dryly, but in the same moment, he found the table way more interesting than my eyes.

A cute blush blossomed on his cheeks, and he hung his head. Would he continue or just stop speaking altogether? Should I say more, or had I already crossed lines I shouldn't have crossed, scaring him away?

He sat on your lap, drinking from a sippy cup. And he still met you for dinner. Stop worrying so much!

Micah interrupted my train of thought by speaking. Even though I had to strain my ears to hear him, at least he spoke. "But I like this. I want this. I just…" He paused. "I'd like to see you again. And text me, and do stuff. Just — I don't think I could handle… other things in public. Not here. But…" There was a hopeful but terrified look on his face. "I'm happy I came."

Nope, I would not answer what was on the tip of my tongue. No sexual innuendos yet. "I'm glad. And yes, I will be a very well behaved dog while we're here." I grinned as his blush deepened even more. Just how red could this boy get? I needed to find out. "Just don't expect me to wear a tail."

He blanched, burying his face in his hands. "I can't imagine you on the floor with the pups," he said, voice muffled. "I think you just broke my brain."

Well, apparently there was a point when he turned from red to white. Good to know. I liked teasing him a bit, especially since it seemed to make him relax, so I'd continue. "You don't think I'd be a cute pup? I think you've hurt my feelings." I didn't hold back my smile.

"No, I meant—" He frowned at me, like it'd taken him a moment to realize what my smile meant. "Oh, that's playing dirty."

"Don't think you fooled me. You still didn't say I'd be cute."

"You'd be… like a guard dog," Micah said, averting his eyes briefly before peeking back at me. He searched my expression then went on, "But a cute guard dog?"

Now I laughed out loud. This boy was too much. "Cute guard dog? Is that even a thing?" At the same time, I finally gave in and reached over to take his hand and squeeze it gently. "Thank you. But would I be a sexy guard dog as well?"

"That's not fair," he complained, squeezing my hand back.

"Do I have to be fair?" I sat back and smiled. "If I do, that's fine. I just like seeing you smile, and I may enjoy it when you blush."

"You *may*," he repeated with a small scoff. He watched me. Currently, he wasn't even red, which was a bit of a shame. "It's okay. You're sort of cute when you tease me. The jury's still out on sexy." He paused then added, almost stumbling over the words, "I mean, not that you're not. You are. I just…"

He blushed again, but this time, he looked helpless, and I took pity on him.

"I understand." But then since I had to be on my best behavior, I sighed. His hand still rested in mine, warm and soft. "I wanted to grab my chest and dramatically complain that you didn't find me as sexy as I find you. But I'm on my best behavior. So I won't do that."

"Wait, what?" he asked, blinking at me. "Sexy?" He laughed, shaking his head. "Maybe cute at best."

With others, I might've thought he was fishing for compliments, but he genuinely didn't seem to believe me.

"You're going to have to trust me on that, because if I gave you any details, you'd end up feeling uncomfortable. So yes, you're just going to have to believe me when I say sexy." Yeah, any explanations on that would end up making me hard and overwhelm him. I'd need some time to get him used to what I really wanted… and that what had happened at the bar was just the beginning. Or a very tame version, depending on how you see it.

"I… Okay," he said. There was that cute blush again. "No one's called me sexy before. Usually they just say I'm cute or adorable. Not something you'd like to be called, when you…" He stopped, looking down at his crisp, button-down shirt. "Well, at least the shirts help. A bit. If you think I'm…" He pulled his hand from mine, averting his eyes again. "I'm sorry. You don't want to hear that. I should just—"

What was up with the shirt? It was a bit overdressed, maybe a bit stiff, but if he liked it, why not wear it? He was young. He could get away with blue hair if he wanted to. A shirt didn't matter in the big picture. Once we knew each other a bit better, I'd have to ask him about it. But for now, I needed to say something else.

"I want to hear anything you want to share with me." That was one of the first things we needed to establish, and it was more important than his choice of shirts. "It doesn't matter if you think it's not something you usually tell a date or if you worry about how it will come across. I won't be upset. I promise."

I wanted to learn everything about him. Slightly stalkerish maybe, but he intrigued me. If he wanted to share about his past, I wanted to hear it.

"You're different," he said, meeting my eyes again. "I mean, I knew you were, but… You really are different." He bit his lip then tentatively offered, "I like that. I like you. Thank you for inviting me here tonight."

"I'm happy you took a chance. I know that wasn't easy." There was still so much about him I didn't know. Why was he so hesitant to date? Was it me? I doubted it. Somehow, I had the feeling I was an exception, even though I didn't want to flatter myself. I just doubted he'd dated much, and I hadn't even been sure he'd turn up. "I had fun the other night, and I was hoping you'd like to see me again."

"I'm glad I did," he said. He seemed about to speak again, but he paused when the waitress returned. He murmured a quiet thanks, took a sip of his drink, then looked back at me. "Tell me something about you?"

I tried to think of what to say. Most of my life was boring, but the more complicated parts were probably oversharing... even though I wanted to get everything about me out there. "Let's see. I teach adult education classes for people getting their GED and sometimes classes on learning English as a second language. So I have entirely too much free time during the day, but my evenings are usually pretty busy. Thankfully the weekends are day classes so going out at night isn't too hard." I paused. That was enough for now. It was a safe topic, nothing to scare him away — but it would show him there was more to me than the BDSM life. "Now, tell me something about you."

From the look on his face, I could tell he hadn't expected me to turn the question around, but he recovered after a moment. "I..." He considered. "I'm a student at the university."

I'd figured that much, but I nodded, gesturing for him to go on.

"I work at an animal shelter." His lips twitched. "With real animals. And I'm majoring in computer science. Programming."

"Is this something we can talk about once we know each other a bit better? I bet you have a few naughty fantasies about what a professor would do to you." I gave him my best innocent smile and picked up my glass to take a drink.

His eyes went wide, but he let out a breathless laugh. "Only about one," he said, blushing hard. "He was just..." He cleared his throat. "Anyway!"

I was surprised he actually admitted that much. The shy guy I'd met seemed to have more than a few layers.

"Programming sounds interesting. A lot of my students want to move in that direction."

"It's pretty cool," he said with a smile. "Just takes a neurotic sort of person to be good at it, I think."

His answer made me smile. There were a thousand jokes I could make about it, but I bit my tongue. As much as I wanted to see him blush and squirm, getting to know him and putting him at ease had to come first. "Any crazy hobbies like rock climbing or something that will completely overwhelm me? I'm hoping you say you're a homebody who likes watching movies, because that's pretty much my level of adventure lately."

It sounded boring, even to my own ears, but at the end of the day I simply liked being at home, especially if I had someone to spend time with. Then I'd be perfectly happy. The problem was that that hadn't happened in a long time. Nicholas had left a void that was hard to fill, if not impossible. I hadn't managed it, and if Micah was a candidate remained to be seen. For now, I'd enjoy his company, get to know him, then we'd see. Pushing away the memories, I focused on Micah.

"Skydiving," he said, his expression solemn.

Really? Or was he messing with me? I couldn't tell. Not even his lips — nice, full, sexy lips – twitched.

"Are you trying to see how good my heart is?" I lifted one eyebrow. "I'm not quite an old fart yet but telling me things like that will add years to my looks."

He couldn't keep a straight face for long. He laughed, and I found myself smiling along with him. "The most exciting thing I've done in the past year is going to a random bar, missing a sign, and meeting this really nice guy. Beyond that… Netflix."

"First of all, I'm going to say I'm relieved that you're not jumping out of planes. But second, I'm just going to say that eventually you and I are going to have a discussion about what happens to a naughty boy who teases his Daddy." I was assuming he was still interested in that part. It might have been bold, but the way he blushed and squirmed told me I wasn't that off course.

"I can be a lot naughtier," he said, but his blush deepened until his cheeks were a deep red. They couldn't get any darker. "I mean… Well." He stumbled over his own words, burying his face in his hands, even though he let out a little laugh. "I have no idea what I'm doing. It just felt like the right thing to say."

Reaching out again, I took his hand. "I love seeing the little glimpses of the real you. Don't be afraid to let that Micah out. I find you sweet and funny, and it wouldn't surprise me at all to find a wicked, teasing side just waiting to get out."

The man next to me had so many layers, and I couldn't wait to figure them all out. I just needed to remember that he might not be comfortable with moving too fast, considering he was a newbie to the scene. He was still very nervous about the date, so he most likely hadn't had that many good experiences. His friends had set him up, too, and he'd indicated he'd been bullied or at least pranked a lot. I needed to be careful.

"But there's no rush. As long as you're enjoying spending time with me, I'd like to keep seeing you." He stared at me with wide eyes. I wanted to pull him into my arms, but that would've been too soon. Holding hands was all I could do right then.

It took him a moment, but he never let go of my hand. "I… I think I'd like that. As long as *you* promise not to take *me* skydiving. I think I can handle the… you know, the Daddy thing," he said, his voice dropping a little in volume, "but that would give *me* a heart attack."

"I promise no skydiving." I squeezed his hand. "I'd kind of like to keep you in one piece."

I knew it was the Daddy side of me, but the idea of watching him do something like made my heart stop. I wasn't the most overbearing Dom I knew, but I had a protective streak slightly bigger than most traditional partners might have.

"I'd kind of like to stay in one piece, too." Micah found the table more interesting again, but he murmured, "I'd kind of like you to stay in one piece, too."

"Thank you." I let my fingers caress over his, trying to hold on to the moment.

It was a little awkward right now, with him stumbling over words and blushing all the time, but I'd take honest and awkward over smooth and practiced. I wanted to see the real Micah, nothing fake and nothing hidden.

The rest of the meal was filled with mundane chatter. The tension had drained from his shoulders, and his lovely eyes had brightened. By the time I paid the bill, he was stumbling less over his words.

I hadn't been sure at first how he'd feel about continuing the date, but he'd opened up enough for me to at least offer. As we sat inside, finishing our drinks, I asked him, "Do you want to see a movie with me?"

He blinked. "Um, sure. When?"

"Now?" I smiled at him.

"Oh." At first, I was afraid I'd pushed too far, but his cheeks flushed pink and he nodded to me. "I think I'd like that."

"Do you want to meet at the theater?" I would've been happy to drive us there, but I didn't want to push him too far. He might've gotten more comfortable with me, but there was always the chance he'd revert to the awkwardness he'd shown when we'd met up.

He nodded. "Okay."

If it bothered him to drive separately, or if he was relieved I hadn't offered to take him, it didn't show. "Then I'll meet you there."

I wanted to lean in and kiss him, but I wanted him to show up at the theater more. There would be time for kisses later.

Hopefully.

"See you there."

"You know, eventually I'm going to pester you until you let me pick you up." I walked up to meet him in the theater parking lot, worried that he'd have had too much time to think as we drove over from the restaurant. But he seemed fine.

He glanced up at me, looking startled. "You think you'd have to pester me?" he asked. "I mean… Did that sound too…" He fumbled over his words. "Um. Let me try that again. You're welcome to pester me about that, if you want to."

Smiling, I slowly reached out to take his hand. "Then you don't mind if I…" I wanted to word it right, but nothing felt perfect. Lacing my fingers through his, I tried to continue. "Take a little more control over things like that? I don't want to overwhelm you."

Micah swallowed hard. "I don't… I don't think you'll overwhelm me. It's kinda nice." He glanced back up to me. "I mean, if you really want to."

"I do." I squeezed his hand. "There's something about you that just pulls me in. I should probably be a bit more subtle, but all I want to do is to wrap you up and keep a smile on your face."

Yeah, I should've played it cooler and not reveal so much, but he'd somehow managed to run over my defenses. It had been years since I'd tried to hold my emotions back, and Micah had a way that left me without a choice. I couldn't hide from him. The last person who'd done that to me had been my partner a lifetime ago.

"I've never thought about someone taking care of me like that before," Micah said, not letting go of my hand. "It's just a little strange. Not bad-strange, just… different." He hesitated, then squeezed my hand back.

"Different isn't bad." I gave him a smile and pulled him closer so his shoulder brushed against my arm. "I just want you to let me know if something makes you uncomfortable, or if my taking control frustrates you. I don't want this to be all about what makes me happy. You're my priority."

"I…" Micah hesitated. "This is okay." He pressed against me. "I just… I don't want you to feel obligated or anything."

As we stepped up to the sidewalk at the side of the building, I stopped and pulled him into my arms. I kept my hold light, but I drew him against my body until he was flush against me. Looking down at him, I pictured the sweet, shy boy who'd curled up on my lap and tried to color the perfect picture. I remembered how he'd cautiously flirted at dinner and had slowly tried to open up.

I brought one hand up and combed my fingers through his hair. "Does this feel like obligation to you? I won't push for more and I can control myself, but I don't want you to question how I feel."

"No, it doesn't… But I'm not really the best judge of character," Micah said, looking up at me. "So I'm going to just have to assume you're telling me the truth. Because you are, right?"

His expression was so earnest. Why did he even have to ask? Had his past experiences been that bad?

I cupped his face, still holding him tight against me. "I will always tell you the truth. No matter what. No matter if you're the man I'm dating or the little boy curled up on my lap, that will never change."

"Thank you," he said, offering me a faint smile.

That confirmed my suspicions. Someone had really hurt my sweet boy. From his uncertainty and fears, probably numerous people. I just hoped he'd eventually understand that I'd never be one of them.

"I don't want to push you, so I want you to tell me if this is none of my business, but… it seems like you've had some bad relationships in the past."

Micah paused then slowly shook his head. "Not really…" he said hesitantly. "I don't have much experience with those, or um… you know… any. I just don't have a whole lot of luck with people in general."

I nodded, trying to read between the lines. "Well, I don't think luck has anything to do with how we treat each other. That's based on someone's personality. Our meeting might not have been the most traditional experience, but I'll always treat you with respect."

"How did I find someone like you?" he asked softly, pressing his face against my hand. He turned his head, lips brushing my palm.

"Because I needed something wonderful in my life and you were obviously the perfect person for that." Running my fingers through his hair, I leaned down, bringing my face closer to his.

He tilted his head, taking a deep breath, but he didn't pull away. If anything, he moved closer, looking at me through those long lashes like he was expecting something — like he knew something was about to happen but wasn't sure what to do about it.

Taking his stillness as permission, even though I probably shouldn't have, I let my lips brush over his. It wasn't even a kiss, more like a caress. Reluctantly pulling back, I ran my finger down his cheek and over his beautifully full lips.

His breath caught, but he didn't pull away. He made a soft sound, like he wanted to continue, but I didn't want to push him too fast.

"The movie's probably about to start," I said. He nodded, and I wrapped my arm around him. I didn't want him to think I was pushing him away at all, especially not after he'd kissed me just as lightly as I'd kissed him. "I'm looking forward to the movie. You want to know why?"

"Yeah," he said, a little tentatively. "Is it supposed to be really good?"

"I have no idea." I kissed his forehead. "I'm just looking forward to holding my boy in the dark for the next two hours. And if I'm lucky, there'll be some scary scenes where you jump into my arms."

He scoffed. "I'm great at watching scary movies. You'll probably be the one jumping into my arms."

Laughing, I nodded. "Will you hold me if I get scared? Are you going to protect me?"

Grinning at me, he said, "Yes, I'll protect you from the big bad movie screen."

"That means you're going to have to hold me tight and be prepared to kiss me if I'm scared."

"Promise," he said solemnly, though his lips twitched into a smile again.

"Let's go claim our seats before all the good ones are taken," I told him. The ones in the back. Where no one could see us.

He nodded, and I squeezed his shoulders before letting him go. I pushed back the frustration that started to grow when he moved away. No matter how right it felt, he needed space and time to decide what was happening between us. Besides, I wouldn't have to let him go for long. Soon enough, he'd be back in my arms.

It might have been our first date, but I knew it wouldn't be our last.

CHAPTER FOUR

MICAH

It had been a romantic comedy, and there hadn't been any scary parts at all — at least, I didn't think so. It had been impossible to focus on the movie when Carter was there next to me. His hand kept sliding to the back of my neck then the small of my back, massaging and caressing until I boldly put up the armrest between us so I could snuggle against him.

I probably shouldn't have been so surprised when he'd texted me asking for me to join him for a picnic, but even after our few soft, sweet shared kisses, I hadn't known what to expect.

It had been so long since I'd been on a date, let alone one I'd enjoyed as much as I had the other night...

My smile faltered, threatening to fade, and I forced myself to stop thinking about that particular occasion. I had Carter now, at least for a little while. Until he grew tired of me, like all the others.

I shook my head a little, scanning the park in front of me. I didn't want to get out of the car first and try to figure out where he wanted to sit. I was too afraid I'd choose wrong and upset him, and I didn't want to ruin what we'd started to build up.

It wasn't until I saw him stride up to a spot under a tree and lay down an honest-to-gods blanket that I took the key from the ignition. Really? I couldn't help but smile again. He was such a romantic. It felt impossible that he could even be real.

I finally got out of the car, locking it behind me, and headed over to him.

It was a warm, sunny day, perfect for a picnic, though not many couples were around. I'd expected more people, but aside from a few lying on the green, reading and enjoying the sun, the park was surprisingly empty. Nice. At least we couldn't be overheard if the conversation turned to more... sensitive topics.

I paused a few feet away from him, offering a tentative wave.

He looked up and smiled at me. Immediately, he stood up, closed the distance between us, and pulled me into his arms. My breath caught. I may have tensed up, but when I felt him starting to pull away, I wrapped my arms around him and snuggled closer. I inhaled deeply, resting my cheek against his shoulder. He always smelled so good.

"Hi," I whispered.

"Hi, back." Carter spoke just as quietly, his lips brushing against my ear.

I shivered as his hot breath moved over my skin, wanting to turn up my head to get a proper greeting, but I didn't dare. Yes, he'd kissed me once at the movies, then again to say good night, but... he'd initiated it both times.

So I leaned my head on his shoulder, just enjoying his embrace.

For a moment, we stood there, then he gently nudged me back. "Okay?" he asked.

I offered him a smile.

He looked so gentle and sweet at me, like he thought I was the most precious thing at all. Crazy, that thought.

Resting one hand on my cheek, he drew me closer, raising my face a bit more. Would he — yes. He would. Carter leaned in and kissed me, and I melted against him all over again. It was short and sweet, just like the others we'd exchanged at the movies, and I caught myself aching to chase his lips as soon as it was over.

But Carter had other plans. He pulled me toward the blanket he'd spread out then offered me his hand.

"Such a gentleman." I couldn't help but tease him, but a grin stretched my lips as I took his hand and he helped me down onto the ground.

The warmth of his body pressed against my own as he followed, sitting beside me — way too close than two friends would sit, but it was perfect for me. His warmth radiated from his leg to mine, and we both faced the spacious green of the park. Here, no one sat, so we were basically alone.

"What do you want to start with? I have fresh fruit, something to drink, sandwiches, sweets…"

"Um…." Drinking first? Would he have a sippy cup for me? Did I *want* him to have one? "Something to drink, then some fruit, I'd say."

Again, he took over, handing me a couple of cups. Regular ones, with no sippy cup in sight. Was I disappointed about it or relieved? I couldn't pinpoint the feeling inside, but Carter didn't give me any time to think about it, because he poured juice in both cups.

He took one from me, and I sipped slowly from the other. I couldn't tell if he didn't want to do anything in public like we'd done… that first night in the bar… or if he was just going slow, but I didn't want to bring it up. So I just smiled and drank, trying to sort out how I actually was feeling. It was something I'd done a lot since meeting him. More than the past few years, when I'd actually tried to *not* feel anything at all.

A quick glance at Carter revealed he was watching me, an unreadable look in his eyes.

I tilted my head a bit more, looking at him. What should I say now? I had no idea what he was thinking.

"We said we'd be honest with each other, right?" I asked slowly. Or something like that. I couldn't remember exactly, but it felt like a good rule… as long as I was asking him the questions, anyway, which felt a bit hypocritical. Something to think about later. "So…" I hesitated then shook my head. "Never mind. I'm sorry. That was… not okay."

Carter smiled at me, the way a… a daddy would smile at his kid. Fuck me.

"What wasn't okay? And yes, we said we'd be honest with each other. You can ask me anything, and I expect honesty in return from you. You can let me know if you don't want to talk about something, but don't lie to me." He sounded stern, really like a daddy.

It did strange things to my insides, since he wasn't hard and cold, but… caring? How was that possible? He laid down rules, explained what he expected from me, but it still sounded so warm. This man was messing with my brain. And my body. And everything.

"I just… I want to know what you're thinking," I admitted. "You look like you're so deep in thought, and you keep looking at me. I don't know enough about you to figure things out yet."

"We'll get there. And it's really okay to ask me whatever you want to know." He looked away for a second, but then his eyes met mine again. "I was thinking how beautiful you are. You're so sweet and innocent-looking, but I'm sure there are a lot more layers I haven't seen yet. I'm looking forward to getting to know all of them. The sweet boy, the funny boy, the naughty boy… you get where I'm going." He smiled at me, slowly wrapping his arm around my waist. He wasn't really pulling me closer, just letting it sit there and showing me he was holding me.

I rested against him, unable to keep myself from blushing. "I'm not sure there's really a naughty boy here."

Then again…

"It's gonna be fun finding that out then. I think there is, but if not…" He shrugged. "I don't mind. As long as I get to know you, I'm good."

"Why are you so keen on getting to know me? What do you see?"

He pulled me a little closer. "I like you. That's all. I like not only your looks, but your humor, your personality, everything. Just the way you are."

I really doubted that. No one ever did. "Even though I'm a nervous wreck?" I asked him, not looking at him. "I know I'm a mess."

"You aren't. I haven't seen anything that's a mess."

"Are we talking about the same person here?" I still couldn't look at him.

"If we're talking about you, yes."

"I still don't get it." The well-known blush crept over my face, and I knew I sounded like I was fishing for compliments, but I honestly wasn't. I just didn't understand him. And I waited for him to realize there was nothing there to get to know and to drop me.

He squeezed me tighter. "Look at me, Micah."

I slowly turned my head, now burning even more. My eyes met his, even though it took me a moment to work up the courage.

Carter raised his hand, caressing my cheek. As always, he moved slowly, giving me time to pull away. I didn't. I leaned closer, welcoming his touch. The tenderness was what threw me off. He was older, more experienced than I was — as if that was a hardship to find — and good-looking. Hell, he was sexy.

"I want you to see how I see you one day. If you let me, I'll try to show you. For now, can we try to stick with the *no lying* rule?"

I nodded. Where would this conversation go?

"Okay, the honest answer? I find you beautiful. Inside and outside. And until I can show you, try to believe me."

I shook my head, then nodded. "I'll try, okay?"

Carter's brown eyes were still so warm and kind. How could anyone have such deep eyes? "Thank you, my sweet boy." He leaned down, brushing yet another kiss over my lips.

I wanted a real one, one with tongue and all that, like you saw in the movies. I wanted to get at least that done so I could stop freaking out about it.

But no. Not with Carter. He seemed to be content with those simple, barely there touches. And I surely wouldn't be able to initiate a kiss like that.

Carter picked up a strawberry, holding it up. "Is that okay? Any allergies?"

I shook my head. "No. And is what okay?"

He moved his hand, holding the strawberry to my lips. Oh. Oh. *This*. I couldn't answer. But I could part my lips, and while it probably looked everything but sexy, I managed to take a bite of the fruit. It was sweet and juicy, a fully ripe strawberry. Tasty. Licking my lips, I met his eyes again, trying to appear sexy. This was what he wanted, right?

"Good boy. Just like this. I'm gonna feed you some more, okay?"

Good boy.

It sent a shiver through me, and I knew he'd be able to see it as much as feel it.

"Okay," I whispered, setting down my cup. I stared at the fruit he had in a small bowl, with everything cut up into small pieces. *Perfect for feeding someone.*

Words were lost somewhere, because my brain needed time to process the *good boy* and the fact that he liked me, and that he was feeding me, and I was allowing him to feed me, and—

He held up an apple slice, interrupting my train of thoughts.

I ate it, managing to touch his fingers in the process. That was way sexier than I'd thought, and I wanted more of it.

"You okay?" Carter held up my cup. I took it and sipped from it.

"Yeah. Strange, somehow, but nice." There, I'd managed to speak.

"Good. If anything isn't okay, tell me." With that, he picked up a cherry, so dark it was nearly black. "Let's feed you some more, my sweet boy."

I could so get used to this.

I knelt in the grass, calling Snowflake over. The big white dog bounded toward me, stopping just shy of barreling me over, and happily licked my nose. I made a face, laughing, and pulled back enough to keep him from getting spit all over my face. He tried again, and I scratched him behind his ears. "Down," I told him.

Reluctantly, he got down, but his tail began wagging when I urged him onto his back so I could scratch his belly. His tail thumped against the grass, one of his legs starting to twitch, and I grinned as I worked to get it to move properly.

This was the best part of helping at the animal shelter, and the worst. I got attached to the animals, and seeing them go to different homes could be hard. Snowflake was a little special, and he'd been here for over a year. I wished I could take him home, but I didn't have room for a small dog, let alone a big one.

Maybe when I got a place of my own…

Reluctantly, I stood up, patting Snowflake. He looked at me with big, mournful puppy eyes, whining. I shook my head. "It's time to go back inside," I told him even though I wished we could stay out longer. He didn't get nearly enough attention, no matter how many times I brought him out. I had others to take care of, too.

I took him back inside and grabbed the next dog, taking her out, and I enjoyed the feeling of the sunlight on my face. I didn't get to go outside much. I spent most of my time at a computer. I liked working here, though. I got to play with animals and call it work, and I didn't have to deal with many people. My coworkers were friendly, but I kept my distance and they kept theirs.

I didn't usually mind, but in the wake of my date with Carter, I found myself wishing I had company. The dogs were great, but there had been something wonderful about just getting to talk to another human being.

Then again, I didn't think my coworkers would understand…

I finished out my day and went to my car, grabbing my phone and sending a text to Carter.

"Just wanted to say hi."

His response came back quickly.

"Hi, how was work?"

I smiled, leaning back in the driver's seat.

"It was good. How are you doing?"

A picture came back, making me laugh. A little dog seemed to be yawning and looked terribly bored.

"I'm in a staff meeting. Normally these aren't bad but this one is killing me."

I took a moment to think, typing out one reply after another before finally just hitting send.

"Wish I could keep you entertained. :-) I can think of a few ways to make the meeting more interesting."

Like sending him funny memes. Or telling him jokes. Or maybe making plans for the next date. There were several long seconds before Carter's reply popped up on my screen.

"I'm trying to tell myself you didn't mean that like it probably sounded, but I have to tell you that this meeting has just become a lot more interesting. Because of you I can no longer stand up without shocking people. Naughty boy. ;-)"

For a moment, I sat there, baffled. I hadn't meant it that way, not at all. But now I could see how I'd done it. I blushed even though Carter wasn't there to see it, trying to figure out what to say. There had been a winking face though…

I wanted him to feel comfortable enough to tease me. He treated me like I was made of glass, and while I liked it to a point… I didn't want to be treated that way forever. Maybe it was a good thing I'd unintentionally had more of an effect than I'd thought I would.

At the same time, though, I wasn't sure what I was inviting.

"Maybe later? To reward you for behaving during your meeting?"

What was I *doing*? I knew better. I had no idea what I was getting myself into.

"I mean dinner or something?" I quickly added.

Carter must've understood I had no idea what I was doing with the sexy flirting.

"That sounds great. I'm going to be here at least another hour. Does that work for you?"

There was a part of me that was disappointed Carter had backed off so quickly, but I didn't know what to say to get the playful man back. I sighed, leaning back in the seat.

"That'll give me time to get the smell of dog off me. Unless you like that."

Carter was back to cautiously flirting when he texted back.

"Not really my thing, but if that's what you like, then I might be willing to talk about it. If I'm being honest though there are other things I'd rather do with you."

"Like what?"

A picture of a man lying on the ground popped up on my phone with a short note.

"You're killing me."

Then a slightly more serious response.

"Do you want the PG-13 version or the R one?"

I was touched by the thoughtfulness of the reply. It was strange to have someone so determined to look out for my best interests, and I was torn. On one hand, I wasn't sure I could handle the R-rated answer. On the other, my curiosity was killing me.

I paused for a moment, taking in a deep breath. I squeezed my eyes closed, trying to figure out just what I wanted to say — or do.

"I'm too curious to pass up the R-rated one," I admitted.

Carter's next text had me laughing.

"This is the best meeting I've had in ages. Just an FYI. We're putting my next one on your calendar."

I grinned, but I wasn't quite as prepared for the sexy text that followed — even though I'd encouraged it.

"I would much rather be kissing your neck, working my way to much lower places if I was with grown up Micah... and if I was with my boy I think I'd rather be giving you a bath. I bet you're a dirty boy after being around all those puppies."

What had I gotten myself into? I rubbed a hand across my face, hoping no one would pay attention to the guy in the car who was blushing his ass off. I'd wanted to know, but at the same time...

At the same time, I was fascinated and terrified all at once. The idea of being bathed by someone else was both enticing and odd, but I could imagine his hands on me as he ran the cloth along my skin... That sounded tempting, whether I was his little or not.

Well, now he was no longer the only one who'd have a hard time standing up in front of people.

I had no idea what to say, but if I left him hanging too much, he'd think I was upset — and I wasn't. Just... surprised.

"All I can think of is other kinds of puppies... I think I've been ruined. :-)"

Not great, but it was better than letting him think I was mad or not replying at all. And I had no idea how I really wanted to respond to his words.

"LMAO some of them would hump you until you were dirty, too, so be warned."

Blushing furiously, I had to think again before replying.

"You're not even here to see me blush!"

That didn't seem to bother him.

"But I can picture you pink and squirming as you try to decide what to say. You look so innocent, but that's just hiding the wicked side wanting to come out."

Did I have a wicked side? He'd implied that before. I'd never thought of myself that way before, but I'd enjoyed teasing him a little. I loved the idea that I could have that kind of effect on him.

It was flattering and arousing, and I wished he was there so I could kiss him until he stopped teasing me.

"You just want to see me pink and squirming from other things."

My own boldness surprised me, and I groaned. What the hell was I doing?

His reply came back so fast I could only imagine that everyone in the meeting had to know he wasn't paying attention any longer.

"I like the way you think. Is that a hint about what you're curious about? Have you been so naughty by texting me dirty things that you need to be punished?"

I had no idea what he meant by punishments, not at first.

My punishments had always been a skipped dinner or time in my room alone. I didn't see them as something I wanted, not at all.

It dawned on me after a moment. What would you do with a naughty child? Spank him. The idea should've had my erection wilting, but I squirmed even more at the idea of being over his lap...

"Now who's being naughty?"

Carter eased off a bit but seemed to understand I wasn't too uncomfortable, just a bit confused.

"LOL You because you started this conversation and got me all worked up. I was just sitting here in a boring meeting."

Why was it easier to text these things than it was to say them in person? I felt bolder, more self-assured... probably because I didn't have to see his face. I could wonder what he was really thinking, but it was different.

"#sorrynotsorry. :-)"

Carter's next reply took several long seconds to come back, making me nervous again.

"Okay escaped earlier than I thought. Evidently I was not the only one who was bored because my boss just kind of wandered off lol."

Then before I could figure out what to say, another message popped up.

"Since you're not sorry does that mean you want to continue this conversation in person or is this a text only thing? Don't forget you promised to have dinner with me."

I dropped my head down, banging my forehead against the steering wheel. How did I get myself into these things? How was it that Carter could bring out such a bold part of me, one that I hadn't even thought existed?

"Maybe we can text in the same room if you want to continue it?"

It sounded pathetic, but it was so much easier this way.

"Deal. Sounds perfectly reasonable."

As I relaxed, another text came up.

"Don't forget food while you're worrying about what kinds of dirty things I'm going to bring up next."

Food. Right. That was a part of dinner. I'd probably end up choking if he continued this, but I wanted to see it.

I wanted to know he really wanted me.

I'd been used before, but oddly, I didn't think he wanted to do that. He was too… earnest, too kind, too gentle. Maybe it was an act, but I doubted it. It felt too sincere for that.

"Are you trying to kill me?"

I laughed at his response.

"If that turns you on then the answer is yes."

I shook my head, even though I was smiling.

"You're so thoughtful and obliging."

Grinning, his next text didn't surprise me at all.

"That's what daddies are for."

Daddies. That was still so foreign to me, but I wanted to learn.

"Shouldn't you get something out of this too? It sounds pretty one-sided."

I may have asked something similar before, but I was still having a hard time wrapping my mind around why this was appealing to him. If he was catering to me, did he really like it, or was it just that he expected something crazy in return?

"I get a lot out of caring for someone. To me it doesn't seem one-sided at all. Think of it as each of us giving the other what they need."

What they needed. What *we* needed. Did I need it?

I thought about the way I'd felt when he'd held me, when he'd taken care of me even the smallest amount. I'd been so relaxed with him as he'd taken charge and let me just... be. I didn't do that often.

"It may take me some time to wrap my mind around that. But... I like it."

I wasn't sure how he would respond but when the message came up, it made me smile.

"I'm glad. I want you to be happy with our relationship as well. I'm enjoying getting to know you and seeing where this goes."

I was too. My erection had stopped being such a distraction, and I breathed out, glancing at the time. I'd been sitting out in the parking lot for a while now.

"Me too. I should probably drive home and shower though so you aren't thinking about puppies when we see each other."

"You know you just put the image of you showering in my head? What am I going to do with a naughty boy who keeps teasing me?"

Then as if the sexy text had never existed, another one came in.

"Where do you want to eat?"

I groaned. I didn't want to have to make the decision. I hated making decisions. I was always afraid that I'd choose the wrong thing, and with him... I didn't want to go wrong. Besides, wasn't that one of the things a daddy ought to do?

"How about you choose and surprise me? :-)"

There. Now I couldn't get it wrong, and we'd get to go somewhere he enjoyed. I could find something anywhere, even if it meant ordering off the kid's menu...

And that thought should not have been so alluring.

"Then I'm going to choose to make dinner for my boy. Will an hour give you enough time to clean up and come over?"

I realized I had no idea where he lived, but it wouldn't take me long — even though I intended to make just one stop on the way home.

"I'm not sure where you live, but probably."

His address and another text came up quickly.

"I'm not far from the university so it probably won't take you long. Chicken okay with you?"

I smiled, nervous but at the same time still excited. Going to his house seemed like a big step, but it would be easier to have a private conversation.

"That's fine. I'd say I'm easy, but your mind is already in the gutter. :-)"

Why had I sent that? I groaned. What the hell was I doing?

"Only because you dragged it there. But that's fine. I wouldn't say you're easy though. I'd say complicated but worth the wait."

His words made me feel warm inside, comforted. He was really good at reassuring me, which was probably why I was bolder than usual.

"Thank you."

I wanted to add a smiley face, but I felt like I'd overdone those. I paused, then added a second text.

"I'm going to head home and shower. I'll text you when I'm on my way."

A little bit cheeky, a little bit sweet, his reply made me smile and squirm.

"Drive carefully. I want my boy to make it over in one piece. And Micah? Not too much fun in the shower. ;-)

What was I getting myself into?

Why was my body very interested in the idea of him giving me an order like that? I'd planned to get myself off in the shower so I wouldn't be distracted… But I had a feeling he wanted me to be distracted.

"See you soon. :-)"

I finally turned the car on, taking a deep breath as I headed out of the parking lot. Okay. This was okay. This was better than okay. He was so experienced, and I felt like I was lost — but he was there to guide me to safety, too.

I stopped at the Walgreens near my house, grabbing one item and feeling more than a little self-conscious. I didn't know if he'd like it or not, or if it was appropriate or not, but I figured it was worth a try.

If I got up the nerve, I'd ask what he thought... assuming he didn't just tell me.

I threw the bag in the passenger seat, shaking my head at myself, but I'd already committed to it. I started the car again, heading home.

When I got home, I got into the shower, the washcloth lingering a little too long on my half-hard cock. But I remembered what he'd said. I wasn't going to disobey, especially when I still wasn't sure just what kind of punishments he'd want to dole out — or if I was really interested in them, or if it had been a fluke.

When I got out, I pulled the baby powder out of the bag, staring at it for a long time before taking a deep, shaky breath and dusting myself with it. It smelled good, if a bit out of place on me, but it felt... right.

I hoped it was.

CHAPTER FIVE

CARTER

"Chicken… chicken… chicken and… what?" When I'd picked chicken earlier, I hadn't thought about what I'd cook. "He's just coming over for dinner. It's not like he expects a four-course meal. He's a college student, for heaven's sake. He'd probably be happy with ramen."

Taking a deep breath, I did my best to stop overthinking and studied the cabinets.

"Okay, I'm going to grill the chicken and then make an alfredo sauce with some pasta." And I was going to stop talking to myself so I didn't look crazy.

With that decision made, I did a quick cleanup through the house. At least I wasn't too messy, so I didn't have to do a thorough cleaning. Instead of waiting inside and pacing around, I headed outside to wait for him. After what must've been hours — even though I knew it wasn't — I spotted his small car coming down my street.

The house was close to the university and not far from town, but it backed up to undeveloped state land and felt like it was farther out in the country than it really was.

As he pulled in, I saw him glance nervously at the house. He seemed to be giving himself a little pep talk so I tried to give him some privacy while he took another deep breath. When he finally got out of the car, I started down the stairs.

"I hope it was easy to find."

Micah nodded. "It was. Thank you." He offered me a crooked, nervous smile as he met me at the bottom of the stairs. "I really appreciate this," he said. "It was nice of you to invite me over."

The confidence he'd shown in the texts had abated, but I'd get him to relax if I gave him time. Once he was relaxed, the bolder side might come out again.

"I'm just glad you're here. While I love texting with you, I like to see you smile, not just imagine it." Stepping closer, I gave him a lot of warning but when he didn't move away, I leaned in and kissed him. "Welcome to my home."

He smelled like he'd just stepped out of the shower… And was that a hint of baby powder I detected?

Instead of pulling away, I leaned down and kissed his neck. Yes, it was baby powder. God, that smelled good. Between that and the feeling of him in my arms, I grew harder in my jeans. I wanted to cuddle him, have him on my lap, maybe even bathe him and put new powder on him. On the other hand, I just wanted to kiss him, draw him closer, and get him off.

He'd known what he was doing when he'd added it. This wasn't a coincidence. He wanted to let me know something. Was he ready for more? Or was it his way of telling me he was okay with the Daddy/little thing in general?

Hell if I knew. But asking him outright would probably make him too nervous to even speak, if he didn't leave my house completely. Despite being way more relaxed than when we first met, his shoulders still showed his tension.

I stepped back, getting myself — or him — to safety before I jumped him. "Come on in. Let me show you around before I get distracted by how good you smell."

His breath caught, and he stepped closer to me again, pressing himself against me before seeming to realize what he was doing. He looked at me with wide, questioning eyes, and I smiled at him. He relaxed a bit, the whole silent exchange taking only seconds.

"Okay," Micah said, his voice stronger. "I'd like that."

Taking his hand, I started leading him toward the house. "Tour first and then I'm going to start working on dinner. It doesn't taste as good when you keep it warm, so it's not ready yet. But it shouldn't take long to put together. I hope you're not in any hurry. I forgot to ask if you had to be anywhere tonight."

He followed me, squeezing my hand as we went through the front door. He shook his head. "No, it's fine. I don't have any other plans."

I gave him a smile. "Good. Then there's no rush."

Shutting the door as we headed in, I led him through to the living room. "It's pretty open plan." I pointed across the room to the kitchen and then toward the back. "The property butts up against some state land, so it has a lot of privacy."

I believed the room was relaxing and inviting with its oversized couch and earth tones throughout the space, but I couldn't read what he was thinking. As we walked over to the stairs, I gestured down a long hallway. "Guest bedroom and bath down there, and the rest of the rooms upstairs."

"It's really nice in here," he said, glancing around us. "I'm used to dorm rooms, so this is just huge by comparison." He laughed, shaking his head. "One of these days, I'm going to get a real house with a real yard so I can have a dog."

"It's more space than I need, but I fell in love with the porch and the property as soon as I saw it." Keeping a hold of his hand, I led him up the stairs. I wanted him to see the house, but I also wanted to let him know nothing was off limits for him. I didn't have secrets I intended to keep from him.

I pointed to an open door as we walked down the hall. "Another small bedroom that I use as an office."

He nodded but didn't comment. Did he like the house? Or was he intimidated by the size? It was spacious, but that was okay, right? I hoped it was. A quick glance at him revealed that he was looking around with big eyes, taking in all the rooms, but a small smile played on his lips. So he liked it, most likely.

"Another bathroom and there's the master bedroom." I paused so he could look through the door. It wasn't huge, but there was room for a king-sized bed and one of my favorite oversized chairs in the corner.

Trying to see through his eyes, I pondered whether the room was too plain, but I liked the simple wood furniture and the navy bedspread stretched across the mattress. "Kind of boring, but I spend more time downstairs than up here."

"It's not boring," he said, shaking his head. "It's really nice."

"Thanks." I squeezed his hand then leaned close again to give him another quick kiss.

Down the hall was the last bedroom. This was the only one I didn't want to show him, but it also was the one I needed him to see.

Familiar sadness hit as I opened the door, but it wasn't as bad. The first few months, I hadn't even managed to open the door. Then I'd just used it to stack boxes in it, sure I wouldn't find someone else to play with. "This used to be a nursery and play-room, but it got packed up in the past few years."

The room was still the same light blue that I'd originally picked, but instead of shelves filled with toys, the room was mostly empty but for a few boxes in the corner. Only the huge crib, the changing table, and the dresser, decorated with blue elephants and yellow giraffes, told the story of the room's past.

"Nursery," he repeated.

"Yeah. I… Um, I decided to add one, when I bought the house. It was easier to play, you know?"

Micah nodded. "I guess?" His eyes scanned the room, no doubt taking in the furniture. I could see Nicholas there, playing, napping, all the happy times we'd had together. Swallowing hard, I turned away. No matter how much time passed, the memories lingered. Maybe Micah would be the one to chase them away, but I wasn't sure yet.

Could they even be chased away? Or replaced? Or would the room forever remind me of Nicholas, no matter what I did?

He looked back at me, a silent question in his gaze, but he didn't ask. It didn't matter. I knew what he was wondering.

"My husband died just over two years ago." I studied the room. "He was my partner and my little for a long time." But no one wanted to hear about ex-lovers or dead spouses, so I forced my emotions back and smiled. "You ready for dinner?"

He looked at me, his expression softening. I braced myself, expecting to see pity in his eyes, but they just showed understanding. He touched my arm and rested his head against my shoulder. The smell of baby powder rose to my nose again. This time, the sad memories mixed with the happier ones I had of the time I spent with Micah… and the time I had with Nic.

"I'm sorry for your loss." He wrapped his arms around my waist and pulled me closer. "It must hurt so much."

He stayed where he was, and I rested my cheek on his head. "Thank you. Yes, it does. But it's gotten better over time."

"That's good."

I pressed a kiss on his head. "But enough of the gloomy past. Dinner?"

"Yes. Can't wait for it."

"Good." I smiled, a little less forced, and the tightness in my chest eased. "I'm starving. Can't imagine you're doing better."

He nodded, not moving away from me. "I haven't eaten since breakfast," he admitted. Micah's voice was a bit muffled because he'd buried his head in my chest, but I managed to understand him. "I got too caught up at work to remember to take a lunch break."

"That's not good for you." Giving his hip a squeeze, I shook my head. "You need to make sure you're getting lunch."

"I know. I still manage to forget sometimes."

"Then let's get you fed." I released him.

Micah stepped back, too. I didn't want his first time here to be sad, but I'd also needed to show him the nursery… and tell him about Nic.

As we headed down the stairs and back to the kitchen, I was finally able to relax a bit. "So what kept you so busy you couldn't eat lunch?"

He blushed. "There was someone looking to adopt a kitten, and I talked him into getting an adult cat instead. It was worth the missed break to see Missy go to a good home."

The blush and shy smile did it. I pulled him into my arms again. "You're so sweet. Just don't forget that you're important too." With a kiss to his cheek, I released him and pointed to the table. "You sit down and tell me more about your day while I get dinner ready."

He hesitated. "Are you sure you don't need any help?" he asked.

"Honestly, I'd rather you talk to me. I'm curious about your week." As I put water on to boil and heated up the pan, I gave him a smile. "How are classes going?"

"They're going pretty well. I'm a senior, so I'm learning the stuff that's actually applicable now instead of the boring classes," he said, fidgeting in his chair.

"That's good." I went over to the fridge and grabbed the chicken and the broccoli. As I moved around the kitchen, I kept up a string of questions that were mostly random. It just seemed easier for him if I kept asking things.

When everything was almost ready and just needed a few more minutes to come together, I started to grab glasses out of the cabinet. Pausing, I looked over to Micah. "Regular glass or do you want to try the sippy cup again? I'm good either way."

"I think…" He paused then nodded. "I'd like to try the cup again. If that's okay."

"I like seeing you relaxed and enjoying yourself, so it will never be a problem for me." I reached for one of the cups I kept around the house for when my friends visited and set it on the counter. "Milk or apple juice?"

He glanced at the cup, pausing again before seeming to gather himself. "Milk, please. I can get it for myself, though. You don't have to get it for me."

Taking a moment, I went over to the table and crouched down so we were at eye level. I rested my hand on his leg. "I want to make sure this is clear. I like doing things for you. I understand this is all stuff you can do for yourself. I know you can make dinner and get yourself a drink and all that, but I like helping you and taking care of you. It makes me feel needed and… settles something in me. It's been a long time since I had anyone in my life. I need to know if I'm smothering you or doing something that makes you unhappy, but I'll never be upset about doing something for you, and I'll never think less of you because you let me take care of you."

Micah's expression flickered from my eyes to somewhere over my shoulder, back to my eyes then away again. It took him a few moments to answer. "I've always been responsible for myself," he said. "I'm not sure if I can let someone take care of me… I like the idea of it, but it's just weird."

"I can understand that." Too tempted by the thoughtful expression on his face, I leaned in and gave him a quick kiss. "That's why I need to know you'll tell me if there's something that you don't like. Deal?"

He kissed me back, less tentatively than I might've expected, and he reached out to touch my arm. "Deal. So far, there hasn't been anything I haven't liked. It's all new, but none of it has been bad."

I loved how he said it hadn't been bad… Coming from him, it was high praise, even though it sounded cute. "You can always tell me what you do like. If I know there's something that makes you happy, or content, or even turned on, I can do it more."

Would that lovely blush ever fade? I hoped not.

"I'm not used to telling someone what I like," he said, and though the words were a little sad, I appreciated them for their honesty. "But I'll try." He paused then bit his bottom lip, adding with uncertainty, "For you."

"That's all I can ask." I gave him another kiss, slower and longer that time. I'd gotten the impression he wasn't used to kissing, but I'd thought he was out of practice. Now, I wasn't sure how much experience he had at all. He came tentatively to the kiss at first, then more eagerly, letting out a soft sound against my lips. It was sloppy, but I didn't mind. "I can promise you nothing that you are curious about or like would shock me. Make sense?"

"Why, Carter, that sounds almost like a dare," he said, batting his eyelashes.

Oh, I liked that idea. "Yes. I dare you to tell me one thing that you've liked so far. Anything non-traditional that we've done or talked about."

"Um…" He tilted his head, thinking for a moment. "I liked coloring."

"Good." I kissed his forehead as I rose. "Now I know to make sure you color again."

He watched me with a curious expression but didn't object, so I headed back over to the counter and poured his milk and some water for myself. The sippy cup was a bit taller than the one he'd used at the bar, and it was green with dinosaurs on it. Hopefully, he'd like it.

Tightening the lid, I brought his cup and my glass over to the table and sat down beside him. "Dinner will be ready in just a minute." I paused, resting my hand on his. "I'm glad you could come over tonight. Once you started texting me, I really wanted to see you again."

"Technically, it was my idea," Micah pointed out, as he took the sippy cup from me. "But you were the one bold enough to invite me over."

"And you were bold enough to accept," I said, grinning at him.

"Touché," he replied. He took a sip from the cup, staring at it and tracing one of the dinosaurs with his finger.

"Besides, I was just too greedy to meet you in a restaurant. I wanted to kiss you more… which might not be that welcome in a restaurant. I think they'd frown if you ended up in my lap."

Now the tips of his ears brightened, and he stared at the sippy cup even harder. "I'm happy you invited me here," he said, finally setting the cup down in front of him. "It's nice to get a home-cooked meal every once in a while. There's not a whole lot I can do in the dorm room, and the cafeteria food isn't that good, especially for how expensive it is."

"You're always welcome here, even if it's just to escape the dorm and all you want to do is study." Most of the time the house was too quiet anyway. He wouldn't make much noise if he studied, but at least someone else would be here. "I like having you around."

He blinked at me. "I appreciate that."

I doubted he'd take me up on it now, but maybe he would in the future.

Giving him another kiss, I smiled and stood up. "Dinner smells ready."

As he drank his milk, I moved around the kitchen and finished up the food. When everything was plated and ready, I went back over to the table. "Dinner is served."

"It smells great," he said.

I set both plates down, close to my place and out of his reach. "You look like you're a little concerned that I'm going to feed it to you." I grinned and picked up the knife. "Don't worry. I just want to cut it up, then you can feed yourself." Then I shrugged. "But if the feeding thing is something you're interested in, just let me know."

His cheeks turned red. "I… haven't had someone feed me since I was a little kid." He paused, nibbling on his bottom lip.

I wanted to be the one nibbling on it, sucking on it, kissing him…

I nearly missed it when he said, "Yeah, okay. You can try to feed me if you want. Just… don't be offended if I start laughing or something."

My heart nearly stopped, then it beat twice as fast. My hand shook, and I put down the knife so he wouldn't notice what his simple offer did to me. "There's nothing wrong with reacting to how things make you feel." I started rearranging the plates again to make sure I could reach everything easily. "If it doesn't work, then we won't do it again, but I'm proud of you for telling me something you're curious about."

I needed to figure out some kind of reward for him, something my boy would love. That way, I could show him how proud I was because he trusted me. Sometimes, the words of praise weren't enough.

Studying the table, I reached over and grabbed a napkin. "I want you to close your eyes for a moment and just relax. There are no expectations and nothing to worry about. I just want you to remember how good it felt to sit in my lap. There were no obligations."

Micah gave me a skeptical look but slowly nodded and closed his eyes.

As he tried to relax, I opened up the napkin to use as a makeshift bib. "You've got a daddy who wants to take care of you. Your job is to let me do that. Nothing else."

"That seems impossible," he admitted. "I know you keep explaining it, but…" He paused, then slowly said, "It feels selfish. You've probably figured out I'm used to taking care of myself. I've pretty much always had to. So this is just… I want to try it, but my mind keeps telling me it's wrong. That's why I'm just sort of… jumping in. I'm afraid I wouldn't do it at all if I took time to think it over."

"If that's how you want to do it, I'm fine with that." I reached out and cupped his cheek. "I'm going to keep repeating this until I know you've understood me. There is no right or wrong here. However it works for us and however it feels right *is* what's right.

No matter if that's jumping right into the deep end or if that's taking it slow."

I pulled back to grab the napkin and tucked it in the neck of his T-shirt. He started to shift, probably worried how he looked. I cupped his cheek again. "Hey, look at me." When I had his attention, I smiled. "I think you look cute. There is one thing that'd be better: If I had you dressed up for me. Maybe a T-shirt that says you're daddy's good boy or something like that."

"Why does that sound so hot?" he asked me, shivering a little. He pressed his cheek against my palm. "I've never even thought about these things before, but coming from you… I just want to throw all caution to the wind. Which is hard. Very hard," he admitted.

"We don't need to be any more careful than you want to be. We're not doing anything dangerous or harmful. Nothing can happen. It's just giving up control in a safe environment, and we talk about what will happen." I traced his skin with the tips of my fingers. "We set our limits together. Then you have nothing to worry about. Even though this isn't like a traditional relationship, there's nothing wrong with wanting something a little outside the box."

"A little outside the box?" he asked, a bit wryly. "I think this is pretty far outside the box."

I shrugged but gave him a grin. "You're not wearing a tail and I don't have a dungeon full of interesting toys to show you, so yeah, pretty mild in the scheme of things."

"Mild," he repeated. He rolled his eyes but pulled away from me long enough to softly kiss my lips. "I'll take your word for that for now. Ease me into this before we start talking about puppy tails and dungeons."

"You don't have anything to worry about." I chuckled. "I don't have a basement."

Sitting back, I grinned as he just shook his head again. Picking up his fork, I speared a piece of chicken.

"No more thinking. No more decisions. I want to feed you

and take care of you for a while." I brought the food to his lips. "Now be my good boy and open for Daddy."

"Yes, Daddy," he said, offering a bashful smile that warmed me down to my toes. He opened his mouth and took the chicken, chewing on it with a hum of approval. "This is really good."

"I'm glad." I leaned across the table and kissed his forehead again. "Thank you for letting me take care of you, baby."

As he shyly smiled and reached for his cup, I sat back down. He hadn't seen how it was to fully sink into the role of being little, but with every step he took, I saw how perfect it was for him. I couldn't wait for him to experience it for himself.

CHAPTER SIX

MICAH

Now that class was over and my attention wasn't completely focused on my work, I couldn't stop thinking about Carter. That wasn't really new or different. I'd thought about him a lot the past few days. We'd sent a few texts back and forth, but none of them had gotten as intense as that one conversation had.

There was a part of me that was disappointed, but I was too afraid to start it up again. I didn't want to promise anything I couldn't deliver on, though when I was with him, it was easy to let go. I didn't know why, but it had gotten easy to respond to those gentle kisses — to want more, even though I didn't know how to say it.

A smile curved onto my lips as I thought about just how good of a kisser he was, and I touched my mouth, unable to stop myself from remembering it in detail.

"Hey, pretty boy," a familiar voice spoke up from beside me.

I turned to see Jacob standing there, and my smile vanished instantly.

"Hi," I mumbled. I'd enjoyed my time with Carter so much that I'd mostly gotten past what he and the others had done, but now that I was face to face with him... I couldn't help but feel the familiar humiliation and shame I'd felt right after I'd arrived at the bar.

I'd been so hopeful that I hadn't even seen the sign — the one that I'd been all too aware of on my way out — and it had landed me in a situation that was far out of my comfort zone. It had all worked out, but I was willing to bet they thought it wouldn't.

I didn't understand why they'd played a joke like that on me, and I probably never would. People... I'd long since learned that people were cruel. I shouldn't have been surprised, and I wasn't — not really.

That didn't mean it didn't hurt.

"We had so much fun the other night at The Irish Pub. You should've been there."

I stared at him. "Maybe if you hadn't told me you'd be at St. Jamison's, I would've shown up," I said with more courage than I felt.

"I don't remember saying St. Jamison's. Do you remember me saying St. Jamison's, Ty?" he asked.

This time I could see the malicious glint in his eyes, and it tore at something inside of me. It wasn't the first time I'd been bullied, and I doubted it would be the last. But it still fucking hurt.

"Nope. I guess our buddy just decided he'd rather go to the kink bar than hang out with us," Tyler said with a smirk.

They'd known perfectly well what they were doing. If I'd had any lingering doubts, the look on his face would've shattered them right there.

"Did you have fun?" Jacob asked, leaning against the wall. "I mean, after skipping out on us, I hope you did."

I wanted to wallow, to sink into the floor and disappear. I wanted to run away instead of letting them taunt me more. I wanted to find Carter and curl up in his arms. I wanted to do anything but stand there, facing two of the guys who had sent me unaware into what could've been a lion's den.

They obviously had known it was a BDSM gathering of some

kind, though if they'd realized they'd sent me into a den of hyper-protective daddies and handlers, they probably would've rethought their decision. Carter wasn't the only one who would've been pissed that they'd sent me there as a joke.

Their lifestyles weren't a joke at all.

Our lifestyles…

The silence stretched between us, but before Jacob or Tyler could throw another stinging comment my way, I gathered my courage and retorted, "Yeah, actually, I did."

It was terrifying to say it, though they'd probably think I was bluffing anyway.

They exchanged a look, knowing smirks on their lips.

"Well, we're glad," Tyler drawled. "Maybe next time you'll decide to come with us."

"Why are you doing this?" I snapped before I could keep the words from coming out. "You know you were just screwing with me."

"Doing what?" Jacob asked with an exaggerated wink. "See you around, pretty boy. Don't let one of the leather-wearing freaks catch you with your pants down."

I had a feeling one of the leather-wearing "freaks" would be a lot nicer to me than they were.

"Fuck off," I muttered, but they were already out of earshot.

I took a deep breath and shook my head, trying to gather myself. I'd been in such a good mood, but now the familiar sadness threatened to spill over me all over again. This wasn't high school, where someone might write it off as a prank. We were in college, and it had just been downright cruel.

Except it had led me to Carter.

The journey may have hurt, but the destination seemed like it was more than worth it — and now I was on a different journey, a better journey, with someone who cared about me and wanted to see me smile and blush instead of cry.

If Carter had been there, he'd have made them run with their tails between their legs. I hadn't managed anything like that, but... I'd stood up to them as much as I could. That had to be enough.

I paused under a tree and pulled my phone out.

"Just wanted to say hi. I can't wait to see you again."

Did it sound too needy? I had to hope not, because I'd pressed send before I'd even thought it through.

I sighed, setting off toward the dorm. I had too much homework to do to worry about all of this.

When I got back, I let myself in and traipsed to my bedroom, flopping back onto my bed. I got my phone back out of my pocket, and I couldn't help but smile when I saw he'd texted me back.

"I'm glad because I'm feeling the same way. Do you work tonight? Maybe we can get some dinner."

The confrontation with Jacob and Tyler was already a thing of the past. They might've thought they'd won, but I was the one with someone like Carter.

"I'm off today. Are you sure though? I know you have night classes all the time, and I don't want to take up all your time."

There were a few things I wanted to do, but I wasn't going to tell him that.

His response came back too quickly for him to be faking his enthusiasm.

"My class tonight isn't late but what about you? How much homework do you have? I don't want you to get behind because of me."

His concern was touching.

"It won't take me long. Promise."

Besides, I was planning on doing other sorts of "research" before I started my homework anyway.

I grabbed my laptop, hesitating before typing in *bdsm baby* into a Google search. I didn't know what else to describe it as, though I was pretty sure there was a proper term. If I'd heard it, though, I'd already forgotten it.

I blinked at the images at the top of the page, slightly in awe at the shameless people who had posed for the pictures. I shook my head and scrolled down, landing on the Glossary of BDSM.

Of course, the very first thing I saw mentioned was *adult baby diaper love*, which they abbreviated as ABDL. Then there was something about DDLG... How did anyone keep all the acronyms straight?

Further down the page, I could see an Etsy store advertising products, and a page with contracts... A little apprehensive, I clicked on the first link.

I jumped as the notification on my phone went off. I looked down at it.

"How about you bring it over and work on it at the table while I make dinner. Then I don't have to worry."

The idea of relaxing around him and getting my homework done while he fixed dinner was more than a little appealing — though I'd have to be finished with this particular brand of research before I went anywhere. I'd probably end up wiping my browser history, too — like there was really anyone who was going to look at my laptop.

I shook my head, torn between amusement and exasperation at my own thoughts.

"That sounds great, if you don't mind me muttering about codes and bugs."

The first thing I learned was that there was a thing for eating food off of someone's body — *nyotaimori*. There were different meanings for the letters in BDSM, too, which I'd never really thought about before. I'd already figured out BDSM was more than whips and chains, but something like what Carter was into seemed so... *mild* in comparison to what my mind kept bringing up.

"As long as it's computer bugs and not real ones that's fine. Come over whenever you want, but I'll get back to the house in about forty-five minutes."

I snorted.

"I'll try not to bring any of the real bugs from my dorm room. It

might be hard, though. We've bonded. I've even started to name the really big ones."

Before he could reply, I added another text.

"Then I'll plan to come over in about an hour and a half? To give you time to settle in? Is that enough time?"

Right. I turned my attention back to my browser, slowly starting to scroll down the page. I clicked on where it said DDLG, and it brought me to a page about age play.

"Do you want me to be honest or just tell you that's fine? If I'm being honest I'd rather have you around the house sooner, but I understand if that's too much for you. I don't want to monopolize all your time."

He wanted me over sooner. It made me feel better about taking up his time and getting in the way. I liked the idea of getting to work with him around, too. Just the idea of his presence after the encounter today would be nice...

My smile threatened to vanish, but I reminded myself that without those two assholes, I never would've met Carter to begin with — and I sure as hell wouldn't have had the nerve to google this stuff if it hadn't been for our earlier confrontation.

"An hour, then, just in case you're running late. :-) I'd rather see you sooner too."

I felt like a giddy schoolboy all over again, thrilled he wanted to spend time with me... and in light of what I was reading, the schoolboy thought made a lot more sense, too. Maybe I really was suited to what he was interested in... Maybe it wasn't just what *he* was interested in, either, because the more I flipped through the pages, the more interested I got.

I went back to the ABDL page, though, unsure of what I thought about *diaper love*. Did people really do that? I tried to imagine myself in a diaper again and laughed nervously. Would he like that? Would *I* like that?

Carter's text back was just like him, to the point and sweet. *"Perfect. I'm glad you're coming over. I'll finish up here and see you soon."*

The more I scrolled through the page, the more I realized that people really did do it. It just seemed… I didn't know. Could I see myself as one of the models on the page, smiling in only a diaper and a T-shirt?

"Sounds good. :-)"

I'd have to hurry if I wanted to find out more before I headed over there. I went out of the page and typed ABDL into the search engine. A few links down was one that said *Things You Maybe Didn't Want To Know About Adult Babies*. That sounded ominous, but I couldn't stop myself from clicking it anyway.

Surprisingly, it was mostly positive, and it even linked to a store that sold gear for people in the lifestyle. Did I really want to go there? I still wasn't sure what I thought about all of it, and the idea of googling this while I waited for Carter to get home so I could head over there made me blush.

But I wanted to know more about what he liked — and to see what parts of it appealed to me.

Instead of bringing me to the store itself when I clicked on the link, it brought me to another article, *Inside The Misunderstood World Of Adult Baby Diaper Lovers*. I was learning more than I'd thought I would, and… Well, it made me feel a little better to see that there was all this information out there — and that it wasn't negative. People did this, and they enjoyed it.

I sat back, imagining what it might be like to wear a diaper. I couldn't imagine it, not really, but I was curious anyway. That was pretty much how I felt about all of this, though: I wanted to know more.

I continued to go through the pages, one leading to another as I explored. The pictures kept catching my eye, and I paused on one.

It was an image of what I was sure was a man, but he was… pretty.

And he was clad in a nightgown, with barrettes in his hair.

I swallowed hard, unable to stop myself from having to shift in my pants. Why was that so appealing? All of this had been so strange, yet…

I clicked on it, looking at it in greater detail even as my cheeks burned. This was the sort of thing that had always gotten me in trouble — why I dressed the way I did, erring on the side of too masculine even though I was always uncomfortable. I'd been teased too many times about being a fag, about being a pretty boy, and if anyone found out I was so entranced by the image of a man in a dress, I'd be beyond screwed.

I couldn't even let Carter know. He'd probably write me off then. He wanted a boy, not a boy dressed in girl's clothing.

What would he even say to me if he was okay with it?

It didn't matter, because there was no way I was going to let him know.

I glanced at the time, realizing a good fifteen minutes had passed as I clicked on one link then another. I hurried to get into the shower, making sure to dust myself off with baby powder again before I got dressed. By the time I was done, I had just enough time to close out all the suspicious links on my laptop and put it in its bag.

I took a deep breath, still seeing those happy people in diapers in my mind, and went down to my car. The drive over there seemed to pass in seconds, probably because I was so distracted by my own thoughts. It was a wonder I got there safely, and I thought guiltily that Carter would probably chide me for not paying more attention on the way.

He didn't have to know… but the idea of not being honest with him made me squirm in a way that wasn't good at all. How had he gotten under my skin like this?

I got out of the car and grabbed my laptop bag, heading to the front door. I hesitated then knocked, taking a step back to wait for him to answer the door.

He must have been waiting for me because it only took seconds for him to open the door and stand in front of me.

"I should feel guilty about interrupting your evening, but I'm just going to ignore that." Carter stepped out the door and wrapped his arms around me, kissing the top of my head. "Thank you for being so generous with your free time."

"You don't need to thank me. I like that you want to spend time with me," I said, stepping into his embrace and snuggling in close to him. "Besides, you're offering me food. How could I refuse that?" I grinned at him. And he'd feed it to me, too, which would let me completely relax in ways I never could seem to at home.

His grin widened and he cocked his head. "So the way to your heart is through your stomach? I'm going to have to remember that."

"I keep telling you that you're spoiling me," I told him. "This sure beats ramen in the dorm room any day. Plus the company is so much better."

He chuckled. "I'm glad."

Kissing my head again, he hugged me one last time and stepped back. "Okay, head to the table so I don't distract you, and I'll get things started."

"You're still going to distract me," I teased him as I reluctantly took a step away. Homework seemed even less appealing than usual with him around, but it had to be done. If I just focused, it wouldn't take long… but his presence sure wouldn't help me concentrate. It was better than sitting alone at the dorm, though.

"There might be a reward waiting for good boys who do their homework, so keep that in mind." Carter took my hand and led me inside. "I've got a few ideas that you might like. But only if you're a good boy."

"I like rewards," I told him as I followed him. Our fingers weren't interlaced, but he was holding me like — he'd hold a kid's, with my hand resting in his. "Are you going to share what they might be? I mean, I'd like to know what I'm trying to earn…"

Carter chuckled and shook his head. "Nope, first you need to show me how focused you can be on your work."

"Unfair," I pouted. "You're going to be right there, and you expect me to be able to focus?"

"Think of it as good practice for later when I want you to focus on following other orders... harder ones." His teasing expression said he was thinking of something naughty.

I could feel the heat on my face rising, but I refused to acknowledge it because I wasn't sure I was ready to hear what he was imagining. I licked my suddenly dry lips and tried not to squirm. "I'll be good."

I had plenty of practice being good, after all. My entire life had been nothing but trying to please other people, and I'd gotten pretty damn good at it. I'd just... never wanted to please someone like I wanted to please Carter. It had always been to avoid punishment before, but now... now it was because I wanted to earn rewards. The difference was like night and day.

He paused at the entrance to the kitchen and pulled me close again. He kissed me tenderly and cupped my face. "You're always a very good boy. Even from the first night, you've been the best little boy." He gave me a knowing smile and kissed my forehead. "Even if you did act like a brat, I'd still find you fascinating and would like to get to know you better."

He cared about me. A lot. And, even more exciting, it might even be unconditional. It touched my heart, reaching deep within me and easing something. "I can be naughty, but I don't think I want to be a brat," I told him, burying my face against his shoulder. "I like being your good boy."

His arms tightened and his fingers started stroking my back. "I like how sweet you are. And I get to cuddle you, so being my good boy is perfect for both of us."

I could've stayed like that forever, feeling warm and safe in his arms... feeling cared for and wanted, too, in ways I couldn't remember feeling in years. It was a bittersweet feeling, but it was one I'd come to crave now that I'd started to get it. I felt like I hadn't realized how much I was missing until I'd gotten it again.

"So I should probably really be a good boy and get my homework done, huh?" I asked reluctantly, stealing another kiss before I took a step back.

"See, there's my good boy." Giving me one last hug, Carter relaxed his hold then released me. "I'll get you a drink while you're working, and I bought something you might like. At the very least you might try and see what you think."

I looked curiously at him then nodded. I felt like a kid on his birthday, eager and anxious to see what sort of present I'd gotten. I was sure I'd like it if he'd gotten it for me, but I had no idea what it could be.

There had been too many things I'd seen on the website: diapers, pacifiers, onesies... and a forbidden part of me whispered so unhelpfully that there had been gorgeous ribbons and cute barrettes, too.

"Okay," I told him. I went to the table and settled down, grabbing my laptop. I'd been working on the project for a while, but it was getting too close to the due date for me to lag behind a lot — even though I wanted to put it off another day. But I had to work tomorrow, and I didn't want to disappoint Carter.

As I got everything laid out and started up my computer, Carter came over with a sippy cup and something small peeking out of his hand.

Oh.

"Here's your juice." He kissed my head and set the cup down beside me. "And here's a binky. It might help you relax and give you something to focus on so you stay on track."

I wasn't sure what I thought about it, but it seemed less surprising in the wake of my searches earlier. I nodded, taking the binky from him and examining it. I experimentally put it in my mouth, and it felt... strange. Strange, but soothing somehow, and I mulled over it as I pulled up my assignment.

At first, it was hard to concentrate with the odd, new sensation and the sounds of him working in the kitchen, but it wasn't long before all of that melted away. I was only aware of my work

— and of the way I could carefully suck on the pacifier when I started to get distracted.

I wouldn't have expected something so small could have such an impact, but it did. And sitting there at his table, pacifier in my mouth and homework in front of me, I found peace I rarely did.

CHAPTER SEVEN

CARTER

As I cleaned my kitchen, I tried to figure out whether I had a good reason to text Micah. Not that I really needed one; he usually just got in touch to say hi, but still. I didn't want to push him. There was a difference between him being bold and me being too pushy, and it might be hard to tell which it was. I didn't want to scare him away. But then, he seemed to welcome it when I took the lead, so texting him might be good to show him I cared.

My thoughts went in circles, back and forth.

Before I could decide, my phone rang, interrupting me. Micah? He didn't usually call, though, and he had classes this morning. A glance at the display revealed that it wasn't my boy, but my mom. Great.

"Hey, Mom. You're up early."

"Don't be so cheeky, young man. I'm not that much of a late sleeper. Your father, though..." She sounded slightly frustrated.

I laughed out loud, knowing very well what she referred to. My dad didn't go to bed until the early hours of the morning, but then he slept in. He'd always been that way, and since they were both retired, there was no making him get up before noon at the earliest.

"To what do I owe the pleasure of the call?" I asked, still grinning.

"I just wanted to say hello. We haven't heard from you in a while, and we figured it was time to call you. Otherwise we'd never hear from you."

Guilt rose in me. I'd been so wrapped up in work and Micah that I hadn't called them in weeks. "Sorry, Mom."

"'Sorry, Mom' is not gonna cut it, and you know it, Carter. You should feel like you need to call your parents every once in a while, you know?"

I scrubbed my kitchen counter, working to get rid of one stain I hadn't noticed before while I tried to ignore the guilt trying to claw its way through my stomach. "I know. I've just been so busy, and had quite a lot of things to do and... I just forgot?"

I scrubbed even harder, as if it could help with the feelings inside.

"It's okay. I'm just messing with you. How have you been? I assumed you were busy, and that's why we didn't turn up and check whether you're still alive. We figured the police would call us if something had happened to you."

I snorted loudly. Typical, my mother and her humor. "Yeah, they would have called you. I met someone, and, well, we've been spending some time together. Happy now?"

"Oh, you met someone? That's great to hear! We're so happy to hear that you're ready to move on. It's been quite a long time since..." She stopped speaking.

"Yeah. It's been quite a long time."

Sometimes it felt like no time at all had passed, and sometimes it felt like an eternity. Showing Micah the nursery had been hard and easy at the same time. It had ripped open old wounds, of course, but on the other hand, I'd seen a future there.

"He's... He's really nice, and I like him very much." I couldn't help myself. My lips curved into a smile when I thought about Micah.

"Tell me more. How did you meet him?"

That was a tricky question. "He came into a bar I was visiting, and we started speaking. Some so-called friends played him and sent him in the wrong bar, but I helped him and his evening ended much better than it started."

"Oh, that's not nice of them to set him up like that."

"Yeah, I know, but there's nothing he could do about it, I guess. At least we met, and… It's too soon to say if it will lead somewhere, but I like him."

"How old is he, if I may ask? If he was set up by his friends, it doesn't sound like he's your age."

I sighed. Always the questions by my nosy parents. "He's younger than me, if that's what you're asking. Quite a bit younger, but it doesn't bother us."

"Same age difference as with Nicholas?"

I breathed out harshly. "A bit younger, to be honest. More like… Half my age?"

"Half your age? Isn't that a bit young?"

I shook my head even though I knew she couldn't see it on the other end of the line. "You're asking way too many questions. We agreed you wouldn't do that."

"I'm sorry, honey. I just want to know about this new boyfriend of yours. We were all devastated when the… thing with Nicholas happened, and your father and I just worry you're going to stay alone."

I swallowed hard as my mother's words hit me. They really worried I'd stay alone?

Of course they did.

I hadn't even been forty when I became a widower. I hadn't shown any interest in dating since Nic's death. Parents worried. It was part of their job.

Well, maybe, just maybe, that would change now… if Micah stuck around. Right now, it looked like it, but I couldn't be sure. If I got my hopes up, only to have them crushed later, I'd be devastated.

"Would you like to bring him over for dinner?" She interrupted my thoughts.

"Not yet, Mom. It's too soon for that, okay? Once we know each other better, I'll make sure to bring him over."

"Then just you? Or are you using all your free days to spend time with him?"

"Umm. Yeah. Well. Mostly, if you put it like that. I mean, not all free time, but…"

She laughed. "I'm only teasing you. I'm glad you found someone. Don't worry."

"Thanks, Mom. I'll make sure to introduce you to him, okay? I just want to get to know him a bit more before springing the *meet the family* at him." Not to mention, it was a two-hour drive to them, since they'd gotten an apartment in some kind of retirement community.

"Sure. And don't be a stranger. Otherwise, we'll have to start visiting you again."

I shuddered at the thought of them standing unannounced on my doorstep again. "Yeah, right. About that. Just… don't do that anymore, okay? Not without calling first."

"Sweetie, it's okay if you haven't cleaned up."

I rolled my eyes. That was *not* the issue anymore. In the first months after Nic's death, yes, but since then, I'd gotten my act together. But if things with Micah went the way I wanted them to, it'd be bad if they caught us.

It had taken them years to get used to me being gay. Then, after they'd accepted it, I had brought home Nic. That'd been interesting. By the time we got married, they loved him and had accepted I just liked younger men. But I did *not* want to find out what they would think about my partner being my little. They'd freak. I could get away with a lot of things, but I doubted they'd understand.

They already looked down at the BDSM community. My dad always claimed they were sick. With my luck, there was some kind of shady club close to them, and, despite me explaining that this was not another name for abuse, they weren't really believing that. This was one of the things we disagreed on, but we all agreed to disagree here. I knew better, but they wouldn't change their views, so I had to leave them alone. They didn't mess with my life, and we had a good relationship. I let them have their opinion.

"I have cleaned up, but still. I might be spending time with Micah, you know?"

"Oh, that's no problem. We'd still like to get to know him."

I groaned. "Mom, stop it. You never did that when Nic and I were together, and while I appreciated it after his death, I'm moving on now. I won't drink myself into a stupor anymore."

"Are you sure? You can tell us, Carter." Concern laced her voice, and even more guilt rose.

Yeah, I had fucked up a few times, drinking so much they feared for me. I couldn't deal with his cancer and his death, and so I'd tried to drown my sorrows in alcohol. Spoiler: that never works, and if you don't want your parents to see you puking your guts out, don't try it when they have a key.

"Yes, I'm sure. I drink a beer sometimes, but that's all. I meant it because you might see more than you want to if you drop by."

"I raised you. Believe me, there is nothing new to see."

I burst out laughing. "No, Mom. Just drop it and call me if you want to stop by."

She laughed, too. "It's okay. I will do that."

We talked some more, about some neighbor of hers who had died in his apartment but no one had known about it because he didn't have any living relatives, about my dad's latest hobby, fishing, my mom's reading circle, the church they went to and their latest scandal — a married man hooking up with another woman and leaving his wife — and all the other mundane things you talked about with your parents.

By the time I got rid of her — I loved talking to her, but it was exhausting sometimes — it was nearly noon. I'd have a couple of hours until I had to shower and leave for class. The kitchen was clean, and so was the rest of the house, so I could maybe pick up something to read.

Or see how Micah was doing. Pulling out my phone, I sent him a quick text.

Hey. How are you today? How's work?

He didn't answer, so I made my way through the house, looking at it. I'd intended to read, but no. I didn't want to. I looked at my living room, trying to see it as Micah would see it. Did he really like how it was set up? Should I change something? I'd done some redecorating since Nic's death, but would he feel more comfortable if it was completely different?

Did it matter to him at all?

With a sigh, I went upstairs to my bedroom. Same game there. What did he think? He said he liked it, but...

I was worrying way too much. Definitely. I could ask him, do something, or wait until he said something. Worrying about it wouldn't help me at all.

My gaze fell to the closed door at the end of the hallway: the nursery, the room where so many memories rested. With a deep breath, I went to it and slowly opened the door. The boxes looked so wrong in there, like they sucked all the life from the room. It'd been ours, one of the cores of our relationship, and it was one of the most painful reminders of what I lost.

With a deep sigh, I started closing the door again. My last look fell on the dresser with the elephants and giraffes. Nic had loved them so much.

This was wrong. The room was wrong that way. It shouldn't carry the sad memories, but the good ones. The times we'd laughed, played, when Nic had built his towers and they'd fallen over. When we'd been carefree and simply happy.

I wanted that again. I wanted this room to be filled with laughter again, with new memories. What I'd had with Nic had been beautiful, and it wasn't right to downgrade our room to storage.

I pushed open the door.

The boxes needed to go first, then I'd see to the rest.

Two hours later, I'd wiped away a couple of tears, carried a lot of boxes to my office, vacuumed the carpet, cleaned the windows, and dusted. I wasn't done yet. I wanted to give the room yet another thorough cleaning before I'd be happy with it, but now it looked like it was supposed to again.

I needed to get ready for work, or I'd be late. Just one more thing needed to be done before I could call it a day and hop into my much-needed shower. With a screwdriver, I removed the elephants and giraffes from the dresser. Maybe one day, I could pick up other animals for my little. These were Nic's and only his.

I stared at the wooden animals in my hands as a tear dropped on them. It darkened the wood of the elephant, but I wiped it away.

Maybe I'd put them next to his picture, since I didn't want to lay them on his grave. Pressing them close to my heart, I left the room. The door remained open behind me.

By the time I finished work, Micah had answered.

"Sorry, today was incredibly busy. Half of the people coming here wanted to adopt animals, and the other half dropped some off for various reasons."

I answered before driving home.

"No worries, I was just trying to distract you, that's all."

By the time I was at home, I had another text from him.

"Well, in order for that to work, I would probably need to read your texts. But you can distract me from studying now."

As if. He had to study, even if he didn't want to.

"Be a good boy and learn and we can meet during the weekend as a reward. Maybe go somewhere? If you want to?"

His answer came so fast that I knew he was glued to his phone, waiting for my text.

"You don't have to ask, you know? I'd love to meet again. Just tell me where we're going so I have the right clothes."

Now I couldn't wipe the grin from my face.

"I'll pick something and let you know. And now get to work, my boy. Or do you want to come over to study?"

Was that overkill? It was past 10 and he needed his sleep. But then, to just hold him a bit, especially after the day I'd had, would be wonderful.

"I'm sorry, but I have an early class tomorrow, so I'll probably go to bed really soon. But I'll be off at 1. Do you want to meet for a bit? I have to work at four, but between then, I'm free?" Then, a second later, *I'm really sorry I can't come over today."*

I'd already expected that, and, while I was disappointed, I understood.

"Don't worry, baby. It's okay, and I expected it. I just wanted to offer. Meeting tomorrow sounds wonderful. Do you want to come over, then I'll have lunch ready? Or meet somewhere else?"

This time, he needed a moment to reply, but then his words popped up.

"Are you mad now?"

Why would I be mad? I pressed the button to call him.

Micah answered immediately, but his voice was small. "Yeah?"

"Hey, baby. Can you talk?"

"Yeah, I'm alone."

"Okay, good. I just wanted to ask why you think I'd be mad at you?" I tried to sound calm, but it upset me more than I wanted him to know.

He hesitated a moment before he replied, "Because I didn't want to come over now? Or rather, I want to, but I need to get up early, and I need to sl—"

"Baby, I'm not upset at all. I just thought we could hang out a bit, but I absolutely understand your reasons. And, by the way, if you just say, no, not today because you don't feel like it, that's fine, too."

"It is?" He still sounded like he expected me to blow up.

"Yes, it is. I love spending time with you, but you're under no obligation to be here when you don't want to or can't. Just tell me and it's okay. I won't get mad, I won't yell, and I won't ever make you do something you're not okay with. That includes coming over if you don't want to."

He paused, and then his voice sounded stronger. "Thank you. I wasn't… I wasn't really sure how it would go over."

"It's okay. Just ask if you're insecure, okay? I promised you honesty, so that's what you'll get."

"Thank you. I appreciate it. And, in all honesty, lunch tomorrow sounds lovely. If I can stop by at your place, it'd be nice."

"Are you sure?"

Micah laughed, even if it was a bit hesitant. "You promised to be honest. I'm doing the same. So, yes, I'd like to come over, have lunch in private, and maybe relax a bit afterward or study before I go to work."

"Then I'll take your word. Lunch will be ready for you, my sweet boy."

We chatted a bit more, but it became clear how tired he was. I'd love to have him here, bathe him, make him relax and put him to bed, but if we ever managed that, it would need a lot more time.

Though, when he'd said he wanted lunch in private, that meant he was okay with me caring for him. Otherwise he'd have worded it differently. I'd take that and just enjoy what I could get… and plan for the weekend.

CHAPTER EIGHT

MICAH

Carter was patient to the point of it being ridiculous. I might've been a virgin, but that didn't mean I wasn't a hot-blooded twenty-one-year-old male with definite interest in the guy who was showing me there was so much more to dating and sex than just… casual interest.

When I'd gone over to his house, he'd made me study while he fixed me lunch, letting me relax in his lap as he fed me. I hadn't wanted to go to work, and he hadn't seemed to want me to either.

By the time I'd left, he'd been as hard as I'd been. It all felt amazing — the way he'd pulled me closer to him, the way he made me feel like I was precious and valued. I'd wanted nothing more than for him to slide his hand down my pants and get one of the virgin things out of the way.

Feeling his hard shaft against my ass, resting where I wanted to take him someday — maybe even soon — brought me to the point of begging. But aside from a few very hot kisses, nothing had happened. His fingers had stayed in safe regions, and I wasn't bold enough to initiate something like that.

That wasn't the only issue. I liked it when he took the lead, and I'd rather have him make me wait then tell him to get me off.

I'd hoped he'd do that, but no. He'd moved me from his lap when I'd needed to leave and kissed me thoroughly, but that had been it.

And now it was the weekend and his promised date.

Of course, I hadn't expected a barbecue with a few of his friends to be what he came up with. My shoulders were tight, even though he gently rubbed them, and thoughts raced in my head.

Finally, he drew me into his arms, pressing his lips to mine. This silenced my panic for a moment, but only until he released me.

"I don't know if I can do this," I admitted in a small voice.

"What exactly is worrying you, baby?" He kept me close, on his lap again.

I rested my head on his shoulder, enjoying his massaging hand on the back of my neck. My face burned as I told him what bothered me. "I'm just... Those are your friends. What if they don't like me? What if they think I'm weird? What if they—"

He stopped me with a kiss to my forehead. "Two things: One, you've already met them, so they're not really strangers. Two, because they're in the lifestyle, nothing we say or do will surprise them." He kissed me again as his hand started playing with the hair at the back of my neck. "I know that's part of what makes you uncomfortable, but I think it's also what could make this so easy."

He gently placed a hand under my chin to raise my face and pulled back just enough to see into my eyes.

"If you're honestly saying this is too much, then I'll send them home. If you're trying to tell me you're overwhelmed and frightened and you want to make sure I don't leave your side, that's fine too. I just need to know how you're feeling."

I took a deep breath, mulling over what he'd said. I tried to look away, but I couldn't bring myself to avert my gaze from his beautiful brown eyes. "I don't know," I admitted. "I don't think I want to cancel... I just..." I paused. "I guess this is my way of saying I don't want you to leave me alone. Please."

What if they laughed at me? I was dressed more casually than I normally was, wearing jeans and a comfortable shirt — not one of my usual button-ups, but one that showed my body much better, or at least I thought so.

It felt like wanting him to stay at my side was too much to ask, but he'd mentioned it first. Of course, he'd been utterly perfect, so much so that I couldn't help but feel like he was too perfect. But I was enjoying it too much to question it.

"Then that's what we'll do." Carter smiled and held me close again. "If you change your mind and want to hang out with Sean on your own, that's fine." His smile softened. "No matter what you want to do, whether it's drink a couple of beers and relax or even get your coloring book out. They wouldn't find it strange."

I nodded, wrapping my arms around him and staying close. I inhaled deeply, smelling his soap and the smell that was just uniquely him. "I'll let you know," I told him. "I'm not sure I'm ready for... What would it be? A playdate? I don't think I'm really ready for those yet."

"I agree, but I want you to know it's an option. If you want to be little or need to let everything go for a while and curl up in my lap with your sippy cup, there's nothing wrong with that." His hands stroked up and down my back, and he relaxed his hold on me. "How about we head out back and start the grill?"

I let myself enjoy being close to him, then finally nodded after I gathered myself. "Okay," I told him, releasing him. "I think I can do this." I hoped I could. I felt ridiculously shy, especially at the idea of anyone seeing me with my sippy cup and anything else. Was he going to feed me with them there? What if it...

I forced myself to stop thinking about it.

"I'm ready," I said after a pause, nodding to him and taking a step in the direction of the back door.

Carter's hand moved to my shoulder and stopped me. "If you change your mind, you need to let me know."

I nodded. "I will," I promised. "I think I'll be okay, though. It's just so new."

"Not as new as you think." He smiled and kissed my head. "The last time you saw them, Sean was arguing with you about the coloring book. This time he has to behave."

I couldn't help but smile at that. "Is he used to behaving?" I asked rather dryly. "He seems like the type to invite the punishments you're always threatening."

Carter laughed. "Oh yes, but he's the type who enjoys the punishments, no matter if he's big or little."

Punishments. How would that be? He wouldn't take a… whip or something, right? He'd said something about a spanking. I knew Carter was sure I wasn't ready for something like that, and he was probably right. At the same time… I was curious. I was curious about so much, and we were moving so slow.

Maybe too slow.

I had to get through this barbecue and show him I was ready for more… with him, even if in nothing else.

"Maybe one day I'll see if I do too," I told him, flashing a grin at him. As uncertain as I felt, I wanted to try it.

Carter's gaze heated and the smile turned… wicked, almost. "I don't think you'll ever be a brat, but I'll be honest and say I think you'd look sexy bent over my lap, squirming as I make your cheeks all pink."

"Which cheeks?" I retorted, already starting to blush. My smile didn't fade though, and I hoped it would reassure him that I could take his teasing. "Besides, I don't need to be a brat. You'd do that if I asked you to."

I was pretty sure he would, anyway.

"You're right." He kissed me, fast and hot. "Because I love giving you everything you want and need."

I let out a little whimper against his lips. "That's totally not fair." I pouted a little, testing to see what I thought of it — testing to see how he'd respond to it.

His hands reached down and grabbed my ass, pulling me flush

against him. "Maybe I need to find another way to distract my worried boy."

I was already getting hard, already beyond distracted, and I was sure he'd be able to feel it with how closely I was pressed against him. "Unfair," I croaked. "Your timing sucks."

"My timing is perfect." He leaned down and started nibbling along my neck. "When talking doesn't work, I think I've found another way to help you stop worrying."

I tilted my head, giving him access to my throat. "I kinda like this way." He nibbled on, raising goosebumps. His hard-on pressed against mine. Damn, maybe I needed to let him know something... something I should've said sooner. "I... um..."

Carter stopped, looking at me. "Everything all right?"

I shook my head, then nodded. "Um... Yeah. I just... I need to tell you... I haven't been with anyone. I mean... I'm kind of..." I trailed off, then whispered, "a virgin." I hid my head in shame, my cheeks burning.

He tensed for a moment, then drew back. Would he be... turned off? "Look at me." Softly, he placed his fingers under my chin, raising my head.

I didn't want to look at him, see his reaction. His pity. His—

"Micah. Look at me, baby." Carter's words were soft, almost a whisper — and kind.

I swallowed, then finally tore my gaze away from his t-shirt, making my way up to his eyes.

"Are you listening, baby?" he asked, still in that soft voice.

I nodded. It was impossible to form words right now.

"Thank you for telling me. I figured you didn't have much experience — and before you get that wrong, I like it. It wasn't obvious, but I put a few pieces together. Anyway, it's nothing to be ashamed of."

"You knew?" That was the only thing I could think about. He'd known and not dumped me?

"Guessed. Yeah. What reaction did you expect, if I may ask?"

He still held my head up, making it impossible to hide from his questioning gaze.

"Uh… that it'd turn you off? That you'd rather have someone who knows what they're doing?"

He smiled at me, pressing a soft kiss on my lips. "Do you want to know the truth? I think it's hot. I love the idea of showing you how good it can be. I love the idea of being your first, getting to teach you all the ways to find pleasure. Get pleasured. And I love the idea of exploring all the ways to make you come."

"I— You're not— I mean—"

Smooth, Micah. Really smooth.

"No, I'm not disappointed at all. Like I said, it's making me hard. Hell, everything you do makes me hard, so how can something like that turn me off?" He kissed me again, this time longer. "Okay? If I'm moving too fast, let me know."

"I… thank you."

"Nothing to thank me for." He started nibbling along my neck again.

"I love that. Makes me want to come immediately."

He chuckled. "I can feel it. Why do you think why I love doing it?"

"I shouldn't have let you see the effect it has on me." I groaned. Not that I really thought I could hide it, especially not from him, but I could at least tease him a little.

Carter laughed quietly and the sound sent shivers down my spine. "I can feel exactly what kind of effect this has on you." More nibbles along my neck and me squirming against him. "What does my boy want?" His hands kneaded my ass and rocked me closer. "You're always such a good boy. Maybe you need more rewards for being so good for your daddy."

The idea of getting more rewards was more than a little appealing. "Mhm," I agreed. "Definitely." Of course, he could've said anything right then and I would've agreed with him. After he'd handled my little confession the way he had, there was nothing I wouldn't give him. I still couldn't believe it wasn't an issue at all — but considering I apparently had given myself away already… maybe it really wasn't a big deal.

"Then once everyone leaves and I have you all to myself again, we're going to explore what kinds of rewards my boy likes best." He kissed the point where my neck met my shoulder. "There are all kinds of ways to reward my sweet boy."

My hands slid to the small of his back, keeping him close. "I'd like that… Daddy." It still felt strange to call him that, but it felt perfect in that moment, just right. I wasn't even self-conscious about it.

He moaned low and rocked his hips against me, making it clear that he was just as turned on as I was. "Such a good boy for your daddy." Then he groaned and slowly straightened. Giving me a tender smile, he glanced down between us. "Not too obvious. Let's go."

I whimpered, not wanting to go just yet. I wanted to feel his hands on me, wanted to push and see how far we were both willing to go — and I didn't want to stop there. But there was the barbecue, and I couldn't ask him to cancel it just because I thought I was ready to take the next step.

I lowered my hands, experimentally touching his ass before drawing back. "Stop turning me on, or I'm going to be dealing with this problem the whole time."

Carter laughed. "Good, because I certainly am."

I rolled my eyes. "You're so bad… Daddy," I said again, wanting to see the effect it had on him.

That wicked smile flashed back again. "I'm starting to think you'd like that." He stepped closer again, brushing his body against mine. "Maybe my sweet boy wants a rough, bad daddy once in a while."

The thought had me biting back a moan of my own. My body wanted everything he had to offer me — rough, gentle, and otherwise. "We're never going to get outside at this rate," I said with a soft laugh, stealing another kiss.

"Someone's trying to change the subject." Carter gave me a

quick kiss, smiling at me. "That's okay this time, however, because you're right."

"Of course I'm right," I informed him loftily, taking a step back. I bumped my hip against him then headed for the back door.

Carter chuckled as he followed me to the yard.

I'd never been in his backyard before, and I paused, taking in the sight. It was as neat as the house was, with a nice grill and even a picnic table with an umbrella over it. "Grill often?" I asked.

"When I have people over."

I nodded, glancing at the table then back at him. "Do you need help?" I asked.

"It's all right." He ran his hand up and down my back in long strokes. "But if you'd like to help, that's a different story. If you're not going to be little this afternoon, then I'm going to treat you like I would any other man I was dating."

"What would it mean for you to treat me like someone you were dating? I mean… I like being little with you, but I'm curious."

I was curious about so much.

He smiled and leaned in to kiss me slowly. "That means I don't get to feed you and I have to let you help if that's what you want. Depending on what you want, I'll also do my best not to bring up that side of our relationship when Sean and Rick are here."

That didn't sound as appealing. "I think I'm getting spoiled," I admitted.

"Good, because I like spoiling you." After another lingering caress, he stepped back and went over to the grill, starting to stack up the charcoal before lighting it. "Looks like it'll heat up well." Glancing down at his watch, he nodded. "I'm going to go grab the burgers. They should be here any minute." He looked at me and smiled. "Do you want anything from inside?"

I shook my head. I still hadn't really answered his question on what I wanted… but I still wasn't sure what that was. Maybe it'd be easier to go into this not being little, but at the same time, it had been fun to play with Sean before. The good thing was that I could change my mind at any time, and he wouldn't hold it against me.

I was even starting to believe it.

I walked over to the table as he disappeared inside, glancing around. The yard really was beautiful, just the way I would've expected from him. I liked being outdoors with the dogs, but I didn't go outside much on my own.

Carter came back out in seconds, a plate of uncooked burger patties in one hand and his other arm wrapped around several bottles of beer and water. He grinned. "I will admit that an extra set of hands would be welcome right about now."

I smiled back at him, getting up to take the plate from him so he could juggle the drinks better. "I didn't think it was possible to carry that much," I told him. "Just tell me what you need me to do."

"If you could grab the beers. If they go down then it will be a mess."

Carefully grabbing the bottles instead of the plate, I juggled a few of the water bottles that had slipped precariously.

He laughed as he set the plate down by the grill and finally grabbed the rest of the water bottles. "Thank you."

"You're welcome," I said, setting everything down on the table. "Is there anything else you need me to grab?"

He shrugged. "Not at the moment. Once the burgers are almost done, we'll need to grab a few things, but they'll wait until the guys get here."

I nodded. I helped him set the bottles on the table along with everything else and followed him to the grill. Maybe I was being a little too clingy, but I was still nervous — and I still hadn't figured out what I wanted. I liked helping him and not feeling useless, and admittedly, what had happened in the house had me in more of an adult mindset.

Before I could decide, voices came from around the side of the house.

Carter grinned and called out, "Back here."

I took a deep breath, bracing myself. This was going to be nice. I'd liked the two when I'd met them that first night, and I doubted that would change. Carter didn't seem like the type to have friends, least of all those who came over to his house, if they weren't solid.

The two familiar faces came around the side of the house with teasing grins and arms loaded down with beer and what looked like brownies. Sean held out the dessert, looking very proud of himself. "We come bearing gifts."

I glanced at Carter, gathering my nerve, then asked him, "Did you make those?"

Sean started to nod but Rick snorted. "Liar. We grabbed them from that new bakery."

Rolling his eyes, Sean shrugged. "I put them on a new plate and slaved over making them beautiful. That counts."

"I'm sure it took a lot of effort," I said, offering a bashful smile.

Sean grinned and glanced at Rick. "See, he's smart. I knew there was a reason I liked him."

Rick laughed. "You mean besides the fact that Carter gives him the best coloring books?"

Sean rolled his eyes again and gave Carter a teasing frown. "I begged for that coloring book."

Laughing, Carter shrugged and then reached over to rest his hand on my shoulder. "Maybe that was the problem." As his hand moved away, he gave me a squeeze. "Thanks for the dessert and the beers. Would you mind throwing them in the fridge? There should be room."

I nodded and took the beers from the two, feeling proud of myself for getting to help. It was a little ridiculous just how proud I was of helping, and I could feel myself sliding into that headspace where I was pleasing my daddy.

"Would you… mind helping me?" I asked Sean, wondering if

he'd be okay with helping or if he'd be too… what? Helpless? I didn't quite know what to make of him just yet.

"Of course." Sean followed as I started for the back door. I easily found room in the fridge for the beers, and he set the brownies on the table.

"What do you think?" I asked, dropping my voice. "Should we sample them to make sure they taste good?"

He laughed. "I'm always up for a good spanking, but you seem like the type of boy who follows the rules."

"He didn't tell me I couldn't try them," I protested, though I felt a bit naughty at the idea. "Ah well." I looked at them then shrugged. "I guess I'll have to wait until after dinner."

Smiling, Sean glanced at them longingly. "They look tempting, but I'd rather get rewarded later for being good. I might have been a little bit bratty yesterday, so I probably owe him."

The idea of being… bratty was almost scandalous to me. I could easily handle the idea of sneaking a brownie and maybe getting caught — and I had the feeling Sean would've made sure he was caught if he had — but the idea of purposely riling Carter up seemed like a bit much.

"Besides, Carter might shoot me if I corrupt his sweet boy." Sean smiled. "He's been tight-lipped about everything, so don't worry that he gossiped, but it's clear how much he likes you."

I couldn't help but blush. I hadn't really expected him to talk about me — and really, I was still trying to come to terms with all the things our relationship included. It was nice to know that he wasn't hiding me from his friends, though.

It made it feel realer.

"I like him a lot, too," I said with a lopsided smile. "He's a really great guy. Like… impossibly so." I paused, then asked the question that had been burning in my mind. "Is he really as good as he seems?" I asked a little more quietly.

Sean cocked his head. "What do you mean? Like the whole honesty and what you see is what you get thing?"

"He just seems too perfect sometimes," I admitted. "I keep wondering… I'm not used to genuinely good guys."

Sean's smile faded to something poignant and almost sad. "It wasn't always this easy for him. He told you about Nicholas?"

I nodded. "Yeah. That had to be really hard for him. I just can't even imagine what it was like."

"It was." He sighed and leaned against the counter, looking out toward the back yard. "They were really good together, but in the beginning they had trouble talking about things. Nothing dramatic, but neither of them had been used to an age play relationship. There was so much emotion involved, and Nicholas wasn't exactly the quiet type. It took them some time and a few crazy arguments before they both decided that being totally honest was the only way to make it work. I think it taught Carter some valuable lessons."

I felt a little bad for asking. It was like I was getting insight into a relationship I wasn't sure I had the right to know about. I knew more about Carter than he did about me, but I was glad to know.

"Has to be weird for him to go from someone loud to someone quiet," I said to him as much as to myself.

Sean smiled. "I'm not even sure he realizes that. He just wasn't interested in anyone for a long time. We were actually really surprised when he all but dragged you into the bar that night. You were the first person since Nicholas that really made him light up." Then Sean chuckled. "But don't think I haven't been trying to set him up. You're not a rebound or something. He just hasn't had any chemistry with anyone since he started noticing people again."

It was more of a relief than I'd expected it to be. "I didn't really think I was a rebound," I said slowly. "I just… I'm not sure where I fit in. I like him a lot," I repeated. "And I don't want to screw that up on accident."

Sean stepped forward and wrapped his arms around me, giving me a quick hug. "I'm not sure you could screw up even if you wanted to. He's totally gone over you. Whatever you guys have going is making him really happy. So as long as you're happy too, I wouldn't worry about it."

I hugged him back, even though it felt a bit strange. It was good, though. I'd kept myself at a distance for so long, but Carter was breaking down my walls. "I am happy," I reassured him. "Happier than I've been in a long time. I have no idea what's going to happen next, but… it's good."

"Don't obsess over what's next, no matter if it's the daddy stuff or if it's just the regular part of your relationship. Just be honest with him and see where it takes you." Sean's smile morphed to a wicked grin. "Exploring and seeing where you end up is half the fun sometimes."

I blushed again even though I didn't exactly know why. "Rick has his hands full with you," I said, returning his grin with a smile of my own. "Doesn't he?"

Sean beamed then laughed. "Oh yes, and that's what he loves best about me. He'd be stodgy on his own without a brat to keep him on his toes."

I shook my head. "Good thing you're there to help him out." I glanced at the door. "We should probably get back out there before they think we're eating all the brownies."

Sean's grin turned wicked. "Oh no, Rick is probably out there holding Carter back and promising him I'm not giving you the third degree or something."

"So neither of them will suspect I'm the one giving *you* the third degree?" I asked with a laugh.

"Never." He shook his head, still smiling. "I'm going to have to watch you. That innocent face is going to get me in trouble."

"I'll try to avoid getting you into too much trouble." I took a step toward the door, then added, "Today, anyway. Who knows what tomorrow will bring?"

"It's always the innocent ones we have to worry about." He started following me out to the yard again. "But Rick is never going to believe me that I behaved myself for this long."

"I'll tell him," I promised. "Though he'll probably think you coerced me into saying it." I led him outside, flashing him another smile. "But we'll see what happens."

And who knew just what would happen? I knew I didn't have the slightest idea… but I was looking forward to finding out.

CHAPTER NINE

CARTER

"Don't tell Rick, but I think he was right. That third brownie might have been too much." Sean's groan said he was looking for sympathy, but since he'd stolen the last brownie, I wasn't feeling like he'd earned it.

"It'd serve you right if he punished you."

Sean laughed. "Asshole. You just wanted leftovers."

"Damn right."

"So you don't want to hear that I have more at home?" His teasing grin said he was trying to drive me crazy.

"I'm starting to think Rick needs to dig that cage out again for you."

Sean groaned, that time for real. "The one bad thing about having a Daddy Dom as a best friend is when he's pissed at you. That's just cheating."

It was my turn to grin. "I don't know what you're talking about. You said you liked the cage."

But he'd also said not to tell Rick because he had a weird love-hate relationship with the damn thing, as he'd called it.

Sean shook his head. "Cheater. Okay, new topic." He was still wearing that wicked grin, so I wasn't sure what would come out of his mouth. "I like him. I think he's good for you."

"But?"

That grin said there had to be something else.

Not that it would matter.

I valued Sean's opinion on a lot of things, but Micah was special. No matter what Sean thought, I wouldn't deny that.

"But nothing. Well, nothing, but I think you're going too slow." He leaned back against the kitchen counter and crossed his arms, daring me to disagree.

He'd just confirmed he was a virgin, so moving slowly was even more important. But I wouldn't tell Sean, of course. "I don't want to rush him. There's nothing wrong with that." And Micah had been so skittish the first night. I'd known right off the bat that even if he was honestly curious about the lifestyle, it would take us a while.

Sean rolled his eyes. "There's not rushing and then there's hibernating."

"I'm not hibernating."

Was I? No, I wasn't. Right? Even if he *was* a virgin, we were moving forward. A bit.

Sean snorted but quieted as Micah and Rick came into the kitchen carrying what seemed to be the last of the plates. Walking over to the door, I took the stack from Micah's hand and indicated toward the backyard. "Is that it?"

Micah looked up at me with a smile. He'd been tense when he'd heard Rick and Sean were coming over, but after a while, he'd started to relax. He'd even volunteered to help Rick clean up the back. "Yeah, that's everything. Good as new."

Maybe Sean had a point. As nervous and new as Micah was to the lifestyle and relationships, he embraced everything after just a little bit of hesitation.

"Great." Leaning in, I kissed him quickly. "Thank you." Heading over to the sink, I set the plates down and glanced around the room. "I think that's it. I'll get these later, but everything else is put away. Thanks."

"You sure? I can do the dishes if you want," Micah offered.

Walking back to Micah, I wrapped my arms around him. "I have better plans for us than dishes at the moment. Maybe later." Then I gave Sean and Rick a pointed look and grinned. "Hint, hint."

Sean laughed. "So subtle."

Micah chuckled and I could see a faint blush on his face, but he didn't seem overly embarrassed.

Ignoring Sean's teasing, I reached out for Rick's hand. "Thanks for coming over."

Shaking his hand then getting a hug from Sean, it wasn't long before I watched them head out the front door. Sean fell behind and whispered something to Micah that had both of them giggling and the blush coming back to Micah's cheeks, but I didn't butt in. Sean and I had been good friends for years, and I was glad they were getting along.

Calling out a final goodbye as they got in their car, I turned and wrapped Micah in my arms again. "See, that wasn't too bad."

"It wasn't bad at all," Micah said, looking shy all of a sudden as he gazed up at me. "It was pretty fun. I like both of them a lot."

"I'm glad." I kissed his forehead and smiled. "It's nice having people who understand you."

"It really is. I mean… I'm still getting used to all of this, obviously, but seeing how happy Sean and Rick are…" He shrugged, burying his face against my chest as he pressed in close to me. "I'm glad I took the leap."

"Thank you for trusting me." I ran my hand over his hair and pulled him closer. "I know that wasn't easy."

"Easier than I expected," he admitted. "I thought it would be harder." He looked up at me again and rolled his eyes. "So you were right. Again. That's gonna get old real fast."

Laughing, I shrugged. "What can I say? Daddies are always right."

"Don't let that go to your head," he grumbled, leaning up to steal another kiss. This one turned lingering, intense, and he moaned against my lips.

"Of course it won't, because I already knew it." Grinning, I kissed him slowly, letting the heat build.

He offered no hesitation or reluctance, kissing me back every bit as eagerly. He drew back just enough to murmur, "Yeah, yeah…" But he didn't seem like he really cared about our conversation anymore.

"I think I've got a naughty boy here." I started kissing along his jaw and down his neck. "Talking back to your daddy. I might have to make sure you remember how to be a good boy."

Micah squirmed and pressed closer to me. He made low, needy sounds as I nibbled on the sensitive skin below his ear before coming back to his lips to kiss him again.

"Promises, promises," he whispered against my mouth.

I arched a brow.

If he was willing to tease and push for a spanking, Sean was probably right. I'd been taking things too slow. "Daddies always keep their promises. Sometimes we just don't go as fast as needy little boys want."

He tilted his head, meeting my eyes. "Maybe," he said, looking like the shy boy I'd had on my lap the first night he'd come to the bar.

I moved my hand up to cup his cheek and leaned in to kiss him again, soft and gentle. "Then we go slow." Pulling back, I decided to push things in a different direction without easing up completely. "Come sit down with me on the couch. I want to show you a few things."

He gave me a questioning look but nodded, for all that he seemed reluctant to pull away. His hand found mine, and when I started toward the living room, he followed close behind me.

I led him through to the couch, grabbing my laptop off the side table near the couch. As I sat down, I pulled him close so he'd be able to see the screen too. "I thought we could look at a few things, like the diapers, so you can see how they look… and maybe get an idea about what you might want to try."

"Diapers," Micah repeated. "Like… to just wear? Or to use?

Or…" He didn't look as worried as I might've thought. Instead, he mostly just looked… curious.

"That can go either way." As I started pulling up the internet, I paused and turned so I could wrap Micah in my arms. "I want you to remember two things for me. I will never make you do anything you don't want to, and if there's something you're curious about, we'll try it. No questions asked. I want you to be happy."

"I am happy," he said, snuggling close to me. "And I'm… not sure how I feel about things. I want to try them, but I don't know what I'm doing."

"You don't have to know right now. This is all still very new, and that's okay. We'll try things together, and I want you to ask questions when you're confused or concerned. Otherwise, I'll make the decisions if you want me to." He was already nodding. "It's always okay to simply realize that making a decision is too hard."

"I don't know enough to make a lot of decisions," he admitted. "And I want to see what you like. I feel like I'm… fumbling a little, but I want you to guide me." He looked up at me, uncertain, but he pressed in closer anyway. "Please… Daddy."

His words warmed my heart. I kissed his forehead then hugged him closer. "I love taking care of you. There are so many ways to do that. Then you don't have to worry about pleasing me or that I'll be disappointed. If I get to bathe you and wrap you up in a diaper that you just wear around the house for fun, that's fine. If you want to use it and let me clean you up, that's something that I'd love to do for you. But only if it makes you feel loved and cared for."

"I should probably want to go for baby steps," he said with a small smile. "But I… um, I want to try everything. All at once." He let out a shuddering breath. "I trust you, Daddy."

I gently touched my lips to his in the lightest of kisses. "Thank you." I tucked him close to me as I turned my focus back to the computer. "I want you to tell me which designs you like best. I'm going to buy some, and you're going to try it. No decision there, no figuring out what to say. All you have to do is pick which prints you like."

"You don't have to buy anything for me," he protested, burying his face against my arm. His words were muffled as he added, "I don't want you to feel obligated or anything."

"No. I already decided what I'm going to do." I ran my hand over his hair and kissed his head as he hid. "I just need to know what you like."

He nodded, pulling back enough to peer at me. "Okay. I can do that."

"Good boy." I gave him a quick smack of a kiss to make him smile.

There weren't as many pattern choices as I would have liked, but since up until recently there had only been white, I probably couldn't complain. "There are diapers with some trains and cars on them."

Micah slowly turned his head, peeking at the screen as I pointed to more options.

"And shapes and blocks. There are even some plain white ones if you like those better."

"But I can choose anything I want?" His voice was more uncertain then, and he trembled in my lap. It was like he was on the verge of saying something, only to falter, and I frowned.

"Anything you want," I promised. We were already talking about diapers. What was it that had him spooked then? I was worried I'd pushed too far, but he spoke slowly.

He pointed silently at the screen, but I couldn't figure out which ones he was gesturing to. "The trains?"

He blushed harder, and I could see him gathering his courage. I couldn't figure out why he'd be okay with diapers, only to be tripped up on designs. "Um. Does it have to be… you know…" He looked up at me and bit his lip.

I wanted to be the one nibbling on his lip, but I didn't want to interrupt him. "It doesn't *have* to be anything in particular," I reassured him.

He nodded, his eyes flicking back at the screen before he looked back at me. He sighed, then finally asked, almost inaudibly, "So even those?"

This time I saw what he was pointing to: the princesses.

Now that was unexpected. He dressed so masculine that I'd never— I stopped. He dressed so masculine. Way too much. Where I wore t-shirts, he wore button downs. Where I had jeans with holes — unless I was teaching — he had pressed jeans or slacks. Did he do that on purpose, to cover something up? To hide something?

"Of course. The princesses are pretty." That was all I could say as I looked at him with new eyes. Why had I never noticed before? Why did I never see...

He was used to hiding it. Micah didn't let anyone see the real him, not even me — until now. I leaned closer and kissed his forehead again. "I think there's another company that even has ones with some pink patterns that would look really cute, if you want to see those."

Relief flooded his face, and he nodded. "Please."

"Can I ask you something?"

Micah tensed, probably expecting me to ask stupid questions.

"Don't worry, baby. I just want to ask you to tell me when you would like something like that. If you want to wear diapers with princesses, then it's fine with me." I saw him in my mind, wearing a nice diaper, maybe with painted fingernails. My cock jerked. Damn, I'd never explored that with Nicholas, but it sounded... tempting. "Besides, I think it's really hot, so if you want to experiment around with it, I'm very much game."

He stared at me with wide eyes, and it obviously took him a few seconds to grasp what I'd just told him.

I cupped his face and pressed a soft kiss on his forehead. "Never be ashamed for what you like. I want to get to know the real you. It's just the two of us. No one else needs to know," I whispered.

Finally, he nodded. "Just us?"

"Sure, baby. It's just us."

Relief flooded his eyes and a small smile played around his lips. "Thank you. It means a lot to me. I'll try to let you know, okay? I'm not used to… any of this, but I want to. So, let's look."

I brought up a new page and started searching. I couldn't remember the site, but it didn't take long to find it. There were only so many options when you were looking for adult diapers with printed patterns on them.

"Found it. They have a lot." Scrolling down the screen, I pointed to one. "The pink pony is cute. What do you think?"

"I like them," he said, nodding against my arm. "Will you pick from these? Please?"

"Of course, baby." I leaned into him and rested my head against his. "Let's get some of the pony ones and a pack of the purple ones, and I think the fish are kind of cute."

Micah relaxed even more against me. Looking at the more feminine diapers made me even harder, but I would show him that soon enough. For now, he needed to get comfortable with telling me about what he wanted.

There seemed to be more traditionally boy styles than more girlish ones on the site, but I thought we'd made a good start. We'd find different pages if he wanted to explore more.

Adding them to the cart, I quickly checked out. "Perfect. That will be enough for us to try them and see what you like. They'll be here in just a couple of days. I think the pony ones will be very cute on you." Setting the computer down on the coffee table, I turned and pulled Micah into my arms until he was draped across my chest as I leaned against the arm of the couch.

Carefully, he wriggled against me until I loosened my arms, but before I could worry about him, he was firmly planted in my lap.

"Thank you," he said, leaning up to kiss me.

"I don't know what I did, but you're welcome." I wrapped my arms around him and tucked him close again. No matter what he was worried about, I wanted him to know nothing would change how I was starting to feel about him.

"You helped me more than you might ever know. I felt comfortable enough to ask for what I wanted," he said, closing his eyes. "And you didn't get upset. It's… an awesome feeling." He offered me a smile as he opened his eyes again. "But I guess we've kinda passed into the realm of 'anything goes,' haven't we?"

"You're right. This is a place where you can be whoever you want. If one day, that's a prince and the next day you're the princess, that's what we'll do. I bet we could even find some cute panties for when you're little."

"You're going to spoil me rotten, aren't you?" he asked, a smile twitching back onto his lips.

"Of course." I gave him another quick kiss. Had that been his way of trying to change the subject? "I like spoiling you and seeing you smile just as much as I like kissing you and seeing you blush."

"Uh huh." Micah laughed, shaking his head, and it was like a weight had been lifted off of him. "I think you like seeing me blush most of all." He poked me in the arm.

I tightened my grip, trapping him against me, and grinned. "Yes, I do." I nuzzled against his neck and then nibbled on his ear. "No, wait. I like seeing you turned on even more. Because you're so cute when you're hot and shy at the same time."

"I'm totally not turned on," he said, loftily enough to where I was sure he wasn't being honest with me.

"Only naughty boys lie to their daddies," I told him.

"Maybe a little," he allowed. "Or maybe a little more than a little."

I rocked my hips up and pressed my thigh against his growing erection and grinned. "I think someone was being very naughty. That doesn't seem like anything little to me."

His breath caught, and he tilted his head up, eyes half closing. "Not fair," he whined.

Chuckling, I shook my head. "I'm being fair. I just can't have my boy lying to me. I've got a sweet good boy who's always honest with his daddy. Isn't that right?"

"Yes," he said, leaning up to kiss me again, hard and desperate. "I'm your sweet good boy, Daddy."

Letting my hands wander lower down his back, I slowly palmed his ass. When he let out a low moan and I felt a shiver race through him, I started kneading his cheeks and rocking against him. "Good boys need to be rewarded. Is that what my sweet boy wants? A reward from Daddy?"

He nodded, whimpering as his lips trailed from my mouth to my chin, then to my throat. "Yes," he groaned, hips rocking against me.

Pulling him tighter so I could feel every inch of him as his cock pressed against my thigh, I leaned down and started kissing his neck again. He really seemed to love feeling my teeth against his neck, because he made the most incredible sounds as the pleasure built.

He tilted his head, baring his throat for me, and his hands went to my shoulders. He clung to me, fingers digging into my skin, breathless and needy as he responded eagerly to every touch. He was so desperate to be touched, so desperate to be loved, yet he never pushed. Rather, he waited until I took the lead.

That was perfect for me, even though I might have to move faster than I intended to. I couldn't make him wait any longer when he clearly needed more, and I also couldn't resist.

All that teasing, those looks he'd thrown at me, the way he always melted in my arms... I needed him. I needed to feel him come apart in my arms.

As I nibbled along the column of his throat, I spread my fingers out over his ass. It was firm and round and the perfect size for my hand. My fingertips grazed over his hole. He was still wearing too many clothes for me to actually touch him, which I wanted so much. But as I continued to tease and massage his ass through his pants, encouraging him to rub against me even faster, shivers seemed to go through him with every caress.

"My sexy, needy boy." I flicked his ear with my tongue and then pulled the lobe into my mouth to nibble on it. "I can feel how hard you are and every little desperate shiver that races through you. Do you like your reward, my good boy?"

"Yes," he moaned again, seeming unable to string more words together as I licked his earlobe and slowly shifted down to nip his neck again. "I'm not the only needy one," he added after a moment, shyly reaching between us until his hand found my own hard cock. He palmed it as well as he could with how close we were, and this time, I was the one to shiver.

"You're the only one I'm thinking about right now. I want to see my sweet boy fly completely apart. I want to see how sexy you are when you come. I want to hold you in my arms and show me how good you feel."

He shuddered again.

I kneaded his ass cheeks harder and ran my fingers over his hole. "Show Daddy how good you feel, baby."

"So good," he panted, twisting so he could kiss me again, more desperately, more needily. His hands slid to the hem of my shirt, then brazenly shifted beneath it to touch bare flesh.

Something about the day, the confession about being inexperienced, or our discussion on the diapers had freed a part of him I hadn't seen before. There was a confidence and strength that'd never shone through as we'd gotten to know each other. Did my sweet boy know how sexy his newfound confidence was?

I moaned as his hand skimmed up my chest, slowly moving over my skin. His fingertips were soft as they caressed me. "Is this what you want, baby?"

He nodded immediately, just a second before his fingers found my nipple and toyed with it. "Please," he whispered.

My brain mostly shut off at some point. The way he was

writing on top of me sent all my blood south to my cock. Forcing my brain to join the fun, I started teasing his ass again. My fingers grazed and teased his ass again and again, and I wanted nothing more than to feel the muscle twitching under my fingers… wanted to show him how good it would feel. He moved faster, half trying to get off now. "You're trying to make me crazy, but two can play that game."

A sexy grin curved onto his lips. "You're already crazy," he teased before kissing me again. "So… crazier?"

"Oh yes, very crazy, sexy boy." Taking his mouth in a heated kiss, I brought my hand higher up his back then let my fingers inch beneath the waistband of his jeans. As I teased the top of his ass, caressing the soft skin that would lead down to his crack, he moaned and gasped into my mouth. When he finally pulled back, panting and looking at me with wide lust-filled eyes, I smiled and inched down even more. "My sexy boy, I love how beautiful you are like this."

He whimpered breathlessly as he squirmed and tried to get my fingers to move lower. "You just like watching me suffer," he panted out.

"No, sweet boy, I love watching you, especially when you're only thinking about how good you're feeling." I tenderly kissed him again. "There's no reason to rush to the finish. Sometimes the trip there is half the fun."

"It feels like I've been waiting forever," he admitted, fingers circling my nipples. Goosebumps rose on my body as he played with me. "I've wanted this for… a while now." His cheeks heated in that familiar blush, like he was making a confession.

"Oh, you're not the only one. I wanted you as soon as you walked in the bar with that sad, lost expression on your face. But instead of rushing into something, I wanted to give us time, until it meant something. This right here," I used my free hand to gesture between us, "you and me and everything we're building together… This is the most important thing to me."

"It's important to me, too," he said, palms resting against my chest. "I've never really…" He took a deep, shuddering breath. "I've never wanted anyone this bad before. It made it easier to… you know. But I want you."

My cock jerked at his words. I wanted him too, and I wanted him to want me even more.

"Well, my poor boy can't stay like this." Tilting my head, I kissed down his neck, nibbling and biting along the column of it as he moaned and wiggled against me.

"Please," he begged, and I could feel his hard cock against my thigh. "I'm going to end up coming in my pants like a teenager."

"You really don't know how hot that would be. But if you want to get naked, I'm happy to give you everything you need."

"Really?" he asked, sounding surprised. "You think that would be hot?" His lips parted a little in shock.

Couldn't he see how incredible and sexy he was?

"Oh, I can't wait to get you dressed up in something cute… maybe even in one of your new diapers, and tease and play with you until you've drenched yourself in cum. Of course, then I'm going to have to take my time cleaning up my boy's mess. I can't have a dirty boy, can I?"

"Oh god," he whispered, a full body shudder running through him as he desperately bucked against me. "That's so…" He moaned, his fingers finding my nipples again and tugging hard at them.

I laughed breathlessly as I bucked up against him. "But that's not what my boy wants right now. You want to be naked when I touch you and watch you explode in my hands. Isn't that right?"

"Yes," he whimpered breathlessly. "Please, please, please…"

We both groaned as I removed my hand from inside his pants, but when I gave his ass a pat and started to tug down his jeans, he sighed.

We really should have gone to the bedroom to do this, but I didn't think I could wait that long.

Micah squirmed to help me pull his jeans and boxers down, cock fully erect. He blushed a little more, glancing uncertainly at me. My eyes were soft as I looked at him. He really didn't know how beautiful he was, especially with this mix of shyness and lust. I got him to lie down so I could strip him completely.

After his pants and boxers had been tossed to the floor, I reached down to my own jeans and quickly unbuttoned and released the zipper digging into my erection.

Micah's cheeks heated as he watched me free myself. He didn't look like he knew what to do when I pulled him closer, but when his cock pressed against mine and I took them both in my fist, he gasped and thrust against me.

With a groan, I tightened my hold and started to stroke our dicks. Micah moaned loudly, leaning his head back as the pleasure rose inside of him. I wasn't doing much better. The feeling of the silken skin against my own hard cock drove me nearly crazy.

As curious as he'd been about the more traditionally feminine-looking diapers, I'd almost expected him to be wearing something less obviously masculine under his clothes. Was that what he wanted to wear or what he thought he should?

If my brain had been working better, I probably would have second-guessed the question, but right now, I couldn't think much. "What would you think if your daddy bought you some pretty panties to wear under your grown up clothes? Would you like to look pretty for Daddy?"

He shivered, his eyes a little glazed as he looked at me. "I'd like that," he said, absolutely not shy at all as his lust overtook him.

He kissed me again, fierce and urgent and desperate all at once. His cock was hot against my own, as he pressed forward then rocked back, seemingly desperate for friction.

"Would it make Daddy happy?" he whispered.

"Oh, I think happy would be an understatement, baby." I tightened my fist around him and started stroking in time to his thrusts, letting him fuck my fist as his pleasure continued to build. He was so incredible that I knew I wouldn't last once he finally exploded. "My pretty boy in his panties curled up on

Daddy's lap. You'd look so perfect with your cock straining to fit in your panties and begging Daddy to let you come. I bet you'd beg so sweetly."

He let out a choking sound, shuddering again. "Daddy—" If he was about to say something, it was cut off by his gasp. "I—" He tried to speak again, but before he could, his cum was spilling over my cock and my hand. He looked both stunned and rapturous, beautiful and perfect in my lap as he came.

The feeling of his release on mine and the incredible look on his face brought my own orgasm to the front. Cum flooded over his cock as I kept up a frantic pace, trying to force every drop of pleasure from both of us. If I found the idea of marking him with my cum a little bit too hot, I kept that to myself.

For now.

When he finally collapsed down onto me, I slumped back against the couch and wrapped my arms around him. Kissing the top of his head as he panted and laid there bonelessly, I smiled. "You are beautiful, inside and out."

He sleepily returned my smile, his eyes drifting closed again after he regarded me for a moment. "And you're perfect," he murmured. "That was... amazing."

Kissing him one last time, I let myself relax just holding him. It felt... right, better than anything had in a long time. It was probably too soon to tell him every thought that was running through my brain, but I just hoped he knew that I meant everything I'd said and more.

One day, we'd both be ready to hear me say it out loud.

CHAPTER TEN

MICAH

The idea of being alone in Carter's house was tantalizing and taboo all at once. It sent my heart into overdrive, making it beat madly during the drive from the university to his home. When I stood in front of his door, I wiped my hands on my jeans, trying to calm myself.

He'd invited me, but it still felt forbidden.

I closed the door behind me, making sure to lock it. We weren't in a high crime neighborhood by any means, but I had a feeling he'd want me to be safe no matter what.

I made my way into the kitchen, looking around. I'd seen it all before, but it was strange being here without Carter. He'd told me I could explore, and it might be a good time to do that when he wasn't there to distract me. Because, in all honesty, when he was close, I didn't care for our surroundings one bit. I just wanted him…

But since he couldn't distract me right now, I wanted to know more about him and his life. The best way to do that was… well, poking around his house. I'd talked to him a lot, too, but some things were better seen than told. At least that was what I figured. If he had any issues with me being alone in his home, he wouldn't have told me to come over. He'd directly stated he had nothing to hide, but I'd been burned one time too many to believe that.

Carter seemed to be too good to be true, and half of me expected to find... something. Another boyfriend? I doubted it. He spent all his time with me. Well, aside from the mornings, when I had class and he was off. But I doubted it. What then? Chains? Whips? I didn't know. Still, I'd feel better once I knew—

I stopped that train of thought. Those were my own insecurities, nothing else. I'd still use this occasion to look around. I blushed at the idea of invading his privacy, and I had no plans to abuse it. But there was something I was curious about...

I'd promised I'd cook dinner — over his insistence that it wasn't necessary — but it wouldn't take long to take a peek at the packed-up, lonely room that had been the nursery once.

I set my bag down in the chair, glancing back at the door like someone was going to walk in and catch me doing something I wasn't supposed to do. My parents had always been private, and I was used to ignoring everything that wasn't mine to look at.

But this had been an open invitation, and if I'd learned one thing about Carter, it was that he meant what he said.

Decision made, I set off upstairs, going to the door of the nursery. I had the strange urge to knock, and after casting another look around me, I gave in. I knocked, like I thought the specter of Carter's deceased spouse would be there to greet me.

Nothing happened.

Feeling like an idiot, I opened the door and stepped inside. Most of the boxes were gone, replaced by a neatly-arranged... nursery. Wow. He had to have done that recently, after the last time he'd shown me around.

There was only one reason I could think of why he'd do something like that, and it... made me hard and scared at the same time.

With a deep breath, I went to the dresser, but it was empty. I was both relieved and disappointed — relieved, because this had been Nicholas's space, and disappointed because I'd been curious to see what sorts of things would be inside.

There were a few boxes in the closet, and I went over to them. In one, clothes had been neatly folded. I gingerly reached in, pulling out an adult-sized onesie. I felt like a grave robber from touching the things. I was just... curious about Nicholas. I wanted to know more about him, but I didn't want to risk upsetting Carter by asking. But he'd been the man who'd held Carter's heart, and I felt like I should know him.

From the onesie, I knew Nicholas hadn't been much larger than I was, and I had to grin a little. Carter had a type, obviously, even if that didn't carry over past the physical. From everything I'd heard, I was the exact opposite of his husband.

I folded the onesie and set it back inside the box, poking at another. That one had stuffed animals inside of it, and I pulled out a cute bear. It looked like it had been thoroughly loved, fur that had obviously once been plush and soft having turned harder with wash after wash.

I wondered what had happened to my stuffed animals. They'd probably been thrown away, which seemed like a terrible waste all of a sudden. But my mother wouldn't even think about keeping something like that.

I started to look in another box when I heard footsteps, and I froze as the door opened the rest of the way.

And there was Carter, looking at me with an expression I couldn't quite interpret.

"I'm sorry!" I blurted out, taking a quick, guilty step away from the boxes. "I was just curious, and you said I could look around, but I shouldn't have taken advantage of—"

"Hush," he interrupted me.

I hushed, but I was trembling. I didn't want him to be angry with me.

He crossed the room in long strides and pulled me close, kissing my cheek. "I'm not upset. I told you that you had the run of the house." He smiled. "I would have thought you'd spend the time looking for naughty things under my bed, but this isn't unexpected."

I blushed. "I thought about it," I admitted. For like three seconds. "I don't know… I'm just… curious, I guess. And I haven't wanted to ask."

Carter looked around the room, sadness shining from his eyes as he moved his gaze back to me. "You can ask me anything you want. I won't get upset. Maybe a bit… I don't know… but it's been long enough that the pain isn't as sharp… even in here."

"I'm glad," I told him, cuddling close to him. "I don't want you to be sad. I mean, I know you're going to be, but I don't want it to be…" I sighed. "I don't know how to say what I'm trying to say." But I had a feeling he already knew.

He gave me a teasing grin and kissed me gently. "I get it and thank you."

The kiss and his embrace soothed something in me, and I didn't feel as guilty for snooping as I had before. "You're welcome." I kissed him again, trying to gather my thoughts. There were worse ways to stall than kissing him, after all. "I haven't started dinner yet," I said. "But I will." I eyed him. "I thought you'd be longer."

He shrugged. "My meeting got canceled. Flu's going around the elementary school and several of my coworkers had to leave early."

I nodded. "I'm glad you're home early. Just wish I had dinner ready for my daddy."

Carter chuckled. "Well, your daddy needs to get a shower and change clothes. Will that give you enough time to get started?"

"Definitely. It's nothing fancy." I shrugged. "Just tacos. Mostly it's cutting things up."

I probably should've asked him if he liked tacos, but there was a part of me that knew he'd probably eat it anyway. I wasn't sure if that was a good thing or a bad thing, but… it took some pressure off of me. I'd rather be humored than in trouble for messing up.

"Sounds delicious." He kissed me again, that time smacky and teasing. "Okay, shower and then I'll come right down."

"Don't be too long. I'll miss you," I told him, batting my eyelashes at him — a bit shyly, maybe, but I felt bolder than I usually did. There was something about him that just made it easier to answer his teasing with a bit of my own.

"Hmm." His smile turned wicked. "It sounds like you don't want your daddy to get... distracted in the shower."

My cheeks flushed with heat, and I squirmed a little. I hadn't immediately thought about that, but now that he'd mentioned it... I couldn't get the idea of it out of my head. His naked body under the water, soaping himself up, his hand sliding down to his cock—

"I... I think you broke my brain," I croaked out. "Now I'm going to burn the food because I'm going to be wondering if you're... busy."

"Well, I can't have you burning down the house, can I? I wouldn't be a very good daddy if I let something happen to you." He leaned in and kissed me gently again, but as the passion started to build, he pulled back enough to smile and stare into my eyes. "It seems like I need to keep a better eye on you. What do you think? Should I keep you right beside me to make sure you stay... safe?"

It took me a moment to get my thoughts focused again, and I mentally ran through the conversation to make sure I hadn't missed anything. Nope. He was definitely inviting me into the bathroom with him, which felt even more intimate than anything before. There was something almost... domestic about it, something that *did* make me feel safe.

"I think so," I said breathlessly, my hands going to his hips. "Can't be too safe."

His smile widened. "That's what I was thinking." One hand came up and traced my cheek while he watched for my reaction. "And since there are so many hazards in the bathroom, I'm going to have to keep you closer there as well. Very close."

Now that I hadn't expected, but now that he'd said it, my mind was chanting *yesyesyes*. The idea of saying no never even occurred to me. I wanted it.

I wanted him.

"Hmm... How close are we talking?" I asked, managing a smile that was somewhere between mischievous and a little nervous.

"Well, close enough that you might end up getting your clothes wet, so we might need to take them off. I can't have you walking around all damp." The hand that'd been stroking my cheek started caressing my chest. "And if you're wet, I might as well get you all clean. It won't quite be a bubble bath, but I can think of fun ways to wash my sweet boy... very thoroughly."

The sound of a bubble bath was oddly appealing — but the idea of being pressed against him in the shower was even more so. "Yeah?" I asked, my voice a little more breathless. "Like what?"

"You're going to have to wait and see." Carter smiled and stepped back, taking my hand. "Come on, boy. Let's get cleaned up and then you can make dinner for us — if you want to."

I shivered at the promise in his voice, and my cock hardened even more. I trusted him, which was still strange sometimes... but I did. I really and truly did.

"Do you want to undress me?" I asked him, tilting my head and gazing up at him.

Carter nodded, leading me toward the door. "Generally, that's what a daddy would do. Is that all right with you?"

It was. I thought I might be surprised at that, but I was far from it. "Yes," I said, my voice stronger than I'd expected. "Do I get to help you undress, or do I just get to admire you while you do a strip tease?" I offered a shy smile, unsure of how he'd react to that.

Carter chuckled. "I'm not sure I've ever done a strip tease. I don't think I'm the type."

"Pity." I grinned at him. "But as long as I get to see the goods, I guess I'll let you see mine."

"Deal."

"Then you should probably get me into the bathroom," I said with a quirked brow.

Still smiling, Carter shook his head. "Yes, sir."

I took his hand into mine, slowing my steps as we got to his bedroom. "Good thing we're in the master bedroom. Now I get to snoop there and in your bathroom."

Though really, I'd snooped through what I'd been really curious about, but now… the idea of seeing his private domain fascinated me.

"If you think my patience will last while you look through my cabinets, you're crazy." Carter grinned as he led us into the bathroom. "You'll have to find another time to snoop."

"I think I can deal with that," I told him, pressing up against him and claiming another kiss. I took his other hand in mine, guiding him to the hem of my shirt. "As long as you don't make me wait too much longer."

"If that's what you want." Carter's hands tightened on the fabric and started easing my shirt over my head.

"It is," I reassured him, lifting my arms so he could more easily pull the shirt from me. I felt a bit self-conscious at first, but then I saw the look in his eyes. They were burning with passion, roaming over my naked chest like he wanted to devour me. My nipples hardened in response, even as a shiver raced over my back.

He made me feel sexy, too — wanted, desired… needed.

My shirt dropped to the floor and I tried to figure how to go on. Socks, right. I hurriedly got those out of the way too.

"Beautiful," he told me, while his fingers traced over my chest from one collar bone to the other, drawing a line of goosebumps and shivers of pleasure.

Then he moved down, caressing my chest. He ignored my nipples, no matter how much they begged for attention, and ran over my navel before finally hooking his fingers under the waistband of my pants. "Can I go on?"

I nodded without hesitation. I was ready. I was more than ready.

He unfastened my pants and nudged, sending them and my boxers to the floor. All I could think about was the feeling of his hands on me, on our cocks rubbing together, of the feeling of his seed spilling over me... I moaned as I stepped out of the rest of the clothes, cheeks flushed but my eyes hopeful as they locked onto his.

He leaned in and gave me a kiss before he dropped his hands to his side. "Your turn."

My heart thundered, and I wet my lips with my tongue before pressing in close. I stole a kiss then stepped back enough to let him pull his shirt off.

His chest was as gorgeous as the rest of him, and I drank in the sight of him. "You're so gorgeous," I whispered. For a moment, I didn't even want to continue. I just wanted to stand there and watch him. But the idea of getting to inspect him in full...

Even while we'd made out, I'd never seen him completely naked — which was a shame, when I looked at what was already visible.

He popped open the button of his pants and carefully pulled down the zipper, pausing long enough to meet my eyes. He kissed me again, and I smiled as he tugged down at his pants. I could see his half-hard cock come free.

My breath caught, and I couldn't help but reach out, running a finger along the top of his cock.

Carter moaned and his hands jerked, like he was having a hard time staying still. "No teasing. I only have so much patience, Micah."

"I wasn't meaning to just tease you." I didn't back off. My fingers closed around his cock, weighing it in my palm. The skin was soft, even though he was rock hard by then. "I'm just curi-ous." It still made me nervous that I didn't have any experience, but he knew it, and hopefully, he wouldn't expect me to be as good as any of his past lovers had been.

And I was pretty sure that no matter what I did, it'd be good enough for him. Still, I wanted to try, wanted to learn and get better.

I slowly lowered myself to my knees, watching his expression. I didn't know if he was going to let me get away with this, but I wanted it.

I wanted him.

Carter groaned and one hand came up to rest on my head. He ran his fingers through my hair, then he dropped it. "Only if you really want this. You don't have to do anything you're not comfortable with."

I reached up to grab his hand, placing it back on my head. "Gentle," I told him, even though I didn't need to. "I like when you touch me. And I like… I want to do this."

Before he could answer, I leaned in, taking just the tip of his cock into my mouth. Carter moaned and stroked over my hair, caressing down my neck and around my ear as a shiver of pleasure went through him.

It was enough to encourage me, and I took a little more. Porn really wasn't a good way to learn how to do things, but some internet pages were, and I might have looked up how to blow a man. So I slid my tongue along his slit, tasting him. He was already leaking, and a shiver of pride ran through me.

Another moan sounded through the room, his fingers twitching where they lay.

I'd done this. *Me.* He was moaning like that because of me. And he was every bit as eager as I was.

Lack of skill or not, I gave it my all. I took more of him past my lips. I wasn't going to be able to do anything fancy like take his sizable cock completely into my mouth, but I could do enough. I let my tongue swirl around his cock, bobbing my head up and down as I took as much as I could. His cock felt like nothing else on my tongue, but I wouldn't get enough of the feeling — ever.

Carter's muscles clenched as he fought to stay still, and his body trembled.

It was flattering. I wanted to see that I could get him to come undone. I wanted to know that I could give him what he needed. Imperfect or not, I made up for it with enthusiasm. I wanted to please him, was eager to give him the slightest idea of what he did for me.

When he gently started to urge me back, I knew he was close, but I stubbornly stayed put. I wanted the full experience. I wanted to know what he tasted like and savor it for the rest of my life. I might make a mess, but that was what the shower would be for.

As I started to suck faster, his cock jerked and started to pulse. Cum filled my mouth as he shot, gasping and moaning. It tasted salty and bitter and some other things I couldn't place, but his low words about how sexy I was and how good it felt distracted me from trying to figure it out.

I swallowed, trying to get as much down my throat as possible. When he was finally spent, he cupped my jaw. I licked him a few times, cleaning him up and I let his now softening cock go — but not before I pressed one last kiss to the tip.

Carter smiled, still breathing hard, and reached down to pull me up. "Come here."

His arms wrapped around me, and he kissed me tenderly, not seeming to mind the traces of his cum that were covering my lips. When he finally relaxed his hold and pulled back, he cupped my cheek and kissed my forehead. "That was incredible."

I melted against him, liking the feeling of his warm body against mine. I was hard, but it didn't matter. I was floating on cloud nine after getting him to come for me. He put me first, whatever we did, and it felt wonderful to know I could return the favor.

"It felt pretty incredible on my end too," I admitted, returning his smile.

He kissed me again. "Let's get you cleaned up." He shifted and reached for the shower knob. As the water heated up, he hugged me tighter and kissed my forehead. "I'm glad you came over tonight. I know you were worried about being here alone, but knowing you'd be waiting for me made a long day easier." His hand stroked up my back, and I let my head rest on his shoulder.

"I really liked coming here to wait for you," I said against his skin. "I like getting to see you more. I like spending time with you, and I miss you when you're gone." My words were still muffled, but it was easier to talk when I didn't look into his eyes. I'd gotten better at that, too, but still. Right now, I was too raw to form words when I looked at him. "I'm so glad I found you."

Carter cupped my chin and raised my head. So much for hiding. "I'm glad you walked into the bar that night. I know it wasn't what you expected, and the circumstances weren't perfect, but I think it was meant to be."

"They weren't perfect, but… I think if they'd been perfect, it would've made me skeptical about it." I nudged him. "As it is, you're already pretty damn close to perfect."

And he was. He really, truly was, in ways that I'd never be able to express.

I leaned up, kissing him again, soft and sweet. "Thank you," I said softly.

The words were at the tip of my tongue, three little words that might've changed everything, but I held them back. Instead, I pressed my nude body against his, still tasting his cum on my tongue, and rested my head against his shoulder.

I didn't need to move from there — not then, not ever. That was exactly where I wanted to be.

The boxes were stacked neatly at home. The mailman had dropped them off earlier that morning, and I'd just moved them into the living room. I'd considered putting them into the nursery, but I didn't want to overwhelm him — though he was probably more likely to accuse me of moving too slow.

Still, I didn't want to risk it, especially since I'd gone online again when he was gone and shopped a bit more.

So the boxes were in the living room, and I was in a drug store. The nail polish section was endless, as was the one with makeup and stuff for hair. I might have to learn about all that, because I was totally lost here. I'd thought buying one bottle of nail polish wouldn't be a problem, and the same with some makeup or ribbons or something. But who'd have guessed there were a gazillion choices?

"Hello. Can I help you?" The friendly, though curious voice came from the left.

I looked down at the tiny woman with brown hair. She definitely wanted to know why I was looking lost in front of the nail polishes.

"I… no. Thank you. I just haven't decided which color would be the best."

"What are you looking for? I can suggest a few things?" She offered a friendly smile, stepping closer. "Is it a surprise for your wife or girlfriend?"

I met her gaze. "Uh, no. Not exactly."

"So… Who then?" She stepped closer, and her perfume rose to my nose.

Was she flirting with me? Seriously?

"I… This is for my boyfriend. He loves nail polish, and I want to surprise him. I think I'm going to pick a few different colors for him." My face heated up. While I didn't have any problems with my preferences, I usually didn't broadcast them. Announcing that I was on a beauty product shopping spree for my boyfriend was new, even for me.

She stepped back immediately, and her smile was replaced by something more professional — still warm, but nothing like the flirtatious one she'd shown before. "I see. Anything he likes? Any colors he prefers?" At least she backed off when she heard I wasn't single.

I shook my head. "I'm not sure, to be honest."

"Then I can recommend this brand. It's a good, solid nail polish. Pick the colors you like and surprise him." She pointed to a shelf.

"Thank you."

She nodded. "You're welcome. Can I help you with anything else?"

I shook my head. I wanted to look at the make-up, but no way in hell I'd tell her that and confirm the fact that I had no clue what I was doing. I'd rather fumble through it alone.

Micah stood in front of my door as soon as he finished his classes. He needed to go to work later, and I had a class to teach, but we could both sneak away for a while.

We'd done that a few times, and it was always nice to have

him in my arms and just relax with him. I usually made sure to have lunch ready so I could feed him. He drank from his sippy cup and snuggled close. Sometimes, he napped. Other times, he just sat there, doing nothing.

There had been a couple of days when he didn't want to be little, but wanted to talk about his day and things that happened in college. He also told me about work, about the dogs he cared for, and especially Snowflake, whom he loved, and the cats he had a love-hate relationship with. Micah was a dog person, through and through, but he still loved the shelter cats.

When I opened the door, he smiled up at me. Micah still dressed the same way he always had, though I'd seen the occasional t-shirt on him even when he hadn't been working. It looked way better, and I really hoped he'd get rid of the pressed slacks one day. Not because I didn't like them, but because I knew why he wore them — and that had nothing to do with being comfortable and everything to do with hiding.

"Hey, baby. How was your day so far?"

"Better now. Actually, it was good, but I was looking forward to coming over to you. You said something about a surprise?" He bounced on the balls of his feet, eager like a puppy — or a kid getting presents, which wasn't that far off.

"Is that a way to greet your daddy, my sweet boy?"

His eyes sparkled. "Sorry, Daddy." He stepped closer, wrapped his arms around my waist and rose to kiss me. By now, his kisses weren't shy anymore. He opened up for me, kissing me back with enthusiasm and rubbing himself against my thigh.

A low moan rose, and I pulled him back with me to close the door before the poor neighbors saw more than they wanted.

When we broke apart, we were both breathing hard, and his cock rubbed against me. I wasn't doing any better, but I wouldn't drag him off to my bedroom now. Presents first, even though he seemed to have forgotten about them right now.

I nibbled along his neck, but before we could get carried away, I led him to the living room where I'd stacked the boxes.

"What's that?" he asked as he took the plain brown boxes in.

"Your surprise, baby. Some of that is what you expected. Some of it… not so much. But I hope you'll like it."

His eyes met mine, and while he hesitated, he also looked eager to start.

"Go on, open them. Here's a knife." I offered him my pocket knife.

"Uh, oh. Daddy. Didn't you forget something?" He grinned at me.

I wracked my brain, but I couldn't figure it out. "Um… Help me out here?"

"Giving your boy a knife is a bad idea, Daddy." His eyes sparkled, though.

"Oh, right. Well, I'll cut, you can open. How's that?"

He grinned, bouncing again. "That's better. Now open them! I want to look!" He paused, his lower lip pushing forward. "Pleeease, Daddyyyy!"

I wanted to suck it into my mouth and have my way with him, but he'd probably explode if I forced him to wait any longer. "You need to learn patience, baby boy. But here we go." I stepped forward, cutting open the first box.

Immediately, his hands were there, ripping apart the cardboard. The first box had the princess diapers. He pulled one out, looking at it. For a moment, he was quiet, and I was afraid I'd made a mistake. He examined the diaper, running his finger along the patterns, then he took in a deep, shuddering breath.

"Are you okay?" I asked, reaching out to put a hand on his arm.

He smiled up at me, and I could see my little boy there — shy, but just waiting to burst free. "More than okay." He set the diaper aside. "This later. More presents now."

"Patience," I reminded him with a grin.

He leaned in to kiss me, slow and lingering, and I relaxed.

"Fine," he said with a sigh.

He was doing so well. He might need a minute to get used to the new items, but he was as eager and curious as ever.

I slit the tape on the next box anyway, unable to deny him a moment longer. "My sweet, good boy." I handed him the box. "For being patient, you can have this one now."

I didn't know which boxes held which items, so it was as much a surprise to me as it was to him. It was nerve-wracking. I wanted to see a spoiled little opening his gifts. I didn't want him to revert back to the terrified boy he'd been.

He pulled out a set of baby bottles, examining them as closely as he had the diapers. "It's weird," he admitted. "They look different now that they're... you know... mine." He hesitated. "Are you sure about all of this? I mean..." He gestured at the boxes. "This couldn't have been cheap."

"You let me worry about that," I said, already working on cutting open the next box. "I want to spoil you, and I can, so enjoy."

"Is that an order?" He rolled his eyes.

"That's an order, baby boy."

"Well, if you insist..." He looked at the bottles again. "They're fish," he said, a smile tugging at his lips.

I grinned at him. "Do you like it?" It was my turn to be a little uncertain, though. What if he hated the theme? He'd hate everything if he did.

But his eyes were as earnest and eager as they had been. "Fridge-worthy," he teased, then tucked them back inside the box, as neatly as they'd arrived.

In the next box, I saw what I'd been both worried and increasingly excited about: panties, made for a little his size, with more fish and ocean themes on some. Others were pink, and it was those his gaze lingered on the longest. I'd guessed right when I'd ordered those. "You'll be able to wear some of those over your diapers," I told him.

Micah tilted his head, looking at the way some of the panties were just a little too big, and he swallowed hard. A shiver ran through him, and his eyes flicked from the panties to the diaper to the bottles before his gaze returned to me. "You pick the best presents."

He unpacked the onesies and nightgowns, looking at those with the same intensity he had the rest.

"Now these," I said, pointing to the other stack of boxes, with the bag from the pharmacy on top, "are for my boyfriend, not my boy."

He looked curiously at me, though oddly enough, he looked more wary about this than he had about the other items.

I handed him the bag. "Sorry I didn't get a chance to wrap it."

"How dare you," he said, deadpan, but I could see him trying not to smile.

"Brat," I said. "You've been spending too much time with Sean."

He laughed, but he sobered before long. "Not bratty, just..." He paused, considering his words before he went on, "More confident?"

"Confidence looks good on you." I kissed the top of his head. "But if you want to be a brat, you can be a brat. I'll just have to spank you."

"Promises, promises," he whispered, but I didn't think he was ready to go quite that far yet. He peered into the bag, quiet for another moment. "These are for me?" he asked, his voice trembling a little.

I nodded. "Just for you."

He poured out the contents, a few bottles of nail polish and some eye makeup. All but one of the colors were subtle, though I'd gotten him a bright purple one to reassure him that he could be bold if he wanted to. "These are pretty," he said, inspecting the eye shadow.

"We can watch some YouTube videos together and figure out how this stuff... works," I said.

"You mean there's something you aren't good at?" He mock-gasped.

"Don't tell anyone, but — no. I'm absolutely, completely perfect." I managed to keep a straight face. "This is why I'm going to look at the YouTube videos with you, so you know what to do with the make-up. I know everything about that, of course."

Micah stared at me with wide eyes. They were going to look even more beautiful with the mascara and eye shadow.

"Just kidding, boy. I'm not perfect at all. I have no idea what to do with the make-up, and I also suck at a lot of other things. Though I'm good at sucking." I wiggled my eyebrows.

We burst out laughing, but then he sobered, all mock-innocence. "I think..." He stepped closer and his breath fanned over my skin, "I'm not sure I believe you. You might have to show me..."

"Is that so, baby boy? Are you sure?" I placed my hands on his hips, pulling him closer.

He melted against me, tilting his head so he could meet my eyes. "No. I think I should be thanking you, if I'm honest. But I also... want to, you know." There he was again, my shy boy. He'd been more confident moments ago, but telling me what he wanted was still hard. Still, we'd made huge steps toward opening up.

"I know? I think I know, yes. Come on, let's move this to the bedroom." I released him and offered my hand.

"Nuh-uh," he said, to my surprise.

I arched a brow, glancing down below the waist. He was every bit as hard as I was, if not more, and patience wasn't really his strong suit these days. "No?"

He gestured. "I still have presents to open, and..." He took a deep, shuddering breath and let it out, a smile creeping onto his lips, "And I think you need to learn patience, Daddy."

That boy was going to kill me. "You are a brat. And I guess you'll get to know my hand one day, but in this case, you're right. Just don't think I'm going to forget the sex."

"Never, Daddy. I wouldn't want you to. But first, presents." He bounced forward, handing me another box to open. I cut through the tape, and he all but ripped the box from my hands. "Boy, slow down. Otherwise you'll have to wait until tomorrow." My voice was stern and was answered with pouting lips.

"Daaaaddyyyyy, please. I'll be a good boy now."

I kissed his head and handed him the box. "There you go."

He opened it, no trace of patience left again. But his expression flickered from eagerness to something a little more subdued. This time, it took him a while longer to find a response to the clothes, long enough to where I started to worry.

"Those are for my boyfriend again, not for little Micah. I—" I swallowed. This could go south really quickly. "I thought you might like to wear something like this sometimes. I had the feeling you're—"

"I like them," he interrupted me. "I think. I just never thought I could wear anything like these." He ran his fingers over the fabric, tracing patterns and colors. "They're nice. Thank you." He picked up a flowing top, swallowing hard as he held it against himself.

"You're very welcome." They weren't anything too flashy, but I'd gotten him comfortable jeans, prettier shirts, and things that wouldn't hide his figure.

There was one last box, and I hesitated before I handed it to him.

"And those," I said slowly. "I thought… I thought you might like the option."

He frowned but took the box. When he opened it, he pulled out several pairs of panties, similar to the ones before, but more… adult. His expression was every bit as inscrutable as it had been before, though I could see his breathing had quickened. He'd been excited about the other pairs, but these were different. Those were for grown-ups, definitely sexier.

"I thought you might want to wear those under your clothes sometimes. You'd look hot as hell in them."

"You think so?" He offered me a shy smile, rubbing his fingers over the fabric of a gray pair. "I'm not sure… would this be… I've never—"

My already half-hard cock twitched at the idea of seeing him in panties. How had I gone so long without realizing how hot this was?

Micah finally seemed to find his words again. "Would you like that?" He looked intently at me, fingers still clutching cloth.

I took his other hand and pressed it to the bulge in my jeans. "What do you think?"

He let out a breathless laugh. "Oh, I didn't… Okay." He paused, but his fingers didn't move from the panties — or from my hard-on. "I never expected you to—"

"I told you I didn't realize it, but I find it incredibly sexy. If you do, too. But you don't need to wear them only to please me. I just want you to be comfortable."

"I… No. I like them. I think. I just—"

I gently removed his hand from my cock, then the other from the panties, and drew him into my arms. This last package had thrown him more than everything else I'd gotten him. Was he afraid I wanted him to wear them? Did he not like them and didn't want to say it? Insecurities rose, even though I tried to hide them.

"Talk to me, baby. What is it? I'll never make you wear them. I promise. I really just thought you might—"

"They're nice." He paused, pressing his face closer to my shoulder. "Really. And I like them. I just… people are mean, and I… Those friends — not friends— whatever—"

"You've been laughed at for liking pretty things?" My blood boiled. Those assholes. He was such a nice, genuinely honest and good guy, and they had nothing better to do than making fun of him?

"Hmm." Micah didn't look at me.

"Oh baby." I pressed a kiss to his head, the only spot I could reach. "People are assholes, and I'm sorry you had to go through it."

"They saw me... in a clothing store. When I was in school, back home. I was looking at... you know. I couldn't walk through the hallways after that. They'd call me names, ridicule me, tease and taunt me... I was crying every day, until the year was over. Then the summer holidays started... and they had all day to find me and torture me. That's when I started to learn programming." His lips twisted into an odd, forced smile. "Computers don't judge you like people do."

My heart broke for him. "Oh, baby. I'm so, so sorry. That must've hurt so much. I wish I could spare you this pain somehow." I held him close, trying to reassure him I was there for him. I'd known he'd been bullied, but I'd never expected the depth of it.

"It did. I'm mostly over it, I think, but I never dared to dress like this. I wanted to, so, so much, but what if they saw me? I like the clothes you got me. They look so nice and comfy, but what if..."

"They'll always find a way, if they want to. They didn't call you out on your clothes, but they sent you to the wrong bar, didn't they? Bullies don't stop because you change on their behalf."

Micah slowly raised his head. It took him a moment, but then his eyes met mine. "How do you know?" His words were barely above a whisper.

"I was young in a time where it was way harder to be out and proud. I've had my fair share of bullies."

"How did you stop them?"

"I didn't. They moved on one day. It wasn't easy, but they were never so bad that they got physical. It was mostly name calling. I learned to ignore them."

Micah nodded. "That sounds good. I tried to, but I just... I wanted to have friends, you know? They were nice, and then they turned around and pulled a stunt like the one with the bar."

I held him closer. "I can't even be mad for that because it led you to me, but I wish you'd stumbled into the bar on your own, not because you were set up."

He offered me a more genuine-looking smile. "Me too. But it worked out. So, you guess I could just ignore them? Wear my nice clothes and tell them to go fuck themselves?"

I nodded. "Yeah, you can, though I'd be careful if you tell them to go fuck themselves unless you know how to defend yourself. Some guys react rather badly to that. I don't want my baby to get hurt."

"I was kidding," he reassured me, only to pause, tilt his head a little, then amend, "Maybe. Mostly. So just nice clothes it is. At least I can try how it feels and see what happens. I... I don't want to hide anymore."

A smile tugged at my lips. "I'm proud of you, baby. I would offer to take care of them for you, but that's not really a good idea, considering my position."

"And I don't want my Daddy to get hurt, so no. I can deal with them. Somehow."

He sounded way more confident, and maybe he'd leave his shell even more now.

"I'm sure you can. There's also always the official way, but I'm not sure if you want to go that route."

"Not right now. I don't really want to get anyone else involved." He wrapped his arms around me and hugged me tighter. "Thank you for the awesome gifts, Daddy. You're so spoiling me, but I love it. I want to try everything and see how it feels."

Now the small smile on my lips grew into a big one. "I'm happy to hear that, baby boy. I'm glad you like them, and I'm gonna get you much more once we know what you really like."

"You, Daddy. And one of you is absolutely enough."

With those words, he leaned up and kissed me on the lips. Gone was the shy man who'd just talked about being bullied, replaced by a guy who wanted nothing more than to... What exactly did he want? For now, he was kissing me like his life depended on it, though he easily relented as I took over the kiss. My own cock grew harder as he started grinding against me, and he wasn't much behind either.

Finally, he forced his lips away, breathing hard. "I want to try —" He took a deep breath. "I want to try the panties. Can I, Daddy? Pleeeaaase?"

The way he said please had me melt into a puddle in front of him every time. I'd do everything just to hear him say that, in that voice — not really like a kid, but not like a man, either. Simply like *my* boy, *my* little.

"You can try everything you want, baby. Pick a pair, go change in the bathroom and then get dressed again so I can strip you."

Micah nodded. "I can do that. Go ahead. I'll pick one and be there with you in a minute." His eyes sparkled and apparently, he'd pushed the remainders of the talk we'd just had deep into his mind. Now he wanted sex, and that's what he'd get.

I waited for him in the bedroom. He hadn't picked the master bathroom. It took him more than a minute to get back, but I waited — not so patiently, but I did.

Which pair of panties would he pick? One with a boyish cut, or would he go for pink? My cock jerked at the images my mind came up with. I'd love both on him.

Finally, the door opened, and he slowly stepped into the room. My heart stopped and my breath caught. Instead of putting the panties on underneath his regular clothes, he'd picked one of the onesies. Fuck me. He'd really done that.

A very shy smile wavered on his lips and his face was flushed.

"God, baby. You're so... you're so beautiful. I can't even tell you how good you look."

"Really? I feel a little stupid." He fidgeted, shifting so he partially hid himself from view, but on the other side, I could see how turned on he was. Neither the onesie nor the panties I hoped he wore beneath hid his hard-on, which pushed the fabric out.

"You're looking a lot of things, but not stupid, baby. Come here. Let me show you?" I watched him as he slowly came toward me. The light onesie was one of my favorites, with green and yellow fish on it. I'd seen it online and immediately thought about him.

Micah sat on the bed next to me, even more nervous now. His fingers played in front of him and his shoulders slumped.

"What's wrong, baby? We don't have to do anything. You know that, right? If you're feeling uncomfortable, just let me know, and we'll watch TV or something. No hard feelings." I held out my arms to him.

"It's not that. I know you wouldn't do anything I don't want to do. It's more…" He trailed off, not looking in my direction, but he pressed against me.

Carefully, I pulled him backwards, shifting both of us around until his cheek rested on my shoulder. "What is it, sweet boy?"

"It feels… right. And it turns me on."

I swallowed as my cock jerked. "This… What exactly is turning you on?"

"Everything. The onesie… that you want me like this… that I can wear something like that… that you want me even more… Everything?"

I hid my smile. "Was that *everything* a question?" I tried to get a good look at his face, but he'd buried it against my shoulder.

"Yeah?" His voice was muffled, but he'd wrapped his arms around me, holding on to me.

"Don't question it, baby. As long as you find it hot, and I find it hot, there's nothing else we need to know. Sometimes, you just have to accept it."

"Okay. I guess… It's still weird, but right, too. And especially the panties… I've wanted some for so long." His voice cracked, but I was proud of him for saying the words aloud.

"You're welcome, baby." I kissed his forehead.

Micah was silent and even though I was still aroused, I let him lie there until he came to terms with his own thoughts and issues. I held him close and enjoyed his lithe body wrapped around mine.

At one point, his hand started wandering, up and down my ribs, until it slipped below the fabric of my t-shirt. He caressed me gently, his fingers exploring more and more of my skin.

When they reached my pecs, I turned around to face him. "Don't stop on my behalf, baby. I just want to touch you too." With those words, I pulled him closer and claimed his lips in a kiss.

This time, he kissed me back with all the enthusiasm I'd seen when we'd made out. Our tongues met, and I kissed him deeply. The only downside of a onesie was that I couldn't slip my hands under it like I could a shirt or pants, but I started to unfasten the snaps at the top to reveal his skin. His chest was bare beneath it, and I slipped my hand inside to caress him too. Every touch was answered with a groan, a deep intake of breath and some goose-bumps, especially as I circled his nipples.

Rolling him on his back, I started another exploration — this time with my tongue, from his collarbone to the hard nipples. I drew them into my mouth, sucking and biting, then licking the sting away. I moved down, unfastening the snaps as I went. Fingers clutched in my hair, and every once in a while I heard a low *Daadddy* between the moans falling from his lips.

Finally, I was where I wanted to be. My chest had touched his hard on already, but I wanted to see which panties he'd picked. They were dark red, not really feminine, but definitely not masculine either. The fabric strained to keep his hard cock contained, and a wet spot revealed his state of arousal. I breathed deeply, taking in his scent, uniquely him but mixed with baby powder. I could come like this, without doing anything — maybe taking him into my mouth, but I probably wouldn't have to touch myself.

I drew my tongue over the fabric, teasing him.

"Daddy, touch me! Please! I need you!" He was breathless, his fingers still in my hair and his hips jerking.

"I will. Patience, sweet boy." With those words, I pulled down the panties enough to let his shaft jump free. It slapped his stomach before it stood, pointing straight to the ceiling. Before he started to beg more, I wrapped my lips around the head of his cock, tasting him for the first time. Where I found his smell delicious and tantalizing, his taste was so much more.

"Ooohh." Micah jerked upward, into my mouth, but I held him down. I took him deeper, sucking him into the back of my throat, before I let him slip back out to lick over the head.

He was panting, but his fingers were slack on my head. Most likely he couldn't even hold onto me.

"Daddy! I—"

I let up for a moment. I wanted him to come, but I'd just started. "A bit more, baby, then you can come."

"Buuuut…"

"Shh. Let me pleasure you." I wrapped my lips back around his cock, trying to get one hand into the onesie still under his ass. It wasn't easy, but I wriggled it under the fabric and slipped below the panties. My fingers found his hole, stroking him there too.

"Daaaaddddyyy!"

That was apparently too much. His cock jerked again and precum pooled at the tip, only to be licked away. "Come for me, baby." I sucked him down again.

With a deep shout, he came, spurting down my throat. Micah tasted sweet and salty and just like I expected it to. It was something I could get easily addicted to.

Micah slumped down, his whole body going slack.

"Everything okay, baby?"

I raised my head to look at him. He nodded, too spent to answer intelligibly. "I'll… Give me…"

"Shh. I'll take care of myself."

"On me… panties. Please."

Good thing I'd had the same thought, or I might not have gotten what he meant. But it wasn't hard to guess now.

I knelt next to him, freed my rock hard cock from the jeans, and started thrusting into my hand. It would only take me a few strokes. Just looking at his spent cock, surrounded by the dark red fabric of the panties, was enough to bring me close to the edge.

He was watching me with a rapt expression, his teeth nibbling his bottom lip, but the rest of his face completely relaxed. He looked content. Sated. Happy. Within seconds, my balls tightened, and as my gaze fell onto his face, I came with a groan. I spurted on the fabric, decorating it with white ribbons. It looked naughty, forbidden, yet innocent. Just perfect. But this was Micah. This boy was just perfect.

CHAPTER TWELVE

MICAH

I'd taken a few of the panties home with me — with Daddy's permission, of course. I'd wanted to look pretty for him when I visited him. But I didn't feel pretty at all right now. My mind was somewhere else, even as I rang his doorbell.

I had a key, but letting myself in when he was at home still felt wrong.

Carter opened the door immediately, and I threw my arms around his neck. I hugged him close, burying my face in his shoulder. Tears threatened to spill, but I fought them.

"Baby, what's wrong?" His hands hugged me close, and I heard the snick of the door behind us.

I hesitated. I didn't want him to think badly of me, and it was really selfish to boot. But at the same time, I was upset, and he kept urging me to talk to him when something was wrong.

I inhaled deeply, breathing him in and trying to center myself.

"It's stupid," I told him, my voice muffled.

"Nothing that upsets you is stupid," he said, kissing the top of my head as he pulled me deeper into the house. "Let's sit down. You can curl up in my lap and tell me what's going on."

I nodded, relaxing my grip on him enough to where he could lead me to the couch. I didn't let go of his hand, though, not wanting him to go too far. He sat down then drew me down onto his lap. I cuddled against him, feeling his warmth and listening to his heartbeat.

"It's…" I sniffled, trying to hold back the tears. "There's… There's this dog at the shelter. He's been there for ages. You know, the one I've talked about. Snowflake." I couldn't even get the words out in a way that made sense. "He's… a little special. Doesn't get along with other dogs at all, and he just…" I sighed. "I really wish I had my own place with a yard, you know? I'd take him in a heartbeat."

I was rambling, and I knew it. He just nodded, wrapping me in his arms and letting me talk.

"So this couple came in today, and they were looking at adopting him, but they looked…" I shook my head. "They didn't look like they'd really be good for him, you know? As much as I want him to be adopted, I sort of…" I bit my lip then looked at Carter, afraid he'd think badly of me for what I'd done. "I guided them to another dog instead. And I feel horrible for doing it, but I couldn't stand the idea of him going to people who wouldn't appreciate him."

"Oh, baby," Carter said, kissing me gently. "I know you're feeling bad now. This was a hard choice to make. I'm sure you did the right thing, even if it doesn't feel like it right now."

"But he could've had a home, and I'm not sure if they really weren't the right people for him or if it was just me. You know, my imagination. If I wanted them not to be the right ones."

I loved that dog. I'd have given anything to be able to adopt him myself. I lost my battle with the tears, and a few escaped before I could get myself under control again.

"What if this was his only chance to get adopted? What if I robbed him of his one chance to find his forever home?" Now I was sobbing even more. "What if it's my fault when he doesn't find someone? What if he never feels the love he deserves? He's such a good dog, but no one wants him."

My tears dampened his t-shirt. I tried to keep them back, but I failed. I *had* led the couple to another dog, so it was my fault.

"Shh, baby, it's okay. I know you feel guilty. And maybe what you did was wrong, but you tried to do what was right for him, right? Or did you lead them to another dog because you were mean? No, you tried to find the right dog for the right people. If you would've given them Snowflake, would you've been happy, aside from losing him?"

He gently rubbed my back, but I couldn't calm down. I was so upset, thousands of thoughts swirling in my head, and I couldn't grasp just one. So it took me a while to get my sobs under control until I could speak.

"I'm not sure. I probably wouldn't. I just... They didn't fit. I think. I have no idea. It felt wrong with them and Snowflake."

"Think about it, then tell me what you feel." He kept rubbing my back, and slowly my sobs subsided as I tried to make sense of what happened. I'd been so upset all the time that I hadn't stopped to think about it. The couple had been nice, but it just... No, it really hadn't been a good fit. And Snowflake deserved the best home he could get.

"I think you're right. But still, now he's stuck at the shelter, and I can't get him, because I'm still in the dorms, and when I graduate, I'll have to work full-time, and then I can't get a dog either right away, because I can't buy a house. And when you rent, you can't keep a dog of this size, and by then I—" My tears took over again, and I sobbed.

"Shh, baby. You already told me about him, but I think I didn't realize what he meant to you. I assumed it was a dog you were partial to, but you love him, don't you? He feels like he's your dog, right?"

I nodded through my tears. "Yeah. It's crazy, because I can't ever get him, and it's not like..." I sighed deeply. "I'm sorry. This was not how the evening was meant to go."

Carter kissed the top of my head and still didn't release me. "Don't apologize, baby. I totally understand you. I had a dog as a child, and Nic and I talked about getting one, but we never did. By the time we were settled, we decided to enjoy our time, travel a bit and all that… and then he got sick."

"I'm sorry. I'm so, so sorry to hear that," I said, trying to get myself back under control. Guilt raced through me as I thought about how I had to sound. It was probably ridiculous. He had real problems, like losing his husband, and there I was, upset about a dog I couldn't ever have.

Most people didn't understand just how special they could be. They didn't understand they were family, just as much as other people. My mother and father didn't really fill that role, not anymore. They'd done their duty, getting me through high school and off to college. They paid most of the bills, and student loans took care of the rest. Now…

Now we barely even talked beyond the requisite visits for Thanksgiving and Christmas. It was always awkward at best, glacial at worst, and it was getting worse. Sometimes I wondered what would happen if I just… didn't go. Would they even notice?

"Baby?"

I realized Carter had been talking while I'd gotten lost in my self-pity, and I felt even guiltier. He had been talking about Nicholas, and I'd totally spaced out. That was rude to say the least, disrespectful, wrong.

Horrified, I sat up a little. "I'm… I'm so sorry. Car— Daddy, I…" I didn't even know what to say. Was there anything I could say?

"Shh. It's okay, baby. I'm just worried about you." He carefully reached out, brushing tears from my eyes.

I sniffled. "You're too good for me. You really, really are. I don't deserve you."

"Don't even talk like that, baby. You're the best thing that has happened to me in a long time. Even though you don't see it, you're helping me move on after Nic's death. I lived with his memories for so long, and no other man has managed to break through those barriers."

"But still, I don't—"

He placed a finger over my lips. "It's okay. I value the gift you're giving me. Even though you don't see it. Maybe, one day, I can prove it to you. Until then, you need to take my word."

With that, he silenced any response I had, in the best possible way. By the time he drew back from the kiss, I was breathless, shaky, but not one worry lingered. My nose was still stuffed up from crying, and I probably looked like shit, but I had to believe him. I'd thought I was doing the right thing, and I still did.

Thank fuck we were a no-kill shelter, or I'd have lost him a long time ago. I didn't even want to think about that. I wanted to think about Carter, and about the fact that Snowflake *was* still there. Day off or not, I'd be going to see him tomorrow. I couldn't stand to wait another day. I knew no one would adopt him tomorrow. That'd be too much of a coincidence. Still, I needed to see he was still there.

And maybe I could figure a way out... to adopt him? If I managed to find a house to rent, could I get a dog? Even if it was a shared one? I wasn't sure. Most likely not. I couldn't ask Carter to take him, even though there was a huge part of me that wanted to beg. I'd go there, I'd take care of him, and I'd do everything for him... just as long as he was safe.

It would be hard to find the time, but it would be worth it. The only other option would be if I moved in with Carter, which was close to completely bat shit crazy. Things were still too new for that, and even though we wanted to be around each other a lot, that didn't mean he always wanted me there.

Plus, that was a huge, huge step. I'd never even had a relation-ship or sex with anyone before, let alone thought about moving in with them. So, while it sounded tempting, I couldn't rush it.

I leaned closer to Carter, breathing in his scent. He'd calmed me down, making it possible for me to collect my thoughts. I'd try to come up with a solution for Snowflake, but right that moment, I couldn't figure anything out. It wasn't like I hadn't pondered the question before.

Right now, though, I was in Carter's arms, safe, protected, loved.

No, not just Carter. Daddy. My daddy.

He was mine, and I was his, even though I didn't understand it. And I'd fallen completely in love with him.

It seemed too soon to say the words aloud, but he probably felt it anyway. Daddy knew lots of things, even when I didn't realize it, like with the clothes. My new clothes.

I shivered. Right. I'd done something this morning. Before everything had gone to hell.

My plan had been to surprise him, to show him how much his gifts meant to me. Well, I'd kind of ruined the fun, but maybe I could still show him.

"I… have kind of a surprise for you," I whispered.

"Oh?" he asked, still stroking my back. He always handled me like he thought I was going to break, especially now, when I more or less had.

I appreciated it so, so much that I couldn't even put it into words.

I nodded. "You're going to have to unwrap your present though." I wasn't in the mood for sex, not after that, even though I wanted to think about something else. "I just… Right now, I would love to distract myself, maybe play a little… or, we could maybe… You know, the nail polish and the… Well, I need eye makeup more than ever." I let out a small, choked, self-deprecating laugh.

"So I get a sexy gift, which I need to unwrap, but then I can't play with it because I have to do your nails?"

I recoiled, trying to find the right words as I started to panic. What had I done? Why had I—

Laughter rose from him, stunning me all over again. "Baby, I'm messing with you." His hands held me close. "That was just a joke. By now, you should know I'd love to make you prettier, and I'd love it even more if you can simply take the time to play. Let me take care of you, okay? That would be the best present ever. Though I have to admit that I'm curious."

"That was not funny, Daddy. Absolutely not. I really thought—"

He again silenced me with a kiss. "I know. It was mean of me. I'll make it up to you, okay? Maybe with a nice bubble bath? I might've gone shopping again, looking for some stuff... especially for little princesses."

"You did?"

"Baby, I'd do so much more for you. I—" he stopped, and instead of speaking, he kissed me. "So, bath time, my sweet boy?"

I hiccuped, then nodded. "Yeah, Daddy. And while you get me ready, you'll see your present, too."

"Now I'm even more curious. Then come on. I'll get you settled." With a squeeze to my ass, he helped me to my feet and led me to the bathroom.

My hand rested in his, just like he'd lead a kid.

The bathroom was warm, like he'd planned this all along. Maybe he had. Given the fact that he'd gotten me princess bubble bath, he'd probably wanted to put me in the tub all along. Right. I'd come straight from work, so I hadn't had a shower. He'd definitely planned that all along.

"Come on, let's get my baby naked so you can play."

"That kinda sounds dirty, Daddy." I cast a teasing grin in his direction. Even though I still wasn't in the mood for sex, that was just too good to pass it up.

"Oh, this is another form of play, baby. This here involves ducks, fish, ponies, and glitter."

I took in the basket he pointed at. There were all kinds of bath toys, more than I'd ever had, even as a kid. Daddy turned on the water, adjusted the temperature, then turned to me. "Come on. Let's strip."

Carefully, he raised my t-shirt, pulling it over my head. His fingers trailed over my skin, drawing goosebumps in their wake. Then he pressed a kiss to my collar bone before he knelt down, tugging at my trousers. I'd worn tighter jeans to work today, and it'd felt good.

Sexy, even.

As the denim slid down, the dark green panties were revealed. I heard his sharp intake of breath, then he kissed me just above the waistband. "So sexy. This is a nice present. Thank you, sweet boy. I love them on you." Daddy's voice had dropped, like he couldn't believe what he was seeing.

It should've been awkward, considering I'd worn them to work, but he acted like he didn't even notice that I probably smelled like a dog. Instead, he was enraptured.

My face grew red. I knew he'd like it, but this much... The kind of effect I had on him still threw me.

"As much as I love seeing that, though, the tub is ready. I'll just dress you later again, after we're done with your hair and face and nails. How does that sound?"

"Really good." It sounded perfect, and my cock twitched beneath the soft green fabric.

He kissed my skin again, then he pulled down the panties. I wasn't really hard, but I couldn't deny that I reacted to his close-ness. With soft movements, he helped me step out of the fabric then guided me to the tub. After adding a bit — and a bit more— of the bubble stuff, he helped me in. The water was hot, relaxing and soothing. It was also purple, and it smelled like berries. I sank down, lying back and closing my eyes. This felt like heaven.

Daddy quietly moved around, and when I finally opened my eyes, I saw he'd added the toys. Now he was sitting on the toilet seat, just watching me.

"You okay?" he asked quietly after a while.

I caught one of the ponies floating around and started stroking its wet hair. "Yeah, Daddy. Better than okay. I feel good, really good."

It was such a relief, especially after the sort of day I'd had, and I loved that he kept spoiling me.

"That's great to hear." He smiled at me, a kind, loving smile.

Giving me a bath made him happy, too — and he'd have to wash me down later. It was something that would be lots of fun, for sure.

He grabbed one of the ponies, letting it prance along the side of the tub, and I grinned before I made my pony start chasing him. By the time I actually managed to intercept his toy with my own, I was laughing so hard I couldn't breathe.

I'd never, ever had that much fun in the bath before. Baths had always been to get clean, not to play in — and I'd been missing out. But no more, because I had my daddy, and I doubted this would be the last time he bathed me.

Hopefully, it was the first of many.

"Time for little boys to get clean," he told me, reaching into the tub to tickle my side.

I giggled, flicking a few bubbles at him.

"You know what happens to naughty boys." He grabbed the washcloth and the soap — baby soap, I noticed, fresh and subtle.

"You keep threatening me," I complained, "But I'm starting to think you won't follow through."

His gaze intensified on me. "Do you think I should follow through?"

In other words, did I think I was ready for him to follow through?

"Maaaaybe. Maaaaybe not," I said, which was as close to the truth as I could get.

He smiled warmly at me, starting to run the cloth down my arm. "That's my good boy. Thank you for being honest for Daddy."

I nodded to him, my eyes drifting half closed as he cleaned me. By the time he got to my cock, I was hard. He lingered just a little too long there, enough to make sure I was fully erect but not letting me get anywhere close to finishing. I whined.

"Well, you wanted to get punished," he teased, urging me to lean my head back so he could wash my hair.

That part was a little messy, and I waited until he was

massaging the shampoo in my hair before I replied, "Not that kind of punished."

"Oh, you don't get to pick the punishment." There was that wicked glint in his eyes, the one I knew meant trouble… but the best kind of trouble. "But we'll get there. Anticipation is half the fun. First we have makeup to do, and nail polish to put on, and maybe…" He studied my expression. "Maybe diapers to try?"

I inhaled deeply, thinking as he started to rinse out my hair. I loved the smell of the soap, so fresh and sweet. "I think so," I said as he reached into the tub to pull the plug. He offered his hand and helped me onto the floor. I was still hard, and he was still pretending I wasn't. I wanted to stomp my foot against the floor like the spoiled little he was turning me into and demand that he get me off.

But the idea of getting me pretty first won out.

"Fine," I said with a huff of breath.

He toweled me dry, keeping me close. The sound of the water going down the drain was the only thing to break the silence, but it was a comfortable quiet. I didn't know how he could have that effect on me because usually, silence felt awkward. Not with Daddy, though. Never with him.

"Come with me," he said, wrapping me in the towel and taking my hand in his. I followed him into the nursery, and he opened the second drawer of the dresser. I could see my panties there, and another thrill ran through me, making me shiver. "You cold, baby?"

I shook my head. "N-no. That's not a cold shiver. That's a… *you're-killing-me-here* shiver."

Daddy leaned in to kiss me. "Good." He grabbed a pair of panties — pale pink, this time — and held them up, giving me a questioning look.

I nodded, a little hesitant but… It felt right, considering we were about to play with some of the more feminine gifts he'd given me. He grabbed a diaper from the top drawer, too, adding, "Just in case." He gestured to the crib. "Would you feel comfortable sitting there while we do your nails and makeup?" His voice was cautious, like he thought he'd be going too far, but I was maybe a little too excited. All of it at once should've been overwhelming, but instead, I was relaxed, eager to see what he did next.

"Yes, please, Daddy," I said, following him over to it.

He pulled the side down so I could sit on the edge, helping me up onto it. "There we go," he said, turning to grab…

I was touched all over again. He'd gotten a makeup bag for the items he'd bought me. "Daddy…"

He glanced at me, and I could see that same uncertainty in his eyes. It made me want to kiss it away, made me less aware of my own lingering hesitation. "Yes, baby?"

"Thank you. For all of this. For everything," I said.

He brought the bag over, setting it down next to me and leaning in to steal a lingering kiss. It left me dizzy, and I wasn't sure we were going to get through this next part before I pounced him.

He teased me, taking his time with painting each fingernail, laboriously working to get it just right, and I rolled my eyes.

Still, I had to admit the silver polish looked beautiful and subtle to boot… something I could maybe wear out, even. He had nail polish remover ready, but I wasn't ready to get rid of it yet.

"You're killing me," I repeated, shaking my head.

"Hold still." He grinned at me. "I watched a few YouTube videos. I think I can get your eyeshadow and mascara on without poking you in the eye or making you look like a raccoon."

"You think?" I demanded, narrowing my eyes at him.

His eyes crinkled around the corners, even though I could see him trying not to laugh. "I'm pretty sure."

I shook my head. We were both new to it, and it wasn't like anyone was going to see me. Even if I turned out looking ridiculous, it would only be the two of us.

I stayed still while he took the same kind of care with the mascara, then the eyeliner, that he had with my nails. I was antsy, though, and I was having a hard time just sitting there. I wanted to see what I looked like, even though I was pretty sure I'd look stupid.

When he brought the mirror to show me, though, I was struck by how… pretty it looked. "Wow," I said, taking the mirror from him to examine my features more. "This is… You did a great job." My voice was rough, and I was on the verge of tears again. "Every time I think you've done the most thoughtful thing ever, you just outdo yourself all over again."

He gently took the mirror from me and pulled me into his arms. "I want you to feel beautiful. I want you to see yourself the way I see you."

"You're gonna make me cry and ruin the makeup." I sniffled, blinking several times to try to keep the tears from my eyes. "Stop being so sweet. Diaper next."

"You don't want me to be sweet?" Daddy arched a brow, unfolding the diaper, then leaned in to tickle my sides.

I laughed, flailing around helplessly. "Dadddyyy," I whined in between my giggles. "Of course I want you to be sweet. I just— Stop it," I demanded, swatting at him.

"C'mon, you," he told me, sliding me up on the crib. "Diaper time for little boys."

Before I could respond, I heard a choked sound from behind him. My head snapped up, eyes widening as I saw an unfamiliar man and woman in the doorway.

And there I was, with pink panties next to me and a diaper in Daddy's hand, ass-naked in front of who I could only assume were his parents.

Well. This wasn't the introduction I'd hoped for.

CHAPTER THIRTEEN

This couldn't be true.

Oh god. Please, please let this be a mistake. A dream. A nightmare. Whatever. Just not reality.

I shifted to shield Micah's naked body with my own, and all I could do was stare as my mother started to lay into me.

"You pervert! Are you fucking kids, too? We knew it all along! You're so sick!" My mother's voice broke from yelling so loudly.

I'd known they would never understand my interest in BDSM and that they thought horribly of the lifestyle, so I'd done my best to shield them from that. Now, they saw a tender, sweet moment as something to be ashamed of.

"You're a disgrace for this family! We accepted all of your strange habits, but this is enough! We will not have a pedophile in the family!" my father roared.

Micah was frozen behind me. I could feel him trembling, and his hand touched mine before he pulled back.

Of course. When we first met, he'd asked me if I was a pedophile because I was a daddy, and now... Now my parents confirmed exactly that.

I let the hand with the diaper sink, staring from a wide-eyed Micah to my parents. Fuck. "This isn't—"

"Don't start with this is not what it looks like! This is... How long has this been going on? Are you dressing men like kids to pretend to— I think I'm going to get sick!" My mother's breathing was so fast that she looked like she was on the verge of passing out.

I took a deep breath, trying to calm myself, in the hope of saving what was left to be saved.

"I'm not a pedophile. That's the first thing we need to settle. Micah is well over eighteen, and this is something we both enjoy. Nothing more." I tried to keep my voice calm, still standing in an awkward angle to protect Micah from their view, but a quick glance revealed that he'd grabbed a blanket — with fish on it — to cover himself. He was shaking.

"Please," Micah whispered from behind me. "Can everyone stop yelling?"

My mother's eyes narrowed, homing in on Micah.

I stepped more in front of him, protecting him from their rage as much as I could. I just wanted to close my eyes then wake up from this nightmare — because there was no way my parents had just walked in on this. It wasn't possible.

"No one's mad at you, honey," she told Micah, her voice dropping in volume — taking on that tone that people use with wounded animals and terrified children. "We'll get you out of here."

Micah buried his face against my back. "I don't want to leave," he whispered.

"Shh, now. We'll take care of you. Of course you don't want to leave. But we'll help you. You don't have to go back to him." She stepped closer, reaching out her hand like she wanted to grab him. Micah pressed even closer against my back, clutching at me with one hand while the other held the blanket to him.

"You will not take Micah against his will. He's free to leave, and I can assure you, this is nothing like what it looks like." Even though my heart still beat like crazy, I was trying to stay calm. What could I do?

"No man would allow himself to be treated like that. This is sick, Carter. And while you might not see it, we do." Her voice softened as she spoke to Micah again. "We'll get you help, okay?" She now spoke calmer, like she was really trying to get him to accept some kind of help.

Why the hell did they have to pick this moment to come in? And into this room? They'd never, ever been in here.

"Can you leave, please? I know you're upset, but I'd like to get dressed. I promise I'm not in any danger. Carter isn't doing anything I don't want him to." Micah's voice was still soft, but it worked. Apparently, he was the victim in this, so they did what he wanted. With a last glance, both my mother and father turned around and left.

Micah's cheeks were burning, but not in the cute blush sort of way. He looked flustered and upset, tears streaking makeup that only smeared more when he rubbed at his eyes. He trembled, glancing at the pink panties with something like longing, but he ignored them.

"I should... get dressed," he said, swallowing hard.

"Probably, yes. I'm so sorry, Micah. This is... I never expected that to happen. They're—"

"You don't need to apologize for them." He tried to blink away his tears, but they only fell faster. "I just... I can't right now."

"What are you going to do?" I could see how he pulled back from me, putting back the mask I'd discovered when he first walked into the bar. Hurt, embarrassment, shame, all mixed together. "Baby, talk to—"

"Don't," Micah whispered. "Not right now." He shook his head. "I just... can't," he repeated. "I need... I need to go. Home. I'm sorry, Da— Carter. I'm sorry. I just..." He shook his head, looking a little frantic, and my heart sank. "I can't."

Had I lost him because of this? Did he believe my parents? "Can we talk? Later, I mean?"

"Yes. No. I-I don't know, Carter. I just need to go now."

With those words, he hurried to get dressed, opened the door, and left, all while I just stood there, unable to do anything.

My mother's voice sounded, though I couldn't hear what she was saying. Micah's voice answered her, but before my parents could speak again, I heard him open and close the front door.

Then silence surrounded me. I sank down onto the bed, resting my face in my hands. What the fuck had just happened?

———

It took me a long time to finally manage to leave the room. My brain replayed the confrontation that'd just happened, and the consequences it'd brought. What if I really lost Micah? He was the man who'd stolen my heart when I'd thought there would be no one in my life again.

Why the fuck had they come over now, when I'd *told* them not to do that?

I sighed again. Maybe I should deal with them first and convince them I wasn't a pedophile, even though they probably wouldn't believe me. But it was better to try than end up explaining it to the police.

At this point, I wouldn't even put it past my parents to have called them already. They'd been so upset. It had always been hard for them to accept me being gay, and this was a part of my life they'd never understand.

Should I hope they were still somewhere in my house or that they were gone already? If they were, I wouldn't have to confront them. If not, I could maybe talk to them and at least let them know I didn't abuse Micah in any way.

I didn't want them to send the police to him. He'd started coming out of his shell, embracing himself and now this. How could we come back from something like that? *Would* we be able to come back from something like that? His last words had been so final. And even if there was hope... Could I do that to him? Could I make him face that again?

I couldn't.

With heavy shoulders, I opened the door of the nursery and stepped out. The house was quiet, too quiet. Micah's laughter was missing. His joy at discovering himself... and discovering us.

I walked downstairs, and there they sat, in the living room. My mother was clutching her pearls like they could save her from drowning. Her face was fallen, like she'd just discovered her only son was a murderer. My father, on the other hand, wore an expression that told me *he* was ready to become a murderer if it meant saving innocent children.

I faced them as I'd face a firing squad. I'd lose them, that much was sure. There was no coming back from this. They were too stuck in their beliefs, too uptight to ever accept it. As much as that knowledge hurt, I couldn't stop the pain racing through my heart — because I'd probably lost Micah in the process, too.

I drew in a deep, shaky breath. "Okay. I'm really sorry you saw this. Micah left, and we can talk. If you want, I can give you his contact information so he can tell you he was never, ever forced into anything. I would love to explain what was up with what you saw, but I'm not sure you're ready to hear it."

My mother was silent, but my father spoke. His voice was low, dangerously low. "What did we do wrong? Was it not enough love? Should we have done something different? No, we're not going to understand... this... but where did we go wrong? And how can we help you and this young man?"

"I don't need help, okay? There is nothing wrong with me, and there's also nothing wrong with Micah. You didn't do anything wrong, either. I just discovered that it's... It gives me a lot of satisfaction to care for someone."

The look on my mother's face turned even more strangled, fingers firmly latched onto her necklace.

I hesitated, then went on, "Micah wanted someone to care for him. He has a lot of weight to carry on his shoulders, and his parents never pampered him. Added to that, he got bullied a lot, because he's more feminine. That, by the way, explains the nail polish and the make-up. We wanted to explore his feminine side." I paused again, not knowing how to go on or if it would make any difference. For now, they were calm and listening, but did they believe me? "I encouraged him to wear what he's comfortable in, to try and figure out who he is."

"But you… He… There was… Why?" My mother's words didn't make sense at all. "Diaper."

Ah, okay. Yes. That was the worst possible moment they could have seen, and the timing… It had been my first time putting a diaper on Micah, and what should've been an amazing, freeing experience was now tainted.

"I can't even… Well, this is about taking responsibility off Micah's shoulders. He likes that he can play like a little kid, without a care in the world. He colors, he builds blocks, he dresses his dolls. I care for him, for everything he needs. That includes, sometimes, diapers." I stopped. It sounded lame, even in my ears. But how could I get across the thrill, the pleasure of him giving me this gift? "It helps him relax and let go. It's not about the diapers themselves, not really." Well, there was a bit of a sexual thrill with them, but my parents didn't need to hear that. "It's just easier to forget the real world when he has… props. It's a… It's really hard to explain."

"I guess you don't need to try. I would love to say I understand, but I don't. And I guess neither does your father. This is just sick. There's no other word to describe what you're doing. My only hope is that this Micah is really just the only person you're playing with, and that he was, in fact, here of his free will. I don't… I don't want to have to report it to the police, but maybe we'll have to." Tears spilled from her eyes.

My heart twisted. What had I done that was so wrong that she thought I was capable of being such a monster?

My shoulders drooped. It had been just as hard to tell them I was gay, and that had been more controlled. "If you have to, go ahead. They won't find anything, but please consider I'm a teacher, so try to at least keep it quiet. The police are welcome to look around, interview me, search my house, whatever. There was never a kid involved, nor will there ever be one. I'm not a pedophile, Mom. I would never, ever touch or hurt a kid."

I couldn't be sure if she was listening or not. My father still glared at me, stony-faced, looking at me like I'd sprouted horns. I couldn't stop trying to explain it, though. We might've had our differences in the past, but I loved my parents. I didn't want to lose them because they couldn't understand something that was… well, almost impossible to explain to those who didn't enjoy it.

"I like men," I said softly. "I'm simply gay, and I like to care for my very much grown-up partners. I don't get off on the idea of raping a kid. That's one of the most despicable acts someone can do. Micah and I play. This is like a role play. Some would play thief and police, or teacher and student. We play this. Nothing else."

She was still dabbing her eyes. "Your father and I will think about this. I want to believe everything you said, but right now… I just have no idea what's the truth."

My heart broke at her words. She didn't believe me? She really thought I was some kind of monster? "Mom, please. You don't have to understand—"

"I can't even talk to you. While you nicely tried to explain what you did, this is just a way to justify some sick perversion. Even if no kids are involved, you are dressing someone up as a child. That's just sick, Carter. No matter what you say."

"Mom—"

"No more 'Mom.' This is not the son we raised, Carter. I can't even look at you. We tolerated so much. You being gay, which was a shock. You being with Nicholas, which was even worse. People talked so much because he was so much younger. And then… no, Carter. This is too much. I can't… no." With that, she stood. "Don't call us. Don't get in touch in any way." With those words, she left the living room, heading toward the front door.

My father gave me one last look. "I have never, ever, been this disappointed in my life. You're not the man we raised. No matter if it's okay for you, it isn't okay for us. It's just wrong, and I pray you'll see that one day. Otherwise, we're done."

I sank down in my reading chair as I watched them go. I wanted to beg, to tell them to come back, but I couldn't. This was over. Maybe they'd come around some day, but right now, I doubted it. Micah was gone, probably hiding somewhere, ashamed to no end. My parents were gone and would most likely never speak a word to me. And I was back at the point where I'd been after Nic's death. Alone in a dark hole.

I rubbed my hands over my face, got up and went to the liquor cabinet. I didn't drink much these days, but I needed it. Badly. The bottle of Jack called my name. Glasses were unnecessary. I just raised it to my lips and waited for the alcohol to burn the pain and the shame away.

He didn't call.
He didn't text.
Nothing.

It had been a day since I'd left Carter's house, my face burning and tears streaming down my face. His parents, of all people, had seen me naked — just as Carter was about to put a diaper on me, while I wore eye makeup and nail polish and had a pair of pink panties ready to put on.

I still had a hard enough time admitting to myself that I liked those things, and when they'd walked in, I'd just... freaked out. Listening to them yell was like being at home again, and no matter how badly I'd wanted to defend Carter, I hadn't been able to get the words out.

I'd barely left my bed since I'd gotten back, only moving to check my phone for the thousandth time. Was he going to contact me? Could I even contact him without making the situation worse? His parents had seemed so convinced he was doing something wrong, something *illegal*, and my cheeks flushed all over again as I remembered what I'd asked him when we'd first met.

How had he still welcomed me into the bar, into his lap, after I'd asked him if he was some kind of pedophile?

I didn't know how it had all gone so wrong. It had been perfect, like we'd been in some happy bubble together. The bath, the nail polish, the makeup, the tickling…

The promise of my first diaper.

And that had all come to a screeching halt in the most traumatic way possible when his parents had barged in on us. I clutched my phone to my chest, tears welling up in my eyes all over again. They thought so badly of him, and it had been staggering. How could anyone think so poorly of Carter? He was the most amazing man I'd ever met.

All I'd wanted was to be his little prince or princess and for him to be my daddy — my everything. He'd wanted it too, just as much as I had, but now… Now I had to wonder if it was really that wrong. How could something so tender be demonized like that? I was so happy when I was curled up in Daddy's arms, when he stroked my back and teased me… when he'd gotten me clothes that felt more natural than the button-ups and ironed trousers ever had… when his eyes had gone so wide when he'd seen me in the onesie for the first time.

How could it be wrong?

Why was it wrong?

I didn't know.

I couldn't claim to completely understand why he loved this so much, but when it so perfectly meshed with what I wanted, what I *needed*, how could I see it as the loathsome thing his parents did?

I unlocked my phone, my hands trembling. I'd needed time to pull myself together. Otherwise, I would've fallen apart on his floor. If I'd stayed a moment longer, I'd have collapsed, and he didn't need to have to take care of me on top of everything else.

As it was, I still wasn't sure how I'd managed to get past his parents and to my car — let alone back to my dorm. In retrospect, it had been pretty fucking stupid to run, but I'd been so desperate to flee an all too familiar situation.

"Daddy? Are you okay?"

I didn't even know if he'd answer. I didn't even know if I should call him that, or if everything had been ruined. I just didn't know. But I had to talk to him. I had to make sure he was okay. If I'd reacted this badly, I could only imagine how shitty he had to be feeling. Guilt raced through me. I should've checked on him sooner, but I'd been so caught up in my own hell.

If anyone understood, it would be Carter — Daddy.

At least, I hoped so.

He didn't answer, though. I checked my messages about ten times, but he didn't reply. Why? He'd always been quick, always made sure I knew he read my messages. I checked my phone again. It usually showed me when he'd read my messages, but even after ten minutes, there was nothing. I nibbled on my bottom lip, hesitating a moment, then called him. It went straight to voicemail.

My heart sank. Why was his phone off? It was never off. When he worked, he put it on silent, but he didn't shut it down. Had something happened to him? Worry gripped my heart, squeezing it tight. Had his parents called the police after I'd gone? Fuck, what if he was sitting in jail right now? What if they thought he really did something to kids? What if they thought he was some kind of criminal? What if they hurt him? What we had was so kind and caring, but what if the police made it into something bad and immoral?

Or...

He'd told me he had issues with drinking. What if this pushed him over the edge and he drank? Drank too much? I called him again, but it still went to voicemail. "Hi, Car— Daddy. I just... I wanted to know if you're okay. I... please call me back?"

I desperately wanted to go over and check on him, but at the same time, my stomach got a little queasy at thinking about showing up unannounced. The last time he'd had unexpected visitors, it had been his parents. And I...

I didn't know if he was going to want to see me after that.

Nothing had changed for me, not really, though my anxiety about trying a diaper again was through the roof. It didn't matter right then, though. Daddy would never make me do something I didn't want, and we could take our time.

Assuming he'd talk to me.

I waited another fifteen minutes then tried to call again, leaving another voicemail. By the time two hours of crying had passed, I was in a panic. What if he hated me? What if he never wanted to see me again? It had been all my fault that he'd gotten into trouble, and now I didn't even know if he was okay.

He'd always taken care of me, and I wanted to take care of him now that he needed it... now that he needed me.

I slumped back against the bed then scrolled up in my messages, sniffling as I read the sweet and naughty texts he'd sent me. I should've tried harder to make sure he was okay before I'd left.

All the regrets in the world couldn't change the fact that I had freaked out and left, too afraid his parents would really call the police if I stayed, too afraid that my own issues with my parents would come to the forefront.

It had been so stupid.

Hours passed, and I went back and forth between crying and clinging to my phone. I lost track of how many times I called him, but he didn't answer me. I started to panic, and I couldn't stay in my dorm any longer.

It was a bad idea, I just knew it, but I had to see if he was okay. I just had to see.

Even if he didn't want to see me — and the thought threatened to break me — I had to be sure he was all right.

I had to blink back tears as I drove to his house. His car was in the driveway, but no lights were on.

I swallowed hard, and while I'd intended to just drive by, I found myself parking behind him. I drew in a shuddering breath, feeling it deep in my bones, and I went to the door. I rang the doorbell. Once, twice.

Nothing moved, but his car was there. He wasn't answering.

I knocked, tentatively at first, then a little harder. I was getting frantic. This wasn't like my caring daddy. This wasn't the Carter I knew. Even if he was upset with me, he wouldn't ignore me without a good reason. If he was home, I had to check on him. If he wasn't... Where was he without his car?

I didn't know what to do.

I knocked again, desperate, and called out, "D-Carter! Please come to the door!"

Nothing.

I sobbed, my forehead resting against the door as I pounded my fist once, uselessly, against it. He had to be okay. I couldn't stand the idea of him *not* being okay.

I didn't hear anything from inside the house, and I thought about the key I had on my keychain. I almost laughed, half-hysterical, at the idea of just walking in on him after what had happened.

But could I live with myself if I didn't try?

"I'm sorry," I whispered, bracing myself. "Please don't be mad at me."

I put the key in the lock and turned it.

It was dark, and I squinted. My heart pounded, and the idea that he wasn't here was as terrifying as the idea that he was. This wasn't like him, not at all, and while he couldn't have gone far on his own...

Panic flared again. What if he was in jail?

What if he was drinking?

What if he just couldn't stand to talk to me?

There were so many possibilities, and none of them were good.

I crept into the living room, terrified to make a sound, then I realized that wasn't good either. I closed the door behind me, making sure to make noise and let him know I was there — assuming *he* was there.

"D-Daddy?" I stammered, blinking back tears all over again. I had to keep myself together. I couldn't lose it, not when he might need me. I'd never been needed before, but that was… something I hadn't understood about this until right then. He might've been taking care of me, but I was always taking care of him, too. Just in a different way.

I made my way through the house, turning on lights as I went. Finally, I found him in the nursery. He sat there, slumped over on the crib. His shoulders were bent forward, and he clutched a bottle between his hands.

Strong stuff. I could smell it even from the door.

"Daddy?" My voice was thinner than I'd have liked, but to see my strong daddy like that just broke me.

He didn't even look at me, just took another swig of his bottle, his eyes unfocused and empty. He stared right into space, like he lost himself somewhere down the line, like he'd broken inside.

I should've come back sooner.

I shouldn't have left at all.

"Daddy?" This time, I managed to get my voice stronger.

Daddy still ignored me.

That wouldn't do. The man I'd fallen for would never ignore me, but this was exactly what he'd done for the past several hours while he'd been drinking himself into a stupor. He'd ignored my messages, my calls, me knocking and ringing his doorbell and now me talking to him. This was enough.

With a deep breath, I stepped in front of him. "This is enough." My voice didn't waver like I expected it to as I reached for the bottle and yanked it out of his hands. "You need to go to bed, sleep this off. Then we'll talk. And don't think for a second that you'll keep ignoring me."

Slowly, like it took all of his energy, he raised his eyes. They were bloodshot, like he hadn't slept at all last night, but spent the hours crying instead. I probably looked the same.

"Baby?"

"Yes, it's me, Daddy. Ready to come to bed?" I grabbed his hand, trying to get him to his feet.

"You're here? Why are you here? Is that… I don't want to lose you. I need you. But you— I'm just dreaming, right? You'll be gone when I wake up, but don't do this. I can't lose you. Not again. Please stay with me, baby. Please stay, Micah."

My heart broke at his slurred words. Maybe he'd seen his late husband in his sleep a few times, or when he'd been drunk. Realizing Nicholas had been truly gone must've broken his heart again and again. Thinking I was gone…

"I'm here to stay, Daddy. I won't leave you, okay? Just come with me. We'll lie down in your bed." I tugged at his hand again, trying to keep my tears at bay. This had hurt him so badly. I'd known it would, but I'd still left him to deal with it on his own. He was the one who took care of me, but sometimes, he needed to lean on me. I hadn't been there, but now I was. And I wouldn't leave him until he was sober and ready to talk.

Then, and only then, could he tell me to get my ass out the door. That would be the only way I'd go. Unless he did that, I would stay where I belonged — at his side, in his bed, curled up against him.

But first, he needed to sleep this off.

Finally, he gave in to my tugging and staggered up to his feet. I struggled to keep him up as I wrapped an arm around his waist. He was a lot heavier than I was, but he seemed to be just aware enough of his surroundings to at least try to walk — try. I wished I could just scoop him up in my arms and take him to bed, but we had to stumble toward the bedroom together. I wouldn't have managed it if it had been farther away.

I was breathing hard by the time I got him to the bed, having supported more of his weight than I'd even thought I could.

"You are never going to do this again, Daddy," I chided him, even though I knew he was too out of it to really understand me, let alone to remember. "Not now, not ever, for no reason."

I sighed, pulling the blankets around him. Right. Water, grab a bottle of ibuprofen for when he got up, go dump the damn booze down the drain... Maybe I was going a bit overboard, but I was furious — at him, but mainly at myself.

How had I just... left him here like this?

I had to blink back tears again, but I steeled myself. He needed me. He was my daddy, and he needed me, so I was damn well going to be there.

I took a step back, only to feel his warm hand around my wrist. "Baby, don' go," he slurred, but there was an edge of panic to the words.

"Shh," I told him, leaning in to kiss his forehead. "I'm just going to get you some water. Okay? Then I won't leave your side. I promise."

He didn't let go, and I lightly brushed my lips against his.

"It's okay, Daddy," I said softly. "I'll be right here for you."

Maybe it was the kiss that did it, or maybe he passed out, or maybe he understood more than I thought he did. Whichever way it was, he released my wrist. I watched him for another long moment, biting my lip. I wanted to just crawl into bed with him, but he'd never put aside my needs like that — and right now, I had to start with a few other things to take care of him.

I went to the kitchen, pouring him a glass of water. On a whim, I grabbed my sippy cup and filled that, too. I found the medicine in the cabinet and set that close by... then I went hunting for the booze.

The bottle I'd left in the nursery was still there, the strong stench of it testimony to just how potent it was. I grabbed it, set my jaw in stubborn determination, then went back to the kitchen. I had to hope he wasn't going to get pissed for me dumping a bottle of liquor down the sink, but I did it anyway — and I'd do it again, even if he got mad.

I threw away the bottle, hunting for more. He only had a half-bottle of vodka, which had been there long enough to collect dust, and I grabbed that too. This was all my fault, but I wasn't going to give him the chance to hurt himself again. I just *wasn't*.

I took a deep breath, washed my hands and sniffed my shirt to make sure I didn't smell like alcohol, then grabbed the glass and sippy cup, tucking the bottle of ibuprofen under my arm. I went back upstairs, setting the sippy cup and the medicine down first.

"Daddy?"

He stirred a little.

"Daddy, you need to drink this. Okay? Can you do that for your boy? Please?"

"Baby?"

"I'm here. You need to drink this, for me, okay? Please. Then I'll come to bed and sleep with you."

"Mmmhh." He didn't make any motions to sit up.

Okay, then we'd do this differently. He needed to drink some water. Otherwise, he'd be totally done for in the morning. "Come on. Raise your head." I wriggled my arm under his head, raising him up. The sippy cup was mine, but I would always share it with my daddy. Always.

Though what he'd think about drinking out of it once he'd sobered up... It would've been a funny thought if the situation hadn't been so shitty.

I put it against his lips. "Slowly."

He drank, though it was messy. His coordination wasn't what it usually was, and he spilled more than a couple of drops even from the sippy cup — I hadn't even known that was possible.

Damn it. I was just glad I hadn't tried with the big glass.

But he managed to get most of the sippy cup empty, and with a sigh, he released the spout.

"Thank you, Daddy. Now let me get this t-shirt off you, then we can sleep." It took some tugging and wiggling, but I managed to get it off. He'd spilled enough water on it that I couldn't leave it on, and I also wanted to feel his skin when I laid in bed with him. I needed to be able to touch him.

I stripped down to my very boring briefs, not the nice panties

Daddy had gotten me — because I hadn't been able to bear wearing them when I'd gotten dressed in the morning — and slid into bed next to him. "Now you can sleep, Daddy. I'll be here until the morning, and then we can talk, okay? I— I love you, Daddy." The last words were just a whisper. I was sure he wouldn't have caught them even if he wasn't in this state, but I needed to say them. I needed to hear myself say them. And, even though he didn't hear them, I needed to tell him.

"My baby," he murmured. Then he wrapped an arm around me, pulling me close.

I rested my head on his shoulder, my arm wrapped around his waist, then I closed my eyes. His jeans made cuddling a bit uncomfortable, but I didn't want to take them off without his consent. I probably wouldn't have managed anyway, since he wasn't really capable of helping me.

"My Daddy." With those words, I closed my eyes and relaxed in his arms. I hadn't slept much the night before, so I drifted off to sleep in moments.

I jerked awake when he pulled away, blinking blearily as he stumbled out of bed.

"Daddy? What's—"

Before I could even finish asking, he was on his way to the bathroom, where...

Oh, I understood. My heart ached for him. All I could do was stay close by to make sure he was safe, give him more water when he got back to bed, and help him wipe his face down. It wasn't much, but I got out of bed while he retched.

I tried not to pay attention to the smell or listen to the sounds, afraid I'd get sick too, but I found a washcloth and his mouth-wash, too.

After what felt like a small eternity, he was flushing the toilet and struggling to get back to his feet.

"C'mere, Daddy," I told him, wrapping my arm around his waist like I had earlier. It was a little easier this time. He was still out of it, but he was at least upright. I led him over to the sink, helping him splash his face and wiping it clean for him before offering him the mouthwash. He took a moment to seem to understand what I was after, then took a swig, only swirling it around in his mouth for a moment before spitting it out. "Good," I said. My arm went back around his waist, and I helped him back to the bedroom. "Up you go."

It was easier to get him into the bed that time. He looked at the sippy cup when I offered it with a blank look, but I urged it to his lips and got him to finish it off. I wanted to give him the glass, but I also didn't want to go back to sleep in a wet bed.

I refilled it, just in case, and set it back down.

"Get some more sleep, Daddy," I told him, snuggling close to him when we were both in the bed again. I pulled the blankets up and around us. "We'll talk in the morning."

I couldn't be sure if his answering groan was one of acknowledgment or simply pain from the killer headache he had to be sporting. Either way, I kissed his shoulder and snuggled back up to him.

I'd clean up the bathroom when I woke up…

CHAPTER FIFTEEN

CARTER

What had I done? What the fuck had I done? My hair hurt. My brain hurt. My eyes. My face. Every fucking cell of my body.

God. I groaned, not even bothering with opening my eyes. That'd just hurt more. My stomach swirled, cramping badly as I tried to remember what I'd done. I drank... too much, apparently. Because— yes, Micah.

There it was, and reality came back crashing around me. Now my heart hurt just as much as my brain.

With a groan, I threw an arm over my face, trying to block my throughs out — not that they made a lot of sense anyway. Fuck, even this movement hurt like crazy.

"Hey, Daddy."

My head whipped around at the quiet voice, setting off movements in my brain and a stomach I'd rather not have. I swallowed, hard, trying to keep myself under control. It rolled for a few more moments, and white light exploded behind my eyelids before it slowly stopped.

I pried open one eye, looking at the most beautiful sight ever: Micah, rolled up under my sheets. His hair was messy from sleeping, and there were dark circles under his eyes, but he was in my bed. Here, with me.

"Baby?" I croaked. "Are you—" I swallowed. My throat hurt, like I'd — fuck. Had I?

"I'm here to stay, Daddy." He offered me that familiar, crooked smile. "If you want me, anyway. I hope you'll at least let me take care of you... Then we need to talk. But I think you need to take some pain meds and a shower first and maybe sleep some more." His words were soft and a bit uncertain, but I guessed he was right. I should do that, in about that order.

"How bad was it last night?" I murmured. I didn't dare to touch him before I had a shower and a toothbrush.

"Let's just go with... You're not going to drink again."

I raised my hand and hid my face. This was not how my boy was supposed to see me — how anyone should see me. "I'm sorry. I'm so sorry you had to see me like this."

"It's okay. I..." He swallowed hard. "I should've stayed or checked on you sooner. I'm..." Micah hesitated again, looking at my chest instead of my face. "I'm sorry for failing you and not being there for you. But I'm here now. I got you into bed, and you slept. Now, how about some painkillers so you can get a shower?" He still spoke quietly, like he knew how bad my head hurt. "Talking can wait until you feel better."

"Thank you, baby." I tried to smile, but I hurt too much. "Painkillers sound good." I opened my eyes and tried to fumble for them, but Micah was faster. He opened the bottle and pressed a few into my hand. I popped them into my mouth, trying to swallow them dry.

I stopped when he said, "Here. Drink some water." Micah held a sippy cup in front of my lips. I looked at him, arching a brow, but he didn't relent. "It's this, swallowing dry, or a wet bed. Your choice."

I took the sippy cup. What choice did I really have?

The cool water ran down my throat, and I swallowed greedily until he took it away from me.

"Enough, or you'll get sick again."

Again? He'd seen… oh no. Please no.

"Baby, did you— Did I really get sick?" I watched his face.

"Yeah, you did. I think your hangover would be much worse if you hadn't. At least, that's what I've heard from around the dorms."

"I'm so sorry. This is— I'm so ashamed. You shouldn't be here. You shouldn't have seen me like that." I tried to sit up, but my arms didn't cooperate.

"What do you mean, I shouldn't be here?" His voice had dropped even lower, his shoulders slumping, and tears glistened at the corners of his eyes.

"You shouldn't see this, see me like this. I'm not the man you deserve. And you sure as hell shouldn't have to take care of me."

"So you don't want me to leave? You're just ashamed?" Why the hell was his voice hopeful?

I was seriously too hungover to have this kind of discussion.

"I don't want you to leave, baby. I drank because I thought I lost you. And yeah, I'm ashamed you saw me so weak." I nearly didn't get out the words, but I managed. Shame burned in my stomach, closing off my throat.

"Then I'll stay. We all have our weak moments, and you take such good care of me. It's my turn now. I don't mind, but I meant what I said. We *will* talk about this, but not as Daddy and boy. As Carter and Micah."

Uh oh. That meant I was in even deeper shit than I'd thought. Discussion as grown-ups didn't sound like fun, and it didn't bode well for me. "Of course, baby. Can you wait to yell at me until after I get a shower and brush my teeth?"

"I won't yell at you," he said softly. "I just didn't like drunk Carter at all. With all respect, I don't think that was a good reaction, even if what happened was pretty horrible."

I couldn't do anything but nod. "You're right. I just thought… I thought I lost you. And I couldn't stand it, not when—" I stopped. I couldn't tell him, not like this. Not hungover, reeking, in pain, and with Micah possibly still mad at me.

"You didn't lose me. I just needed some space. I'm sorry I left you. I shouldn't have done that." He still avoided my eyes, but I could see he was just as miserable as I was.

"You had every right to do that. Okay? Look at me, baby."

He slowly raised his gaze to meet my eyes. He nodded. I'd have to find a way to get him to believe me later, but for now...

"But how about I take this shower we keep talking about, and then we can talk over coffee, maybe? The painkillers should kick in by then."

Micah smiled softly at me. "Sounds like a plan. Off you go then. I'll start the coffee." With those words, he rolled out of bed.

I got a glimpse at him, finally noticing he'd been nearly naked. He was so beautiful, so sexy. And if I didn't fuck up the upcoming talk, he would still be mine.

By the time I was done with a long, hot shower, had brushed my teeth twice and made sure the bathroom was clean — and it was, which meant Micah had taken care of it and I owed him even more — my headache was just a nasty, but tolerable, pounding instead of the head-splitting pain I'd had earlier.

Now it didn't distract me from the shame that rose even more as I tried to put the pieces of the last couple of days together. A lot of it was gone, but I had some fragments that didn't really fit. It didn't help with my self-esteem, but I needed to face Micah and have the grown-up talk he'd just threatened me with. I didn't look forward to it, but Micah was worth it. He'd be worth everything — even swallowing my pride and admitting I'd fucked up with drinking so much. Then I would do a lot of groveling, and even more spoiling, and maybe we could move past this. Hopefully. I couldn't stand to lose him.

I would stay on my knees as long as I had to.

Wrapped in a towel, I came back to the bedroom. Micah sat

on the bed with two cups of coffee on a tray, along with some toast. I should've been the one waking him with coffee and breakfast… then feeding him, maybe giving him some juice in his sippy cup, then making love to him.

Not the other way around, with him taking care of me. My face grew red, and I hung my head in shame as I approached the bed. His expression didn't change, still soft and worried — which was far more than I deserved.

"Here you are. I brought milk and sugar, too, since I have no idea how you drink it."

I took the offered cup and wrapped my hands around it. "Black is okay. Thank you." I took a careful sip, hoping my stomach would agree with it. When it didn't revolt, I took another one before I put the cup to the side. "Let me get something to wear, then we can talk, okay?"

Micah nodded, but he didn't reply. He was busy playing with the sheets, pulling at them and rearranging them.

He'd gotten dressed, so I threw on some sweatpants and a t-shirt too. Then I was back at the bed.

I took a deep breath, trying to steel myself for the conversation. "So, here we go. First, I'm sorry. So, so sorry for everything. My parents shouldn't have walked in here like that, but that's not something I could change. My mother knew better, but they didn't listen, apparently. I couldn't control that, but I'm still sorry you had to witness it. I…" I sighed. "I probably should've changed the locks, but I thought telling them would be enough."

"It should've been," he replied, taking a sip of his own coffee, which was pale with the amount of milk he'd added.

I'd have to remember that was how he liked it, even if I didn't yet know how much sugar he took.

"Everything else, though, was completely my fault. I should've stayed here, thrown them out immediately, and cared for you. I handled that completely wrong." I paused, trying to word my next sentence. "It just threw me. I know what I'm into, and I know what you like, and I know there's nothing wrong with it. But to hear them say this is something perverted, to accuse me of hurting you, of being a pedophile even... I just couldn't deal with it. And for that, I'm sorrier than I can ever tell you."

Micah interrupted me with a hand on my wrist. "Carter, it's okay. You were as shocked as everyone else. We both know what's between us. My parents wouldn't understand either, but frankly," he shrugged, "I don't care as much about them as I care about you. There's nothing to be sorry for. The situation was completely out of control. I did the only thing I knew how to... I ran. I should've stayed with you, checked on you, but I didn't. So I'm sorry, too." He smiled at me, but it was sad. "How did things with your parents end, by the way?"

"Well, about how you probably guessed. I tried to explain, but they don't understand. In the end, they left, telling me not to ever contact them. It... hurt, to put it lightly."

Micah crawled over to me, took the mug from my hand to set it on the bedside table, and wrapped his arms around me. "I'm so sorry. This is just wrong of them, even if they don't understand."

I closed my eyes, enjoying his warmth, but it was all wrong to have him hugging me. He needed to be in my arms, not the other way around. "Thank you. I hope they'll come around, but right now, I doubt it it'll be any time soon. Time will probably tell, but for now, it's what it is."

Micah nodded against me. "Yeah. Maybe we can talk to them in a few weeks, try to explain some more."

"Maybe. Maybe not. We'll see how it goes."

Micah rested his head on my shoulder and squeezed me, then he pulled back. "Well, that was the part we both couldn't do much about. But there is something else, and this is something where I will draw a line."

He took a deep breath, and I could see how he pulled his shoulders back. My baby was gearing up for a fight.

"The drinking. You drowned your sorrows instead of calling me, texting me, coming to me. If you'd sat at home, thinking about what to do, that would've been one thing. I know I left pretty abruptly, and… I'm still so sorry for that."

"Shh," I told him, though the look he gave me made it clear he didn't appreciate being interrupted.

"I'm still allowed to be sorry. But you didn't think about choices, because you couldn't even say your name anymore. No way in hell were you planning anything."

My lips twitched as I heard him, even though it wasn't funny at all.

"So this is something we need to work on, together. You're my Daddy, so you're responsible for yourself and for me. This won't be the last issue we have. We'll probably fight sometimes, or bicker, or whatever. But there are other ways to deal. Drinking like that can't be one of them." Micah took a deep breath as he was done.

I just nodded, even though I had to hide my face. He was, of course, right. I should've handled it differently. "I'm sorry, Micah. I'm truly sorry. I promise not to do it again. I'll get rid of what I have at home, so I won't be tempted, okay?"

He coughed, then mumbled, "I kinda did that already. I was so mad last night."

Now I had to laugh. "It's okay. And I would be mad, too."

I paused, looking at him. I could only imagine how upset I'd be if he'd been the one in a drunken haze. I'd have been furious, and he had every right to be upset.

"If you can forgive me, can I make it up to you? I don't want to lose you, baby. I— I really like you, and I think we could have something beautiful. I'll do anything to earn your forgiveness." I wanted to say something else, but I couldn't. Not like this, when we'd just had such a big fight. Well, not a fight, not really. But it had been one hell of a mess.

"No need, Daddy. It's okay. Just…" He sighed. "Just promise to not do it again. If we fight, we'll talk it out. And if something else happens, we'll deal with it. No more heavy drinking."

"I promise, baby. That's the least I can do." I could feel the weight leaving my shoulders.

"Good. Now hold me." With those words, Micah dropped into my lap. "I missed you." He snuggled close, like nothing had ever happened.

I wrapped my arms around him, just holding him close to my body. "I missed you too, baby. So we're good? You'll stay?" I sounded too fucking needy, but I couldn't help myself.

"Yes, Daddy, I'll stay. I-I love you. I didn't want to say it yet, but… yeah. I guess I should probably say it, since it's true." He blushed again, that nice, charming blush I loved.

"I love you too, baby. So much. And I promise to do better and be the daddy you deserve."

"You do?" He looked at me with wide eyes. Obviously he'd gotten caught up on the first few words.

I chuckled. "If I didn't, I wouldn't have drank that much to deal with the pain. So, yes, I do."

He swatted at my shoulder. "Next time, show me you love me, not the bottle. It works better."

"Are you angling for a punishment, baby?" I pressed a kiss to his head, still holding him close and breathing in his scent.

"Punishment? No, not right now. But I could go for some loving from my daddy. You know, since I didn't get much the last two days, and he promised to make it up to me." His eyes sparkled, the tense moments between us forgotten — or at least pushed aside for a little while. The little brat was actually teasing me.

I dug my fingers in his ribs, making him laugh out loud. Micah giggled, a happy, free sound. "Stop it!" He giggled again, trying to squirm away.

I held him close, not giving up.

"Stop it, Daddy! Another kind of loving!"

I tickled him again, then I finally gave up and tried to kiss him. He was still laughing so hard, he couldn't even kiss me back. I joined him, laughing with him. Joy shone from his eyes, the pure happiness I'd seen in him once in a while when he was truly relaxed.

I wanted to see more of it.

"Are you done torturing me now, Daddy?" he asked breathlessly. "Can we move on to more pleasurable things? I won't get hard if you keep that up, you know."

Just for that, I tickled him again, but before it could escalate, I pulled him into the kiss I'd wanted. This time, he reacted, kissing me back with vigor while he wriggled around on my lap. Someone would definitely end up over my lap if he kept that up.

On the other hand, I loved to see how confident he seemed now with kissing.

Nevertheless, he got off on submission, and I got off on dominance. He could push, but I wouldn't give in. Pulling him up, I maneuvered him to straddle my thighs, facing me. My palm landed on his ass. It was way too covered for it to be really fun, but it would give him the message.

"Baby, you're up for a good spanking, and you know it. You can keep pushing and run that pretty mouth, which will lead to be me putting you over my lap before you get some loving. Or you can be my sweet baby, and you'll get your loving now." I tried to sound stern, but I probably failed.

The thoughts of reddening that perky ass had me twitching in my pants, while the thought of pleasuring him did the same. With the two ideas swirling together in my mind, I couldn't stand it anymore. I kissed him again, before he could answer.

This time, my baby didn't push. He gave in, melting in my arms while he responded to the kiss. I ran my hands over his back, cupping his ass, then traced up over his back. He shivered, pressing closer to me. Both of us were hard, and despite the fabric separating us, our cocks touched.

When I ended the kiss to nibble on his neck, he breathed, "Make love to me, Daddy. Make me yours."

I stopped, looking at him. "Are you sure, baby? I don't want to rush you. We can—"

My boy silenced me with a kiss. When he let up, he murmured, "Yeah, I'm sure. If you want to, of course."

Goosebumps rose on my arms at the thought of taking him. I was more than happy with what we'd done so far, and for me, it had been enough. I never would've pushed him. But when he offered, I wouldn't deny him. I cupped his cheek, then claimed his lips again.

"Always, baby. Always." I started nibbling at his collarbone, then I guided him to his back. He stretched out, his t-shirt riding up and revealing a stretch of skin between his jeans and his t-shirt. Leaning forward, I kissed his hip bones before I moved his t-shirt up.

He squirmed a little, lifting up to help me pull it off of him. It was like I was seeing him for the first time, and I had to stop and admire the expanse of his chest. He was my baby, yes, but he was also Micah — and it was like I was seeing Micah for the first time. He'd been so strong, taking care of me and standing up to me, and even though I wished it hadn't been necessary, I loved him even more for it.

His shirt discarded, I leaned down again, kissing his chin, then his throat, then down to his collarbone. I nipped the skin, earning a startled gasp from him, and he thrust his hips up against me.

I chuckled. "Like that, huh?"

"Don't tease me," he begged. He took my hand, hesitated a moment, then moved it to where his erection pushed against the fabric of his boxers. "I need you too much."

My mouth went dry. I couldn't wait to have his nude body beneath mine, to feel him writhing beneath me as I claimed yet another first from him. I kissed his neck, using my other hand to prop myself up as I kissed down his chest to his nipple. "Are you telling me what to do, baby boy?" I asked him. "Should I stop and punish you?"

He groaned, his hand squeezing mine as he kept my fingers

wrapped around his erection. "Please, please, please. Daddy, I can't… I'm going to come before you're even inside me."

The thought of that had me even more hot and bothered. "And?"

I remembered talking to him about how hot it would be to have him come in his diaper because he was so desperately needy, so ready to climax, and that desire hadn't faded at all.

"Come for me so you can enjoy yourself," I urged him, freeing my hand from his to slide it beneath the waistband of his underwear.

He whimpered, shaking his head. "I want you in me when I come," he said.

"My stubborn boy." I licked and sucked his nipple, drawing it into my mouth then biting down — gently, so gently, but enough to make him gasp.

"Daddy!" he whined, his hand going to the back of my head and burying it in my hair.

"Shh," I told him. "I'm not going to rush this. I want you to enjoy every second of it."

"I am enjoying every second of it! I just want it to happen a little faster." He pouted at me, and I kissed those full lips before going to the other neglected nipple. He gasped out a breath, squirming. "Daddy, Daddy, Daddy…"

How could I resist him? I had to. I couldn't let his first time be rushed. So I kissed on, teasing the nipple that grew firmer and firmer, as his moans grew louder.

"Daaaaddddyyyyy!"

I smirked but didn't let up. He'd enjoy it that much more if he came first, then we could take our time. My impatient baby just wouldn't see it that way. He wriggled below me, trying to get friction on his cock, but my fist remained closed around it, stopping all attempts to get off. This was my job, and I took it seriously.

Releasing his nipple, I rubbed him a few times, giving him just what he needed. Immediately, his moans grew louder, then he started pushing into my fist.

"I want you to come when I tell you to, my baby. Then, I'm going to get you hard again and make love to you."

"But Daddy, I—"

"Trust me, baby. This will be much better when you're not already on the edge." Not to talk about me, but I couldn't come before I was inside of him. I needed to wait.

"I trust you. I just… Promise to make me come again when you're inside me." He gave me a look like this was really important to him, and I guessed it was.

"I promise, baby." I kissed his nipple, then my lips found the skin of his stomach again. I moved lower, kissing toward his cock. Slowly. Very slowly.

He squirmed beneath me, soft, pleading whines spilling from his lips, and I treasured each and every one. I never forgot, even for a moment, how new this was to him. He'd never had anyone kiss him as soundly as I did, to touch him like I did — to show him how much he was loved, as I strived to do each and every day.

And he'd never had this before. No one had ever taken their time reveling in his sweet body before — because he'd never offered it to anyone.

He'd only offered his love to me, and he offered it with absolute, perfect trust.

It went right to my heart — and to my cock. It pulsed in my pants, all too aware that this beautiful boy was giving himself over to me in every way.

I kissed his belly button, then down the thin line of hair leading further down, then to the inside of his thigh. I was so close to his cock that my breath fanned against it, sending heat over it, and he jerked so hard my lips almost touched him.

I chuckled, leaning in to plant a kiss on the head of his cock, and he jerked again, smearing precum across my lips.

"Dadddddy," he whimpered. "You're going to make me come without even touching me."

I wondered if I could.

"Don't give me that look," he said, sitting up a little. Breathing heavily, he chided, "Now is not the time."

"Now is the perfect time, baby boy," I told him.

He pouted down at me, and I swatted his outer thigh. He squeaked indignantly, but he offered me a smile.

"But maybe if you ask nicely, I'll reconsider just this once, baby."

"Pleeease, Daddy?" he asked, his eyes wide and round. "Pretty please with a cherry on top?"

"There we go," I said, leaning down and flicking my tongue against the glistening tip of his cock. I pressed my hands down onto his thighs, holding him in place.

He gasped, trembling. His thighs strained, but my hands kept him from moving. "Daddy…"

I would never get tired of hearing him call me Daddy, of knowing what it meant to him — to both of us.

Instead of answering aloud, I took the head of his cock into my mouth, sucking it in past my lips. He was hard and twitching, the length of him near-bursting with need. I wanted to tease him a little more, but I didn't think he'd last long — and I wanted him to be floating on cloud nine when we got to the next step instead of frustrated by a half-assed orgasm.

"I'm— Daddy—" He couldn't even get a sentence out, and I'd barely started to pleasure him when he jerked and spilled into my mouth. "Sorry!" he panted, but I didn't let him pull away. I kept him firmly in place, drinking down every bit of his cum.

I licked my lips when I'd taken the last drop, planting another kiss on his softening cock before drawing back. I moved atop him, kissing him and pulling him closer to me. "Daddy's good boy," I murmured against his mouth. "You're such a good boy."

He whimpered, and I could feel his cock give a half-hearted twitch against my thigh.

The wonders of youth.

It wouldn't take him long to get hard again, which was good, considering I wasn't sure how good my control would remain. I ached to sink inside of him, to claim him as my own. I pulled back enough to be able to lean over the bed to reach into my nightstand. Rick had dropped lube and condoms into my hand a few days ago, complete with a knowing smirk, and now I silently thanked him. I wouldn't have thought about condoms. Lube was at home, since I did have needs, but I didn't keep condoms on hand.

Well, Rick had apparently foreseen that.

Micah's head turned, his eyes focusing on the foil packets nearby, and a shiver ran down his spine. I expected some hesitation, maybe even a little wariness or fear, but there was nothing like that. There was only need — need, and trust, and desire.

I drank in the sight of him, memorizing the look on his face. They would follow me to my dreams, where we could be together like this over and over again. My hand found his cock, slowly stroking him, and he whimpered against my mouth.

"I..." I breathed against his mouth, "am going to get you hard... Then I'm going to make sure you're ready to take me... Then I'm going to give you what you want. It'll feel so good, baby."

I grabbed the lube, poured some into my palm, then returned to his cock. He pushed into my hand with a soft noise, and I kissed him while I memorized every vein and ridge with my fingers.

When my hand slid down, fingers brushing his hole, he jolted, giving me that same wide-eyed look as his cheeks flushed.

"You are so beautiful," I said, admiring him.

And he was. He really, truly was.

The tip of my finger pressed lightly against his hole, parting for my touch. "Easy. Just relax." I slid my finger inside of him, so slowly I could feel his body twitch around me. I could only imagine how his ass would feel around my cock. I curved the tip of my finger, stroking him, finding that perfect spot inside of him.

Even if I hadn't felt it, I'd have known I was there by the way he jerked in my arms.

"Daddy, wh—"

I smiled at him, satisfied, and stroked him again. "Your prostate, baby."

"No one told me it'd feel that good," he said breathlessly.

"Just wait," I promised him. I hadn't been with anyone since Nic, but it wasn't like you just forgot how to bring pleasure to your lover. I'd always topped, and I'd always been focused on making sure my partner got the best experience they possibly could. It wasn't that I wouldn't bottom, but Nic had never been interested in topping.

With Micah, it was possible he wanted to try it one day, but for now, it seemed to be the way he wanted it.

And, no matter what we did, Micah's pleasure came before my own, so I was slowly sliding my fingers into his ass to open him up while my balls drew tight and my cock hardened painfully. I'd get to take care of my own needs soon enough, but the more important part was that I wanted Micah to remember this moment forever. I wanted him to remember how happy we both were.

I wanted us to share everything.

I took my time, working up to three fingers into him. If I'd had slender fingers like him, I might've had to use more, but my thick, rough digits were good enough to open him for me.

"Daddy, please," he said, his cock straining again. "Please, please, please," he chanted.

I couldn't wait any longer, not when he was begging me so sweetly. I yanked my shirt over my head and threw it to the side, then tugged my sweatpants off. I breathed out a sigh of relief as my cock sprang free, bumping against my stomach.

I ached to slide into him, but I grabbed one of the packets, tearing it open. It was hard to even get the condom onto my cock, but the sight of those bright, inquisitive eyes had me working that much harder to do it.

I drizzled lube on the condom. I didn't want this to be uncomfortable for him, and while I knew it would hurt at first, I wanted him to enjoy it more. I smeared it across his hole, using the excess to grab his shaft and stroke him.

Finally, my cock was pressing gently against him. He was making the most incredible keening noises I'd ever heard, begging me without words to take him. I didn't want to hurt him, and I went slow.

He inhaled sharply when I started to press inside of him, and I froze. "You okay, baby?"

"No," he whimpered. He grabbed me when I immediately started to pull out. "You're taking too long."

"I don't want to hurt you."

"I know." Micah smiled at me. "But I want you. I want to feel your cock... *there.*"

I knew what he meant, and I was damn sure going to give his prostate one stroke after another until his body was too lost in pleasure to remember which way was up. Then I'd bring him to climax with my hand so I could feel his seed against my stomach when I came.

I took a deep breath then started to push. His features scrunched up, but when I stopped, he grabbed my arms. "Don't stop," he whimpered.

"Baby—"

"Please?"

How could I refuse him? I kept going until I was balls-deep in him, and his whimpers turned into moans as he got used to the feeling of me inside of him.

He shivered, pulling me in for a kiss, and I lost myself to it. It was only when he rolled his hips against mine that I started to draw back, to thrust into him a little bit at a time until he was moaning. I angled against his prostate, making sure to hit it on each stroke, and I took him that way — softly, tenderly, making sure he enjoyed every second of it.

He'd still be sore the next day, but I was going to make it worth it.

The sounds he made were impossibly beautiful, and the looks on his face... They had me pulsing, desperate, rocking against him. He lifted his hips as I pressed against him, kissing him deeply.

My hand went to his cock, stroking him in time with my thrusts. Within moments, he was gasping again, the sounds spilling from his lips getting more frantic. "Come for me, baby boy," I whispered against his mouth.

He moaned, bucking as my strokes grew faster, my hand squeezing just a little more. It was all I could do to hold back as I brought him closer to the edge, and I gasped when his seed spilled over my fingers.

"Daddy!" He jerked beneath me, thrusting back against my cock for a moment as the ripples of pleasure washed over him.

I held off for only seconds, then I was filling the condom inside of him.

He kissed me, deep and hard, and I stayed where I was, breathing heavily. I didn't want to move. I never wanted to move.

I just wanted to stay there inside of him.

CHAPTER SIXTEEN

MICAH

I'd left the nail polish on. At first, I wanted to remove it, but then I stared at it and the bottle of nail polish remover, then I couldn't do it. It was too pretty. Too much myself.

Of course, it reminded me a little of Daddy's parents standing in the doorway, but mostly, of the way Carter had looked at me when he'd put it and the makeup on. He'd watched me like I was the most beautiful, most precious thing he'd ever seen in his life. I'd never had anyone see me that way before, and the fact that he did…

It was one of the reasons I loved him so much.

Well, that and the fact that he'd taken my virginity and left only the best memories behind. Last night had been simply magical. He'd taken such good care of me, making sure nothing was painful or uncomfortable. It'd just been perfect. It hadn't been sex, it hadn't been… fucking. It was just making love, nothing more and nothing less.

I couldn't help but smile as I remembered the feeling as I'd woken up, wrapped tightly in his arms as he showed me how much I meant to him. Daddy had held me close all night, spooning me from behind. His strong embrace gave me a safety

I'd never experienced, and the huge smile on my face wouldn't vanish, even though I probably looked like an idiot.

On top of the nail polish, I wore a tight t-shirt, showing my body, and jeans that somehow hugged my ass. It'd taken me minutes to look away from the mirror in Daddy's bedroom, because I still couldn't believe this was me. It felt… right. Strange, yet right.

It'd taken even longer for Daddy to keep his hands off me, though. He didn't succeed until I really had to leave, or I'd be late for my class. Even then he'd been reluctant, his kiss lingering, as well as the hand on my – slightly sore – ass. I'd have given so much to just stay with him. I wanted to curl up on his lap, watch TV, maybe fool around some more — not deal with programs and codes and bugs and all that. I didn't want to go at all.

But Daddy would have none of it. He'd made me sit down at the breakfast table and fed me eggs and bacon while I sipped my coffee. We didn't play, and I also didn't use my sippy cup because I needed some coffee in the morning, but still, Daddy took care of me. Just the simple act of feeding me, making sure I had eaten enough to make it until lunch, brought my heart to a stutter.

Shouldering my bag, I headed toward my classroom. My morning class would last until about one, then I'd have to work, but afterwards, we'd meet again. He had today off, so he'd be waiting for me.

And just like that, the huge grin broke out on my face again. I couldn't care less.

"Hey, Micky! Is that— did you accidentally steal your sister's nail polish?"

My head whipped around as I faced the assholes who loved to tease me. Today, I even gave them a reason, because I was wearing something—

I stopped short. They'd teased me regardless. Whether I wore plain, manly clothes, or not. Whether I tried to blend in or not. Whether I hid myself or carried my head held up.

It didn't matter. *It. Did. Not. Matter.*

Fuck. Why the hell hadn't I— I couldn't think about that now. Right now, I had to deal with them. What would Daddy do now? How would he react? Would he hide? Would he run away? No, he wouldn't.

I took a deep breath to steady my shaking hands. It didn't help, but well. I just had to ignore them then. "Nah, I don't have a sister, actually. That's mine. You like the color, Jacob? I'd offer to share, but I like the color too much. But you can buy some, then I'll teach you how to apply it?"

Jacob looked at me like I'd grown two heads, clearly speechless for the first time ever.

"Hit me up when you find your color, then we can maybe set something up to make you a bit prettier, even though I'm not sure it would help in the bigger picture."

Tyler broke down laughing just as Jacob snapped, "You little shit! How dare you say something like that! You're just a little faggot! Don't ever talk to—"

"Mr. Swenson, to my office, right now." A teacher's voice ripped through the hall, making all three of us jump.

Jacob slowly turned his head, facing the older woman. "I didn't—"

"Office. Right now."

Well, that made things easier, even though his insult stung. But well, this time, he might learn his lesson.

Jacob grew white as a sheet, then slowly raised his backpack.

I didn't know what possessed me, but before he turned away, I winked at him. Walking past him, way too close for my comfort, I whispered, "Let me know when you have your nail polish."

With those words, I nodded toward the teacher, who just stopped me. "Are you okay? I'm sorry Mr. Swenson just—"

I shook my head. "I'm fine." I walked to my classroom. Tyler trailed behind me, suspiciously silent. His grades weren't the best, just like Jacob's, so he probably didn't need any additional trouble.

I tried to still my pounding heart. This sure as hell wasn't the last confrontation we'd have, but for the first time ever, I didn't care. And while I was thankful for the help, I also didn't want to have the confrontation taken away from me. I'd finally stood up to them, then I didn't even get to finish it.

But on the other hand, maybe it was better that way. A guy caught my eye, winking at me. He wore tight jeans, though they had carefully crafted holes in them — at least I hoped they were carefully crafted so nothing important would fall out. "Nice nail polish. And nice take down. He needed it. I'm Finn, but you can call me Sweetie. Or whatever you want."

I stopped short, eying him. Was he another one of those assholes trying to mess with me? But his own fingernails were painted in a sparkling blue, and I wasn't really sure, but his eyes were a bit too dark… was that make up?

With a deep breath, I answered, "Micah. You new here?"

Finn shook his head. "Usually, I'm over in arts. I just had to drop something off. You?"

I nodded toward the classroom. "Mine. I'm in Programming." Why couldn't he be a new student? Finn might be fun to hang out with.

"Shame. And here I'd thought we could get those idiots to reconsider wearing makeup. But we can meet for lunch or whatever. Here, put your number in. I'll text you. I have to leave in a minute, because my class is about to start, but we can hang out sometime. I'm happy to meet new people, and I can tell you're a lot of fun." Before I could even react to some parts of the statement, he thrust his phone in my hand, grinning at me.

I added my number, not sure what to make of him. "I… Okay. Here you go."

"Thank you. Gotta run, but we'll talk." With that, he hurried away, swaying his ass like he was on a runway.

I shook my head. That guy sounded crazy, but a nice crazy. Would I even manage to make friends, now that I wasn't hiding who I was anymore? I might've tried all of this backwards, then. Shaking my head, I walked into my classroom and pulled out my phone to text Daddy what had just happened. I couldn't write everything, but I gave him a rundown.

"Well done my baby. I'm proud of you and I love you. When you get home later, I might have a surprise for you," was his answer.

I couldn't stop beaming during class, even though I managed to screw up a few things because my mind was otherwise occupied.

What had he planned? Would it involve playtime?

I didn't stop smiling all morning.

My smile lasted exactly until the moment I stepped into the dogs' section of the shelter. As always, I checked Snowflakes' kennel to greet him before I started working. It was my routine, something I looked forward to. But Snowflake wasn't bouncing around behind the metal bars as usual. I looked around, making sure I had the right number, because the kennel was empty. Not he's-on-a-walk-empty. It was spotless, like he'd never been there, with his name card and chart gone.

What had happened? Where was my dog? Panic rose, robbing my breath.

I stormed into the office, trying — and failing — to remain calm. "Where is he?" I asked, trying to still my beating heart.

The volunteer looked at me. She had to be new, because I hadn't seen her before. "Who? And who are you?"

My staff t-shirt should've told her that already.

"Micah. Snowflake, the dog from kennel 11. White and big. His kennel is empty and cleaned out."

She slowly nodded. "I think I saw a note. He was adopted earlier this morning, I think."

"What? How— He — Why?" I stammered, not getting out a sentence. Why? My Snowflake? My beautiful dog? Why had he been adopted?

"Because this is a shelter? People adopt dogs here, you know?"

Her tone was bored and slow, like I'd have trouble understanding her otherwise.

"But you— I don't—" I turned around as tears threatened to spill over.

My dog was gone. I'd really hoped to be able to adopt him one day, or talk Carter into doing it, but now, he was gone. Just like that. I hadn't even been there to say goodbye.

Wiping my hands furiously at my eyes, I turned back to her. "Can you tell me who it was?"

"That's personal information, and I don't see why you need it. Susan probably has it since she handled it. I can't tell you more." She looked like she'd throw me out of the office any moment.

I nodded. I'd have to ask our supervisor then, when I came in next time. She usually worked early shifts, so she was gone by now. Why had she handled it anyway? It was unusual for her to deal with adoptions directly, but maybe it was because Snowflake was hard to place? I didn't know. For now, it didn't matter. I had no one I could ask. I had nothing I could do.

Though, even if Susan *had* the contact information, what would it help? The people who got him had wanted him. They wouldn't give him up, and I couldn't take him anyway. But maybe they'd allow me to see him again, to at least say goodbye and make sure he was well cared for?

Tears spilled over again as I hid in the bathroom, trying to get a grip on my emotions. Why? Why today, when it'd just been perfect? Why not any other day? I'd been so happy, and now? Now it was over. He was gone.

I cried for a long time, trying to get a grip on my emotions, but then the tears overwhelmed me again. I couldn't stop them, no matter what I did. My beautiful dog, just gone. My insides felt empty, like something had been ripped out.

Finally, I managed to pull myself together, even though I looked like shit. I took the other dogs out, got the kennels cleaned up, and did all the other things I needed to do.

A couple of coworkers passed me, but I managed to hide my face enough so no one asked what was going on.

My shift couldn't end soon enough.

By the time I stopped in front of Daddy's door, I was a mess. My eyes were red and swollen, my nose was stuffed up, and I couldn't stop crying, no matter what I did. I wiped my face, but it didn't help at all.

I just wanted to feel Daddy's arms around me, have him hold me close and make it all go away. The pain of losing Snowflake wasn't something that some playtime would help with, but at least he could maybe… I didn't know. Nothing would help, probably. But I ached for his arms, for his tender care, for his support.

It was stupid, but even though there'd been the couple there recently, and despite knowing he was a shelter dog, he'd been there for so long that I'd never really thought he could truly be gone one day, just like that.

Or maybe I had and just ignored it. I wasn't sure. In any case, he was gone, and I would spend the next days crying.

I rang the doorbell, wiping my cheeks, but it was useless. Knowing Daddy would hold me, comfort me, be there for me, made me cry harder.

"You have a key. You don't —" Immediately, he drew me into his arms. "Baby, what's wrong?" he murmured, holding me close to his chest. His strong hands ran soothing circles on my back, and I clung to him like a lifeline. "Baby?"

"I— They— He's—" I couldn't speak. Sobs wracked my body, making it impossible to even tell him. It hurt so much.

"Come in, and then you can tell me, okay?" He remained calm, even though his heart beat like crazy.

Without releasing me, he guided me to the kitchen, where he held me until I managed to get a grip on my emotions.

When I was just sniffling, he carefully said, "Can you tell me what's wrong, my sweet boy? Otherwise, I can't help you." He hadn't released me, just let me get it out.

Still in his arms, I murmured, "Snowflake got adopted today. I didn't even get to say—" I sobbed again.

"Oh. Ohh. Is that why you're so upset? It's because of Snowflake?" He sounded… I couldn't place it.

Was he making fun of me? Because I cried for my dog? He couldn't be like this, could he? This wasn't the man I knew.

I jerked my head up, staring at him. "What do you mean, because of Snowflake?"

"I mean… I think I messed up. Again. And big time." He didn't look at me.

What? What the hell did that have to do with me crying about Snowflake? New tears welled up, but this time, I forced myself to stop crying.

"Come on. I need to show you something. If I'd known this would be your reaction, I'd have told you. I just thought you'd be happy." He sounded down, like he really had messed up.

What was wrong? No matter which way I turned that, it didn't make sense. I couldn't figure out what he could've done, especially since this morning, when everything had been perfect. Messed up big time… that sounded ominous, but I was still completely in the dark.

Slowly, he opened the door to the living room. "The surprise I got you… I'm sorry, baby. So, so sorry."

I looked into the living room, just to be nearly toppled over by a huge white dog. It bounced at me, jumping up, trying to lick my face. "Snowflake?" No doubt, that was him. I dropped to my knees, burying my hands in his fur as he tried to lick my face. "Why is— You got— There— Why?"

"I thought… You were so afraid of losing him. And it's soon, but I wanted for you to have him. I thought he could stay here, with you. Or me, and you, when you are here, which I hope will be all the time. And if… if anything happens, it's your dog, but I would make sure he always has a place to stay. It's… I wanted to make you happy, baby." Carter seemed to be at a loss for words, and I couldn't get out any, either.

I just stayed on the floor, caressing Snowflake's fur, until he decided enough was enough and bounced away, only to drop a ball in my lap not even a second later. I looked at it, then at the door to the yard.

"Let's take him outside, then we can talk. I have the feeling that I'm missing something here." My brain was fried.

Carter just nodded and with a hand on my back, he followed me to the door. I threw the ball and Snowflake ran after it, catching it in the air. "So, tell me from the beginning why he's here. Please." My eyes caught Carter's, before I threw the ball again.

"I kept thinking about how sad you were that Snowflake might get adopted. I couldn't shake the look, the sadness in your eyes. I told you that Nic and I actually talked about getting a dog, but then he got sick. Well, I had this… hope, that we could… that I could get a dog, with you this time. It was… it shouldn't mean you're his replacement or anything. Don't get me wrong. It's more like… closure. He's gone, but you're with me. When I thought I lost you, I actually thought about getting Snowflake to have a piece of you left, but then you came back, and I wanted to give you this gift." Carter swallowed and took my hand in his. "I love you very much, Micah. I want to live my life with you, and Snowflake."

I just shook my head. "You could've told me. I was heartbroken."

"I'm sorry. Actually, your supervisor was supposed to plant some hints who adopted him. I had to talk to her, since Snowflake is a bit special and she wanted to give me another dog, one better suited for a newbie. Took me some convincing and dropping your name to get her to give him to me."

I nodded. That made sense, since he definitely wasn't a beginner's dog. I'd known him forever, so I didn't have issues with him, but he'd be wrong for someone getting their first dog.

"I have no idea what to say. Honestly, I'm just stunned. And no, I had no clue at all. I can't tell you how relieved I am to see him here. And I can't believe it." My emotions were all over the place, sadness, happiness, everything wrapped up in a tangle I'd need some time to unravel.

Carter stood next to me, watching me play with Snowflake.

"Thank you. I have no idea how I deserved that, but thank you." I smiled at him, pressing a kiss to his lips.

"Did you... did you even hear what I said?" Carter still looked nervous.

I thought back, to what he said. Oh. Oh!

"Yes, sorry. I'm— today is the day of apologies, right? Yes, of course. I would love to be here, with Snowflake, and you, and I want to see where this will lead. I love you so much, and I can't wait to see where we'll end up." I paused, then I laid my arms around his waist. "And thank you for being honest about your past with Nic. It helps me if you tell me, since I don't feel left out then." I rested my head on his shoulder, breathing in his scent. "I love you so much."

"I love you too, baby."

I lay behind Micah, my arm around his waist and my chest pressed against his back, and watched him sleep. He looked so young, so carefree and so peaceful. I'd seen more and more of that when we were together, when we either played or when I'd just made him come.

Both were my favorite things to do, of course.

I loved seeing him when he let go of his stress, his worries, the pressure studying brought with it. And I loved hearing him laugh.

Okay, well. I plainly loved him. There was no other way to say it. He'd brought light and laughter into my life again, something I'd lost with Nic. The issue with my parents still lingered in the back of my mind, but if I had to pick between not meeting Micah and keeping them, I would always pick Micah. They'd either come around, or they wouldn't.

My fingers traced lazy circles on his stomach, and my eyes fell on Snowflake, who'd somehow managed to claim a spot right next to the bed. For a shelter dog, he was surprisingly well-behaved, and him and my baby had spent every evening since we'd gotten him snuggled up on the couch.

Dogs had no business on a couch… At least, they hadn't until

Micah had looked at me with those huge, green eyes, worrying his bottom lip. Then I somehow ended up with my boy on my lap… and a huge white dog on *his* lap. Somehow, they had me wrapped around their little fingers. Paws. Both.

Snowflake was sleeping, too, flat on the side, his breath deep and even. It wasn't all easy with him, of course, since he did react to other dogs rather badly, but Micah knew how to handle him. I'd gotten better, too. Having a dog in my life wasn't that bad, and maybe I should've gotten one much sooner, but it made me especially happy to give this dog a home, since Micah loved him so much.

Which brought me back to my little. He'd been staying over every night now, sleeping in my bed. Sometimes, he needed to get up before me because he had an early class, and a couple of times he went to bed before I was home at night. But there was no better feeling than coming home, knowing he was there. Some of his clothes had migrated to my closet, his favorite foods were in my fridge, and his toothbrush kept mine company. It was perfect.

Micah was basically living with me, and while we hadn't been together for long, I hoped he'd give up his room in the dorms soon. I didn't want to ask him to take that big of a step yet, even though he'd said yes to staying with me, but in my heart, I knew it would happen.

My baby stirred, rubbing his ass against my groin, and I softly pressed a kiss to his shoulder.

"Mhh."

"Morning, baby."

"Mhh." He wriggled closer, pressing that firm ass against my cock.

I'd sported morning wood since I'd woken up, but now it got more pressing.

"What are you doing, baby? Trying to get some loving?" I held him close, trailing my lips over his soft skin. When he'd just woken up, he was even smoother, all relaxed and cuddly.

"Is it working?" he murmured.

"Have I ever not given you what you wanted?" I asked with a smile.

"A second dog and a couple of cats?"

His words were barely audible, but I managed to hear him anyway. "What?" I dug my fingers into his ribs, carefully since he'd just woken, but this kind of brattiness wouldn't go over unpunished. "You ungrateful little brat, you. Here I planned to make you come until you don't know your name, and you're asking for more animals?"

Micah started shaking, laughing silently. He struggled to get away, but he didn't manage, partly because he'd just woken and partly because I had a good grip on him.

"Or wait, no. You didn't ask. You told me you hadn't gotten them. That's even worse." I tickled him even more, loving the sounds and squeals he made. He tried to pry my hand away, but it didn't work.

"Daddy!" he finally panted.

I gave him a bit of breathing room.

"Daddy, stop it! I'm good now!" He was breathing hard and still giggling. "I'm good, I promise."

"Are you now, baby? Or do I have to spank that sexy ass?" I ran my hand down, over his stomach to his hips and then cupped said ass. Rubbing it firmly, I managed to draw a moan from him. "So my baby would like that?" I waited for him to answer me.

"I'm not sure. I think… maybe, if you need to punish me?"

I chuckled. "It's not really a punishment if you enjoy it, boy. But if I have to punish you, sure, why not?" I rubbed my cock against his ass, showing him I found the idea way too tempting. I wasn't into pain play, but some mild dominance… and afterwards, fucking that reddened ass… Yeah, that I did like — very, very much.

"So you'd enjoy it?" he asked hesitantly.

"I would, yes. If you'd enjoy it too. I don't need it to be satisfied, though, if that's what you're worrying about." I caressed him and realized he'd tensed up during our conversation. One day, he'd learn I was perfectly happy with what we had. I'd suggest things, but I would never make him do anything he didn't want to.

"Nah, I'm not worrying about that. I know you wouldn't do it if I didn't want to. I was more worried about liking it too much and what you'd come up with as a punishment instead." He turned around, his green eyes twinkling. His hands touched me immediately, running over my chest, my abs, my nipples. "Now, about that lovemaking… Do I have to beg?" He pouted, pushing his lower lip out.

That little minx. Somewhere, the shy, blushing boy had gotten lost… because this one definitely said what he wanted.

"I like it when you beg, baby. And I'm not sure you even deserve some lovemaking, since you were a brat…" I tried very, very hard to sound stern, but my roaming hands and my hard cock meeting his probably gave me away.

"Oh, Daddy, that's just meaaan." He pouted some more, but his eyes were still sparkling. "And here I thought I could start our day with something fun."

"You thought that, baby? And what if I had other plans, like doing laundry?" I kissed along his neck up to his ear. His cock already pressed against mine, trying to get friction.

"Now that's really mean." He grasped my ass, pulling me closer. "But I guess I'll have to take care of it in the shower then, if my Daddy doesn't want to help me with my problems."

I looked down at him, seeing the smile on his lips. "You belong to me, baby. No touching yourself in the shower. Or elsewhere." With those words, I rolled him to his back. Looming over him, I took both of our cocks in my hand. "You still didn't beg, if I may say that. So I'm not sure you earned the lovemaking. But I guess you'll have to make it up to me later."

With those words, I started rubbing both of us.

"Daddyyyy, Dadddddyyyyy, please!" Within moments, he

really started to beg, pleading for me to let him come, take him, get him off.

But he wouldn't. I kept myself in check, even though I wanted nothing more than to spill onto his stomach. My lips caressed his skin, drawing moans between his breathless words. Micah clawed at my shoulders, trying to fuck my fist, but I had him below me, caught and unable to move. So fucking perfect.

"Daaaddddyyyy! Let me come! Please!" His last word was a mix between a sob and a moan, and I couldn't hold back anymore. He was so beautiful, so sexy, and his smell drove me crazy.

I came, spilling all over him. My hand moved more easily now, but he still held back, even though tears glistened in his eyes. I kissed them away, murmuring, "Come for me, baby."

With a choked sound, he jerked, then his cock pulsed in my fist. Warm cum mixed with my own, adding to the mess we made.

I kissed him deeply, then murmured how beautiful he was, and how much I loved him. It took a while before he could respond, but then he smiled slowly.

"Now that was nice, Daddy. I guess I don't need to get off in the shower then."

"Oh boy. You're trouble, you know that?" I rolled us both to the side, so his head was resting on my shoulder.

I almost drifted off to sleep again, even though we should get up and take Snowflake for a walk. I hoped to spend a relaxed Saturday with my little before we headed to the bar for play night — if Micah was game, of course. I hadn't told him about it yet, since I hadn't figured out a good way to approach it.

Even though it probably wasn't even something to worry about, I was afraid he'd be reminded of the way we'd met. But I wanted to go, with him as my little. I wanted him to have fun with Sean, and maybe one of the other littles.

"I... I kind of wanted to ask something." I held him close, our mixed cum cooling on us. Grabbing an old t-shirt, I quickly cleaned us up, then I returned to what I was saying. "I… Today is play night in the bar. And I wanted to ask if you want to go…" I trailed off.

"Sure. It's gonna be fun to meet Sean again. He's coming, right?" Micah didn't even raise his head.

"Are you sure? And yes, he's coming. Rick and I usually set up everything, then he goes home to get Sean. He's usually so hyper before a play date that he leaves him at home." I laughed quietly.

"Of course. It's going to be nice. Can I play, too?" Now he was looking at me, his eyes big and deep.

"Yes, baby. I'd love if you wanted to play. I'd love if you'd come with me, as my little. We can spend the evening with coloring, you sitting in my lap, and maybe Sean and you can play with his cars."

He nodded. "That sounds awesome, Daddy. I'd love that." Stretching, he yawned. "What are the plans before that? I need to take Snowflake out, but aside from that, I don't have anything important to work on."

That worked wonderful with my plans. "How about I'll let Snowflake outside in the garden, make breakfast for my baby, and we'll spend the day playing? Except when we go outside with Snowflake, of course?"

"Hmm. I love the way you think." He kissed my shoulder. "Can I have pancakes for breakfast, Daddy? In your lap?"

I grinned. "Sure. And after our morning walk, we could do your nails again? What do you think? Then I can take a pretty princess to the play date tonight."

"I'd love that, Daddy." He leaned over to me, grinning. "Now, how about those pancakes? I'm starving…"

I slapped his ass. "Go take a shower, then wait here while I take care of Snowflake and get started on breakfast. I'll be back to get you dressed." I'd love to bathe him, but then we'd never get breakfast done, and I really needed to let Snowflake outside, too.

"No bath, Daddy?" Micah pouted.

"You just told me you're starving. Either you get a bath now or pancakes. And I figured you'd prefer to get fed." I kissed him one last time, just in the moment as his stomach rumbled.

"I guess so. So I'll go take a shower all alone, then wait here." My baby was still pouting, his lower lip trembling. I nibbled it.

"Be nice, baby, and stop pouting. I'll pamper you all day. And believe me, I want to give you a bath. Maybe we can do that later, or tomorrow." I kissed his lips, then sat up. Snowflake jumped around, clearly eager to get outside. "I'm coming, big boy. You need to go outside, right?"

"Sorry, baby. Daddy's gonna let you out right away." Micah's fingers were buried in the white fur, hugging his dog close.

I let them have their moment, but Snowflake was restless, so I headed outside with him. The water started a few moments later.

Snowflake ran into the garden, raising his leg immediately, and I turned to the kitchen to start the pancakes, cut up some fruit for my baby, and make coffee. One thing Micah absolutely needed was a cup of coffee, no matter if he was little or not, so he'd get one. Then, when he was done, there would be milk in his sippy cup.

Whistling away, I got the breakfast ready, smiling from ear to ear. Taking care of my little felt so right and so perfect.

When everything was ready for my baby, I went upstairs and found him naked on the bed. He was resting, not asleep but apparently deep in thought. What a sight he was, all that lean muscle, the flat stomach and the half-hard cock.

"Now this is a lovely sight." I stepped closer, taking his hand. "But as much as I love it, you need to get dressed. Come on, let's move that to the nursery."

"I've been a good boy, Daddy. Just got myself clean, nothing else." He beamed at me as he followed my lead to the nursery.

"Now that's a really good boy." I opened the door for him, then let him sit down on the changing table.

I grabbed a onesie, pale green this time, as well as some panties in a dark pink. "Then let's get you dressed." Grabbing the baby powder, I rubbed it gently on him, taking very good care to reach every part of him.

He stirred, as did my cock. But my baby's eyes were closed, and he seemed to be completely relaxed as he let me spread the powder, then slip the panties on. They were a nice fit, highlighting his cock and balls, but giving him a slightly feminine touch. I had to adjust myself, despite my recent orgasm.

My hands roamed over him, caressing him and stroking over all that naked skin before I took the onesie and slipped it on. "You okay, baby?"

"Hmm." A smile played on his lips. "Perfect." He fell silent again as I closed the onesie. Then, suddenly, he asked, "Daddy, can you… help make me pretty? For tonight?"

When I just imagined him dressed in his pink panties and painted fingernails, his face all made up even though he'd be facing the world — or at least our world, in the kink bar… now I was hard. He'd be so beautiful. Even more than he already was, even though it was hard to imagine. I swallowed, trying to find my voice. "Of course. You're going to look so hot, my sweet boy."

He offered a small, shy smile. "We'll just see if you can keep your hands off me."

CHAPTER EIGHTEEN

MICAH

I felt pretty.

It wasn't something I was used to, but it was a feeling I *wanted* to get used to.

I smiled up at Carter from beneath eyeshadow and mascara, reaching to touch him with a hand bearing freshly painted fingernails. I could feel my cock threatening to respond in my soft pink panties. It was exhilarating.

Frightening, too, but I loved the effect it had on Carter.

He grabbed my hand and squeezed it. "You okay?"

I nodded. I was terrified, but I was more than fine. "Just thinking."

"About me, I hope." He leaned in to steal a sloppy kiss.

"About what you do to me," I said. About the things he'd done to me. About how beautiful he made me feel even though he easily could've recoiled in disgust at finding out this was a part of me. Instead, he made me feel special and sweet, and it made it even easier to fall head over heels in love with him.

"Close enough." Carter let go of my hand, inspecting me from the front.

My cheeks heated. He'd seen me in the flowing shirt and the tight pants earlier, but it felt like he was really *looking* at me this time. It should've been uncomfortable — and it was, a little bit. At the same time, the way he smiled at me made it clear he liked what he saw.

"I did a good job picking that out for you," he said, grinning at me. "It looks great on you."

Something inside of me relaxed. "Yeah?" I offered him a hopeful look, wanting to hear him say it again, wanting to believe it.

At least he didn't tease me about fishing for compliments. He'd done that exactly once, and I'd been so crushed he hadn't done it again. I wasn't fishing. I was looking for validation, and he was the only one I knew how to turn and look to.

Maybe Finn, when our friendship got a little more stable, or maybe Sean, when I got more comfortable with the other little. But for now, it was just Carter.

"You look beautiful," he told me, tucking a strand of my hair behind my ear. "This is in the way though."

"It does that," I said, grinning a little as I remembered how I'd told him the same thing when we'd first met. My hair still wasn't any better about cooperating now than it had been then, but I liked how it looked more.

This time, he smiled back at me and leaned in to steal another kiss. "I know."

And he did. How many times had he brushed it back into place? Countless. He was there when I first woke up, when my hair was utterly unmanageable, and he was there throughout the day when it got out of place.

He was always there, but it felt like he wasn't there enough. It might never be enough.

Staring into those beautiful brown eyes, I forgot what I was going to say next.

The screeching of a table getting shoved around ripped us out of the moment. "Aren't you supposed to be working, too?" I asked, bumping my hip against his.

"Aren't you supposed to be helping?" He arched a brow. "You said you were coming to help us set up, not to distract me."

"That *is* helping," I protested, pouting.

He ran his finger along my lips. "Try again."

"Do you want me to mess up my nails?" I asked, keeping a straight face for only a few seconds. I couldn't help it. I had to tease him. Maybe I was more like Sean — and like Nicholas — than even we'd known. Now that I was used to Daddy being there, solid and steady, it was easier to joke with him.

I wasn't afraid at all.

"Go sit and look pretty," he told me, pointing to a table that had already been moved into its new spot for the night. "Or I'm going to jump you right here. Wouldn't that be a surprise for everyone walking in?"

There was that wicked smile on his lips, the one I adored every bit as much as he liked my blush.

I pushed at him, my cheeks flaming predictably in response to his words.

"Go do things," I told him. I couldn't meet his eyes, too mortified at the idea of anyone seeing us in the middle of anything.

He grabbed me around the waist before I could go far. "Hey," he said softly, resting his forehead against mine. "You okay, baby?"

I nodded. I liked when he joked with me, and I didn't want him to stop, but sometimes, it was hard. "I'm just not an exhibitionist. You can cross that off my yes/no/maybe list."

I hadn't made one yet, but I'd at least learned what they were. Right now, pretty much everything was in the "maybe" or "no" sections, but who knew? Maybe that would change in time.

So much else had.

No matter how much we joked about spankings, that was still in the maybe list, too. It was something I wanted to explore, but something neither of us was positive I was really ready for, no matter how much I wanted to feel it.

Carter chuckled softly, then let me go. "No more jokes like that in public unless I want to see you blush, then," he said.

"Oh, come on," I complained, stomping one foot against the floor, but at the same time loving how it made me feel. "You always want to see me blush."

He started to reply, but I swatted at him.

"Go do things," I said more firmly. "You're supposed to be showing off those muscles for me." I was still blushing, but I liked the idea of that.

He strolled off with another grin, and I went to the table he'd gestured to. A smile curved onto my lips, and I sat down in front of the ocean-themed coloring book and set of colored pencils he'd left for me there. It was just like him to be so thoughtful.

"I love fishes too," a voice said from beside me.

I looked up to see Sean, and I grinned at him. "I didn't know you were here already."

"Daddy was running late, so he brought me with him," he said. "But he got tired of me nagging him, so he told me to come nag you."

"He didn't!" I said, but I stole a glance at Rick anyway.

Sean laughed. "So maybe that's not exactly what he said... Come on. Are you going to share your coloring book with me this time?" He sat down across from me, already pulling the book toward himself and flipping through the pages.

"It would serve you right if I said no," I grumbled.

"It would," he agreed. "But you're not going to. You like me too much."

He was right. I did. Spending time with him and his daddy had helped me start to feel more comfortable with the idea of other people in the lifestyle knowing a little bit about us. I wasn't going to go shouting my kinks to everyone who wanted to hear, but I wasn't as ashamed as I'd been.

I'd always be self-conscious in front of people like Tyler, but those like Sean and Finn made it clear not everyone was like them. I had more allies than I'd ever thought. I just hadn't known where to look.

Honestly, I still didn't. Sean and Rick looked like just ordinary people, but their dynamic transcended that of most others I'd seen. They were genuinely, truly in love with one another.

Like me and Carter were.

I blushed harder.

"Someone's thinking naughty thoughts," he sing-songed, selecting a green colored pencil. "I don't know why you like these. Crayons are better."

I made a face at him. We'd had this conversation before, and we'd have it again. It was comfortable, and it made it easier to relax even as people started drifting into the bar. "Are not."

"Are too."

"Are—"

Carter cleared his throat from nearby, and I jumped. He was trying to stifle a laugh, but he was failing miserably. "Do either of you want a drink?"

"Yes, Daddy," I told him, fidgeting in my seat like I'd just been caught doing something naughty.

"You're adorable." He leaned down to kiss my forehead. "I love you."

"I love you too," I told him.

This time, he kissed my lips.

Sean made a gagging noise, and I shot an exasperated look at him.

"Like you have any room to talk," I grumbled.

"Not even a little," Rick said as he joined us. He gave Sean a quick peck on the cheek, and Sean — predictably — pouted until he kissed him more thoroughly.

It was familiar.

It was normal.

It was perfect.

It was… my life.

I listened to Rick and Sean banter while Carter went to grab our sippy cups and their drinks. When he got back, I helped myself to his lap, cuddling him close. It was strange to have come back here, full circle from how we'd been. I'd been so shy I'd barely been able to talk to him, but he'd been this strong, soothing presence even then. Now… Now I could talk to people I knew, at any rate, even if I shut down with those I didn't.

But we were working on that.

Carter wrapped his arms around me from behind and rested his chin on my shoulder. "Having fun?" he murmured.

I nodded. It was intimidating, seeing all those people starting to collect here, but I was safe — over in my corner, in my daddy's lap. It made a difference, just as it had that first night. He was a bastion, a light in the darkness…

He was mine.

And I was his.

THE END

ABOUT R. PHOENIX

R. Phoenix (code name: Raissa) has an unhealthy fascination with contrasts: light and dark, humor and pain, heroes and villains, order and chaos. She believes love can corrupt, power can redeem and that the best of intentions can cast shadows while the worst can create light. She agrees with those who say that the truth is best told through fiction — even though fiction has to make sense while reality can be utterly baffling.

She loves chatting with readers, though she often awkwardly rambles. No matter how much she tries to keep her bad and often perverted sense of humor in check, it seems to escape at the most inconvenient moments. (Thanks, universe.) Feel free to friend Raissa on Facebook and chat or send her an email!

Facebook Page | Facebook Profile | Twitter | Join Mailing List

ABOUT CHRIS MCHART

Chris McHart lives in Germany, with her husband, partner in crime, and muse (all in one person, not even she's that kinky!). She loves her husband, men in kilts and Scotch Whisky. Her idea of a perfect evening is to curl up with her laptop and write (the other options are not suitable to post in public).

Visit her blog or friend her on Facebook, where you can join her group. You can also subscribe for her newsletter and receive a free short story!

Email | Blog | Facebook | Newsletter| facebook group

OTHER BOOKS BY CHRIS MCHART

My books on Amazon:
Saving Alex (Gay M-Preg) Unexpected #1 & #2
Unexpected Powers (Gay M-Preg) (Unexpected #4)
Two Ruined Christmas Eves
One Perfect Christmas Eve
Small Steps
From: Lon To: Adam
Truly Yours 1 - Toby & Dalton
Loving History
Never Wrong
Tyler & Jason (Bound in Silk #1) (BDSM)
Max & Pres (Bound in Silk #2) (BDSM)

German books:
Meine Bücher auf Amazon:
Unerwartet Nachwuchs (Unerwartet #1)
Unerwartet Richtig (Unerwartet #2)
Unerwartet Magie (Unerwartet #3)
Doppelt Ruinierter Heiligabend
Ein Perfekter Heiligabend
Langer Weg zum Glück
Von: Lon An: Adam
Wahre Gefährten 1: Toby & Dalton
Arizona Feeling
Tyler & Jason (Bound in Silk #1) (BDSM)

Max & Pres (Bound in Silk #2) (BDSM)

Italian books:

La sorpresa di Alex (Sorpresa #1)

Salvando Alex (Sorpresa #2)

Amami, se puoi (Sorpresa #3)